D0814485

The Day the Angels Came to

DUNNING

*Where Heaven and Earth
Meet Through a Tear in Time*

ROBERT L. IVEY

*It is not known precisely where angels
dwell – whether in the air,
the void, or the planets. It has
not been God's pleasure that we should
be informed of their abode.*
Voltaire

WESTBOW
PRESS®
A DIVISION OF THOMAS NELSON
& ZONDERVAN

WestBow Press books may be ordered through booksellers or by contacting:

WestBow Press
A Division of Thomas Nelson & Zondervan
1663 Liberty Drive
Bloomington, IN 47403
www.westbowpress.com
1 (866) 928-1240

ISBN: 978-1-9736-5147-5 (sc)
ISBN: 978-1-9736-5146-8 (hc)
ISBN: 978-1-9736-5148-2 (e)

Library of Congress Control Number: 2019900510

Print information available on the last page.

WestBow Press rev. date: 6/12/2019

ACKNOWLEDGMENTS

I would like to thank my good friend and artist, Judith Huey, a very talented artist and illustrator, for her art work in the pages of this book. I would also like to thank my wife, Marilyn, for her patience and endless work in editing my manuscript. Without her work and support this book would not be possible.

PREFACE

The idea for this novel, *The Day the Angels Came to Dunning*, was based upon a very realistic dream that came to me. In this dream I found myself standing inside a small wooden church and upon looking up, I saw *angels* in the rafters above. My dream was so realistic, I decided to create a story around it. I hope you find my story interesting and maybe in some way uplifting in the knowledge that God is always present.

Robert L. Ivey

1

Monday morning was hot. Deep-South hot! The morning was so heavy with humidity that one could cut through it with a knife. People living in the South found this weather nothing out of the ordinary and were accustomed to seasons which generally included mild winters and the rest of the year described as "hot and hotter." Visitors often found the summers quite oppressive. Regardless of the heat, by seven o'clock the streets were already busy with people going to work or performing early-morning chores.

Doris Williams drove down the shady, pecan tree-lined street with its older wood framed houses and small storefront businesses. She noticed townspeople beginning their morning rituals, making the city come alive once again after a peaceful night's sleep. The hospital, the fertilizer plant, and the Coca Cola bottling plant, all started their workdays early. It was the same as every other Monday morning—just another hot, summer's day in the making in Dunning, Alabama. Dunning was what one might call a "big, little town" in the southeastern corner of

Alabama. With a population of about sixty-five thousand, it had grown since its origin at the turn of the twentieth century, thanks to the coming of the railroad. In the early twentieth century, the town grew quickly into a center of local commerce as well as a center for shopping and medical services for the many bedroom communities and neighboring towns of southeast Alabama, northwest Florida, and southwest Georgia. Historically, this part of the country was referred to as the "Wiregrass" area named for a type of grass grown in this tri-states region.

Driving down Everwine Street, Doris saw the church on the left side of the street, protected by the shade of the ancient pecan trees that were probably as old as the church. The church was a very traditional, white wood structure with a tall slender steeple. In front of it, stood a lovely pale marble statue of an angel with its wings closed against its back, its head bowed, and its hands folded in the posture of prayer. The little church was reminiscent of the style of churches built in the late nineteenth and early twentieth centuries in the southeastern section of America. Over the years the church had been added on to several times to include a Sunday school wing and fellowship hall.

St. Michael's African Methodist Episcopal Church was a lovely part of Dunning's early history. *It is such a beautiful church,* thought Doris, as she looked with pride at the little white structure. But she felt a sense of loss by its membership dwindling over the years as many people found other things to occupy their time rather worshipping God and thanking him for their blessings in places like this simple, framed church. For many people television, cell phones, and computers now occupied their lives and took them away from the real world of living.

Doris Williams was seventy-five years old. She didn't look her age, probably due to the way she had lived, always staying busy with a host of tasks and living, as she often said, a "clean,

God-loving life." For many years she had seen to the needs of her husband, Amos, and her children, four daughters and two sons. Amos died four years earlier from a heart attack and it left a deep void in Doris's life. They had been very close for fifty-one years of their marriage and had worked hard to ensure that their children had every advantage to succeed in life. Their children had done well—two teachers, a minister, a nurse, one son in business in Atlanta, and one in far-away Germany with the military. Doris filled the void left by the death of her husband seeing to her children, grandchildren, and the many needs of her church.

"In churches, as with anything, if you work hard, they will always find more for you to do," her daughter, Sarah, laughingly said about all the time Doris spent working at the church. It was true, but Doris didn't mind. It gave her purpose and Doris had to feel needed.

"Mamma," spoke a little voice from the back seat of the 1997 Buick.

"Yes, baby," said Doris as she glanced in the rear-view mirror, into the dark eyes of her four-year-old grandson, Tyrone.

"Are we there yet?" came his impatient little voice.

"Almost, baby. Here's the church right now. Can you see it? Can you see the angel keeping watch?" Doris asked, smiling at the bright-eyed little boy in the back seat.

"Yes ma'am. I see where God lives," uttered Tyrone. Doris couldn't imagine a bigger blessing than the voice of a small child.

Again, Doris smiled back at the child through the rear-view mirror. *It is true,* she thought, *God does have a special place for little children. Children have a way of taking complex concepts and putting them into simple ways of understanding.* Turning left onto the graveled parking lot of the little white church, Doris parked her car and got out. She opened the back door for Tyrone and helped him out. Taking his hand, they walked to the side door of the church. The image of the tall slender black woman, slowly walking up the sidewalk and holding the hand of the small child, was a picture that could have been captured in a Norman Rockwell painting.

It felt cool inside the church. Cool and quiet. Turning to the right, Doris walked to the closet that housed the vacuum cleaner and dusting supplies she used in her weekly chores. As she did, Tyrone walked to the left and to the sanctuary of the little church. He liked to sit and play on the soft red carpet as his "mamma" cleaned God's house.

Tyrone pushed open the door and walked into the dimly lit room. He walked in front of the altar, where he sat down to play with the toy truck he had brought with him. The room was quiet and lit only by the sunlight streaming in through the very old, but very beautiful stained-glass windows that had been lovingly placed in the church by its first members long ago. There was a quiet peace about the room that certainly wasn't there during the worship service. Then, it was alive with the emotional worship of the Lord. Tyrone began to move his little blue car along the red carpet, engrossed in his make-believe world. He made car noises as he talked to himself in a quiet little voice that was meant for his ears only.

Doris gathered the tools for her Monday morning ritual as she had done so many Mondays before. She didn't have to think about it; she just gathered the things that she would need to make the small sanctuary look as though no one had disturbed it the Sunday night before. Not that it was too badly disturbed. The Sunday night congregation was usually small. The pews were about half-filled with older ladies, a few old men, and small children. A handful of teenagers sat near the back of the church and did what all teenagers had done in church for generations— giggle and pass notes to each other.

4

Walking toward the sanctuary, Doris struggled with dragging the vacuum cleaner while carrying dusting cloths and furniture cleaner. As she walked, she softly hummed a hymn that had stuck in her head from Sunday night. Over and over the tune went. Still humming, she came to the door to the sanctuary. With her arms filled, she pushed against the double swinging door. It opened without making a sound. Doris smiled to see Tyrone sitting and quietly playing at the edge of the altar.

Suddenly, her smile disappeared and Doris froze as her heart jumped into her throat. She could not move as a chill engulfed her entire body. The hair on the back of her neck stood on end. Every nerve and muscle in her body was suddenly wide-awake. The feelings possessing her at this very moment ranged from disbelief and fear to total incomprehensible understanding.

In the dim-colored light of the morning, she saw figures. These figures were above the exposed beams that crisscrossed the ceiling of the sanctuary. Not birds, not animals, and certainly not the painters who were scheduled to come and repaint the faded ceiling this week!

These figures were like none she had ever seen before. The figures, bathed in a soft light, were either standing or sitting quietly, shimmering. They seemed somewhat suspended in the top of the room. Without looking up, one would have likely missed them. But the figures were there quietly occupying the rafters of this small church as if birds resting after a long flight. For a few moments, Doris stared in amazement unsure of what she was seeing, not even sure they were really there. It was as though an invisible force was separating them from Doris. Were these figures in a separate dimension? She closed her eyes tightly and then slowly opened them again. The figures were still there!

"Oh, my stars! They're *angels*! Doris quietly mouthed the words, unaware that she was even speaking. For what seemed an eternity, she stood frozen, looking at the unearthly figures above her. Tyrone continued playing quietly before the altar as the beings rested just above him, unmoving in the rafters. They appeared to take no notice of Doris or the little boy beneath them. It seemed they were in two separate worlds. Doris set down her load and quietly knelt at the door. Still in a state of shock, awe, and fear she prayed, "Oh God, dear God, please help me to understand what I am seeing. If they are not really here, then, please, Lord, let them disappear." Nothing happened. There was only the quiet in the dimly lit room. God did not answer. After a few moments, Doris felt her body slowly beginning to return to life. Looking up, the figures were still in the rafters. Very quietly and softly she whispered, "Tyrone. Tyrone. Come here, honey. Come here to Mamma."

Tyrone looked at his grandmother and smiled. Slowly, he got up and began to walk toward her. Doris let her eyes drift upward to see if there was any notice from above. There was none. It was as if there existed "two worlds in one" inside the little church—-one, a world of people, activity, and noise below, and another world above which appeared as a *tear in time and space.* The figures above seemed to be resting, almost drowsily, and took no notice of the small boy as he moved slowly toward his grandmother, looking down at the blue car in his little hand. He had not seen the images at the top of the church. As he reached her, she pulled him into her arms tightly and slowly stood, holding the little boy closely. Carefully and slowly, she turned to go, but not before glancing once again at the figures, *angels,* for lack of anything else to call them. They really were there! It wasn't just her mind playing tricks on her. For some reason yet unknown they had chosen to inhabit her little church. They remained just as they had the entire time, moving ever so slightly.

It was at this moment Doris noticed details she had not been able to see at her first notice. There were three of these figures and they did have wings! She could see them! The wings gently moved and only just occasionally like someone's hair blowing in a slight breeze. She could also see that they were pale, very pale figures, ghostly, with long flowing hair and wearing what appeared to be white robes. Was she really seeing this, or was it her imagination, or perhaps a dream of some kind, feeding her mind's images with how angels should appear? These figures seemed to be in a form in which she had imagined angels would be from the time when she was a child. It all seemed so impossible. *How could this be? How could any of this be?* Doris thought, slowly backing out of the room and moving quickly down the hall still tightly holding the small child. There had to be an answer, a logical explanation to what she had just experienced. Reverend Johnson would know. He would explain it all for her.

Doris reached the end of the hallway; the door to Reverend Johnson's study standing open. He was behind his desk, his back to the door, and engrossed in the papers spread out in front of him. The Reverend's study was typical of a man who had spent his adult life in the service of God, having been a minister for thirty years. Thomas Johnson was tall and slender, with graying hair cropped short, and a dark complexion. He wore a dark suit with white shirt, and rimless glasses. A large bookshelf filled with worn books from endless studying filled the shelves along the wall behind him. Papers on the desk, along with financial reports from the past year, gave the appearance he had already been busy this morning. There was also a large, comfortably worn chair placed across from the desk for any visitor who came to see Reverend Johnson.

"Reverend Johnson," Doris said in a tense voice as she entered the room.

He turned to the sound of the anguished voice.

"Yes, Sister Doris, what's the matter?" Saying these words, her face told him that something was wrong. "Sit down now and tell me what has happened."

"There are *angels*," Doris blurted out. "There are *angels*!"

"Of course there are angels, Sister. They watch over us for the Good Lord all the time."

"No, Reverend," Doris said, shaking her head, *"I mean in the sanctuary right now! I saw them!"*

Reverend Johnson stopped for a moment, trying to decide exactly what he should say next. *How could he tactfully tell Doris Williams there was nothing in the sanctuary that could be mistaken for angels?* Although he had not gone into the room since last night, the building had been locked from the outside and no one had entered this morning. Only a few minutes earlier he had unlocked the side door to the building in which he and then Doris entered. No one could possibly be in there.

He began, "Sister, sometimes we see things that aren't really there when we first glance into a darkened room. You probably just saw shadows and thought something moved," he added, smiling, with the look that an adult uses with a small child when trying to explain there is nothing to be afraid of hiding in a dark closet. Her expression told him she was not convinced. She had seen something that she didn't understand and his explanation wasn't changing her mind.

"Okay. Sister Williams, what *exactly* did you see?" Reverend Johnson said, putting the papers down, standing, and with his hand open, offering her a seat.

Doris paused for a moment, only at this moment realizing that Tyrone was still in her arms. Again, she spoke in a quiet, slow and deliberate tone, "No, Reverend, come with me. I have to show you."

Obviously his ploy wasn't working on her. He'd have to go and prove to her what he had said about seeing "shadows in a darkened room" was true. At that moment, the thought crept into his mind that Doris could be ill, or heaven forbid, had taken a little "nip" this morning which was clouding her judgment. He hoped neither of his fears was possible.

"Okay," he smiled again. "Show me what you saw."

Trying to think ahead as to what she might say or do next when they could find nothing, the Reverend said, "Tyrone, you sit here and wait for your grandmother and me. Can you sit here like a little man and keep an eye on my office for me?"

Tyrone nodded and climbed into the Reverend's big chair and again began playing with his car, rolling it along the arm's worn leather. Reverend Johnson drew a deep breath as he and Doris walked from his study, down the hallway, and into the sanctuary. This was not working out to be the Monday he had anticipated. He really had a full agenda today.

Approaching the sanctuary, Doris secretly hoped when she walked in, she would see nothing and Reverend Johnson would say, *"See, it was just shadows playing tricks with your eyes."* They would both laugh about the whole thing and the story of the *angels* would end!

However, reaching the doors to the sanctuary, Doris stopped and touching Reverend Johnson's arm, said, "They're in here. They're in here, Reverend," the tension rising in her whispering voice. Reverend Johnson could feel the tension also. *Is her excitability reaching me now?* Still in a whispering voice, Doris leaned closer to the Reverend and said, "Look inside, just look inside!"

He smiled again and pushed against the door to open it trying not to let his skepticism show. Doris stood behind him moving cautiously to peer over his shoulder as the door opened.

The door slowly and noiselessly swung open. Thomas Johnson looked around seeing nothing except the soft sunlight streaming through the windows into the room. Just inside the door, to the right of the altar, lay the cleaning materials Doris had abandoned as she hurriedly made her exit.

"See, there's nothing here . . .," the Reverend's voice abruptly stopped, his eyes moving side to side and upward above the altar. Surprise and disbelief hit him just as it had grabbed Doris earlier. Standing wide-eyed and open-mouthed, staring speechlessly at the images floating over the beams above the altar, his eyes not believing what they were seeing. The Reverend thought, *they are angels, or what appears to be angels.* For a full minute he stood unmoving and staring upward at them. Slowly he closed his eyes, before looking back to Doris who was standing slightly behind the door with a frightened smile, nodding an "I told you so," as he looked at her. Thomas Johnson turned again to gaze with disbelief and awe at the scene above him. In the open door of St. Michael's they knelt, prayed, and watched an unbelievable event unfolding above them. It was barely seven-thirty. This Monday was not going to be like any ordinary day in Dunning, Alabama.

2

had Simmons slammed the door to his white Honda Civic, covered with WTLA stickers and glanced at his Timex watch. It was seven-thirty and, as usual, he was running behind schedule. He should be in a meeting at the television station now. "Shoot," he said to himself turning the key of the ignition, putting the car in gear, and heading from his apartment to the WTLA offices downtown. In traffic, it was about a fifteen-minute drive. As he drove north, he crossed the Dunning Bypass and headed down South Owens Street into town. The traffic was already getting heavy. With a sigh, Chad accepted that he was going to be late, again, and it appeared that he was going to catch every traffic light in town. Moving through the traffic, he mentally ran through several stories on which he was working: a new facility for the Army helicopter training at Fort Rucker, a new water tower to supply the city of Dunning with its growing needs, and the completion of renovations for an elementary school, were at the top of his list. None of these were the kinds of stories that were out of the ordinary or attention grabbers, but then those stories are few and far between.

Chad stopped at yet another signal light before turning right onto East Main. Driving past the courthouse he turned left onto North Pine and then on toward the WTLA television station. The station was located in one of the tallest buildings in Dunning. Many years ago the building had housed the old Dunning Hotel, but was now home to one of the Wiregrass area's two local television stations. The competition, WDDR, was across town near the bedroom community of Welsley. Chad was continually in a battle with reporter and newscaster, Cynthia Davis, of that station's news department for the best or latest stories. Several times they had out-scooped each other for such stories. He liked Cynthia, sort of. She was very attractive and always professional-looking and acting. *Too professional*, he thought. Had they not been such competitors, he might even have asked her out. But, somehow it didn't seem the smart thing to do since she always kept a distance between everyone else and herself, especially Chad. Maybe the reason being he did generally beat her to the really good stories. Whatever the case, he did not know her very well. Perhaps part of his intrigue with her, in a mysterious sort of way, was her lack of closeness to coworkers and friends.

Chad pulled into the WTLA parking lot in a hurry. Luckily, there was a parking place. Gliding into it, he switched the engine off and slid out of the car as quickly as possible. At almost a run, he moved through the door and into the lobby.

"Morning, Chad," called out Melanie Snyder as he ran past her, the kind of "good morning" that said *"You're late again for the morning meeting!"*

Chad didn't like Melanie. Not only did she have a cynical attitude, but was nosy and critical of everyone. Furthermore, she could be a perfect candidate for a Weight Watcher's lifetime membership. She used three times too much make-up, topped off by cotton candy, teased hair, five shades too light to look natural.

No wonder she was frustrated and didn't have a boyfriend, he thought.

Moving without so much as a nod, Chad rounded the corner to the elevator at a run and pressed the "up" button repeatedly. The elevator was not known for its speed and today was no exception. Finally, the door opened after what seemed to be ten minutes, with Chad shooting through and up to the second floor and into the hallway at a fast walk, heading toward the conference room where Jim Stuart was holding the station's morning meeting.

Just maybe they'll be late starting or not notice that I'm late again, thought Chad. *No chance of that. Face it and go on in.*

Surely enough, the entire staff was present as he entered the room, everyone looking up as he made his entrance. Chad quietly found his seat amid the smiles and elbow-nudging's. Jim was just saying, "We need something to headline the news tonight unless Martians land in Ozark! Anyone got a promising lead?"

No one stirred. There was not a sound in the room as Chad sat low in his regular seat at the end of the table.

"It is nice to have you bless us with your presence this morning, Mr. Simmons. I would assume you were up late last night working on a story for this evening's news."

Chad said nothing forcing a slight, uncomfortable smile at his boss. Stuart knew he had not been up working on a story, but probably out in one of the many night spots drinking and trying to impress the girls with his local celebrity status.

Stuart continued, "We can't headline the news tonight with, **Farmers Battle the Heat and Lack of Rain,** for a third night. And, don't even think about whipping the horse on the State making its latest proposal on improving the county jail. I want a story and I want it before lunch. Now, get moving and don't let 'DDR beat us to it."

With that, the meeting was over. Slowly, everyone got up and shuffled out of the room. Tom Whiddon, the Sports anchor, jokingly nudged Chad as they walked out, "Car trouble again, Chad?" he asked with a mock questioning look on his face.

"Yeah, ain't that just my luck?" piped Chad, not to be one-upped by his friend. "I thought Honda's were supposed to be the best car on the road. Mine just wouldn't start," he said, throwing up his hands in animated desperation.

Tom laughed and shook his head. "You need to look into getting something a little more reliable. Tell you what, I've got this great red Schwinn bike that I'll let you have for a hundred bucks. At least it might get you to work on time!"

"Thanks," laughed Chad. Somehow a hundred dollars seems a bit high for a bike you've only had since third grade."

"Plus, I'm not into riding a girl's bike," he shot back at Tom.

"Okay, but don't say I didn't try to get you to work on time."

"Really? Tom, you're a true friend," Chad said with a sarcastic tone intended to make Tom laugh. It did.

By now, everyone had drifted down the hallway and toward their offices to begin the task of putting together another day's news programming. Chad walked to his small corner office at the end of the hallway. The office looked trashed, as though someone had come in overnight and scattered papers everywhere. Two cups of cloudy, old-looking coffee sat on the desk. Ignoring it all, Chad walked over to the window and looked out across the city. From his window he had a view of the police station, the civic center, and a host of night spots which dotted the street south of his building. It looked as if today was going to be another typical day with headlines reading **Hot, Dry Weather** in spite of what Jim Stuart wanted.

"Now, where's another cup?" Chad unconsciously said to no one in particular looking under the clutter for a clean cup. Coffee was the only agenda at the moment. Then, he'd start trying to look for something to make Stuart's ulcer ease off a bit.

—◊—

Just east of Dunning in Welsley, Cynthia Davis arrived in the parking lot of Channel 7, WDDR. Already her carefully applied make-up felt as if it were dripping from her face in the morning's humidity. *How could anyone look professional, neat, and fresh in this climate?* Cynthia thought. Dabbing her forehead with a tissue, she closed her car door, and started walking toward the entrance to the yellow brick building. She felt the rush of wonderfully cool air as she opened the door. "Thank you, God, for air-conditioning," she prayerfully said to herself. In the Deep South, it was impossible to stay comfortable without it.

Standing inside the building everything was quiet. She glanced at the clock at the end of the hall reading eight o'clock. Nothing seemed to be going on and no one was around. Cynthia walked to her office, placed her purse in a chair, and sat down at her small desk. Looking around the room, everything was unchanged, as neat as ever, just as she wanted it. Taking a note pad from her desk, she began jotting down notes for the day:

- Call the airport. Ask if they will give an interview about the runway extension.
- Check with state trooper's office for details regarding accident on bypass last night.
- Go to . . . . .

The ringing phone made her jump.

"WDDR, Cynthia Davis," she answered in her most professional voice.

It was Sam Newton, her station manager. Newton was a no-nonsense man with a very rough veneer, who always came to the point, never wasting words.

"Cynthia, I just got a call from a source with the city police. Something is going on over at St. Michael's AME Church on Everwine Street. I don't know what it is but go and find out. Make sure you beat WTLA to the story . . . . if there is one."

"What's this about, Sam? Is there any information at all?" questioned Cynthia.

"Told you all I know. Now get down there and find out what's going on." The connection went dead without any further conversation.

Standing up and grabbing her purse, Cynthia headed for the door and out again into the already hot, steaming humidity. *So much for fresh make-up,* she thought, as she climbed back into her car which was feeling like an oven after only a few minutes.

Disturbed from his cup hunt, Chad answered his ringing phone. "Hello, this is Chad," he said as he dug under a stack of papers.

"Chad," the voice on the other end of the line spoke.

Chad recognized the voice as Melissa Ward, a dispatcher with the police department. He had gone out with her a couple times and she liked him more than he liked her, but still it didn't hurt to have a friend at the department who would pass on the latest tips when *news* was happening.

"Hi, darling! How is Dunning's finest this morning?" He was spreading it on pretty thick for this early in the morning. But, seriously now, who didn't need to keep a good informant, especially in the police department?

After a short laugh and flirty giggle, Melissa came to the point. "Chad, you might want to run down to St. Michael's AME on Everwine. Something is going on and I'm not sure what, but we received a call from the minister there and he wants policemen at the church."

Chad knew this would cost him dinner and whatever came with it, but hopefully it would be worth the cost. "Hon, did they say what it was about? Robbery? Break-in?"

That's all I know, Chad, but I knew you would like to know, continued Melissa. Call me sometime when you have a free evening."

Yep, Chad thought, *there was the payment for the information.* "I will. In fact, I was thinking about calling you this weekend, if you weren't busy, that is," he lied. "I'll talk with you later, Melissa. Thanks again," and hanging up before the conversation got any deeper forcing him to make any real promises.

Grabbing his camera and note pad, Chad moved from his desk, out the door, and down the hall to the elevator. "Come on, come on," he said impatiently to the elevator, as he continuously pushed the down button. Deciding not to wait for it, he turned heading down the hall to the stairs and down to the first floor. Pushing through the stairway door and moving into the lobby, he passed Melanie on guard at her desk. Her large form sat perched precariously on a very small stool, as if defying gravity.

Noticing Chad breathing hard from the stairs, Melanie, fired at him sarcastically, "Already worked up a sweat this early? That is so unlike you, Mr. Simmons."

Not to be outdone and without breaking his fast exit, Chad shouted his reply over his shoulder, "Nope, I just get hot thinking about seeing you again."

Melanie shot him a frown for his comeback as he disappeared out the door. She'd get even later.

3

The phone rang twice before it was answered. "Bishop Derrick Brown's office. How may I help you?" inquired the pleasant voice of a young woman.

"Good morning, I'm Reverend Thomas Johnson. I'm pastor of St. Michael's Church in Dunning. Is the Bishop in this morning?"

"Yes, Reverend, he is, but he's in a conference at the moment. May I take a message and have him call you back?" replied the young woman.

"Miss, this is a matter of the utmost importance; I really need to speak with the Bishop now." The urgency in his voice was obvious.

Briefly pausing, the young woman said, "Just a moment and I'll see what I can do, Reverend. Will you hold, please?"

"Yes, thank you," Johnson replied nervously. As he waited, the Reverend glanced out the window of his office. He could see a police car turning into the parking lot. It was followed by another one. The voice of the Bishop on the phone brought him back inside.

"Reverend Johnson, so good to hear from you. I understand you have some sort of a crisis going on."

"Bishop Brown, you can't begin to imagine what has just happened." Taking a deep breath, he related the events as they had previously unfolded this morning. Finishing, he stopped and waited for the Bishop to reply. There was a long silence.

"Reverend, I will be there as soon as I can get to Dunning from Montgomery."

"Thank you, Bishop Brown, I'll be waiting." Hanging up, Thomas Johnson breathed a sigh of relief. By now, two police cars had parked and two officers were standing at the doorway to his office. They had overheard the conversation and were looking at him with complete skepticism.

Thomas stood up and walked to the door. "Thanks for coming so quickly. Come with me, officers, and I'll show you our situation."

The three of them walked down the darkened hallway to the sanctuary doors. No sound could be heard from the empty building except the low hum of the air-conditioning unit. Thomas pushed open the door slowly, and then silently pointed to the ceiling, his face one of joy, admiration, and disbelief. There they were! The scene was completely unchanged. The resting *angels* were still there.

Both officers, caps in their hands, froze at the amazing sight, reacting just as Thomas had earlier when summoned to the sanctuary by Doris. One of the officers crossed himself and whispered something Thomas didn't quite understand. After a few moments, Thomas closed the door slowly and quietly.

The taller of the officers spoke first. "I don't think I'm believing what I just saw."

The second officer added, "Yeah, I saw them too, but I don't understand."

19

Reverend Johnson then spoke, "I don't understand either, Son, but you do see our situation, right?"

Both men nodded. Then the taller officer spoke again. "We're really going to need some serious backup to control this scene, once this news gets out. Serious backup."

That's an understatement, thought Thomas. *How in the world could you control the excitement this phenomenon was going to bring to Dunning?* The minister shook his head unknowingly. There were so many people he needed to call before this all became a major *breaking news* event. Walking outside, the policemen called for assistance to secure the area around the church as Reverend Johnson walked back to his office making his own telephone calls.

Picking up the phone, he first dialed the number of *Dickens' Auto Repair Shop.* Raymond Dickens was owner of the most successful auto repair shop on the east side of the city. He had the reputation for doing the best work, for the best price, in town. The fact he was a black man made no difference to his many clients, thanks to his unblemished reputation for honesty and good work. Dickens' shop, an old converted service station, had once been a Pure Oil service station in the 1950s. The old sign out front, lettered with *Dickens' Auto Repair* in blue, had simply been painted over years before. It was always busy.

Raymond was standing out front discussing a service job with a very old, tiny white lady, Mrs. Daphanie Waddell, when he heard his phone ringing. "Miss Daphanie," as she was affectionately known around town, brought in her 1985 Lincoln for service work. She had been coming to Raymond's for years and trusted no one else with her car. The old car was a deep blue, resembling an aircraft carrier compared to today's newer models, but looked as though it had just rolled off a new car lot.

"Dion! Dion, catch that phone!" called Raymond.

Appearing from around a rack of tires was Dion, a tall, thin, young black man about twenty-five or so. He walked into the office and picked up the receiver. *"Dickens' Auto Repair, this is Dion,"* he answered. Listening for a couple of moments, he took the receiver from his ear and placed his hand over the mouth piece. "Mr. Raymond, it's for you. It's Reverend Johnson and he says it's very important."

Raymond finished the conversation with Mrs. Waddell and turned to go into the office. Taking the phone from Dion, he cleared his throat before speaking. "Hello, Reverend. What can I do for you?" His thoughts were telling him that *the Reverend was probably calling about either some church business needing his help, or another matter involving one of the many committees of which he was chairman. Or, it might be that the Reverend simply needed his car serviced.*

"Raymond, I need you come to the church now. This is something that you won't believe." The urgency in Reverend Johnson's voice told him something was very important.

"Reverend, couldn't you just tell me what the issue is, I'm terrible busy right now and...," he was interrupted by the preacher.

"Raymond, this can't wait. Nothing in your life or mine has ever been this important. Come right now. I'll explain when you get here." With those words, the phone connection ended.

Scratching his head, Raymond pondered their conversation. He was completely puzzled by the minister's words. What did he mean by saying, *"Nothing in your life or mine has ever been this important?"*

Putting down the phone, he walked out of the office.

"Dion, I'll be back in a while. Watch things and keep Willie and Sam busy fixing that car for Ms. Rawls. She's coming at one o'clock to pick it up. You know how she can get if things ain't just right."

"Okay, Mr. Raymond, I'll watch everything," said Dion.

Even as Raymond left the building, Dion was feeling important standing in the doorway of the business that he felt was part his, even if it wasn't. Dion had hung around the shop since he was a young teen. Raymond had always been something of a "father figure" to him. *Too many young men today were in need of fathers or father figures,* thought Raymond, *shaking his head. What has happened to people and family?*

Raymond knew that while he was away Dion would keep an eye on the shop as if it were his own. Smiling to himself, he walked toward his old truck thinking: *Sometimes Dion enjoyed being boss a little too much and tried to give instructions to everyone there.* Generally Willie and Sam just ignored Dion and did their jobs under the hoods of the many cars that came into the shop. Each one had been with Raymond for many years.

Raymond got in and turned the ignition key to the green 1949 Ford F-series pickup truck. It fired to life with a roar on the first turn of the key. Raymond was proud of this old truck. It had been his father's and the truck that he remembered riding in as a child to this very shop started by his father. The old truck looked as good as the day his father bought it, maybe even better.

Pulling out of the parking lot at his shop, Raymond turned north heading up Oak Street. Passing closed store fronts, Raymond couldn't help but feel a deep sadness at the "loss of community" for many in this predominately black section of Dunning. Back in the fifties and sixties there had been numerous thriving, black-owned businesses. Most were closed now and gone. The vacant buildings and homes lining the street, many with barred windows, spoke today of a time much different than the time he remembered as a young boy growing up in Dunning. In those days drugs and violence didn't permeate society.

Shaking his head, Raymond turned left onto Everwine, heading towards St. Michael's. Nearing the church he passed Ms. Sally Wallace's house. Her house was in total contrast to much of the street he had just driven past. The old street looked gray and neglected; however, her property was in brilliant color. Ms. Sally owned a neat little yellow house with a white picket fence around it. Having a manicured yard, flowers, and blue gazing ball, it could have been a cottage out of a children's story book or something brought into Dunning by a time warp from the past. Surely enough, Ms. Sally was in the yard watering her flowers as she did every day.

Passing the house, Raymond tooted the horn of the old green Ford. Ms. Sally waved, not seeing who it was, but waving anyway. Her eyesight was not what it had been once. The driver could have been any one of her "children" as she referred to all of them. Ms. Sally was the resident grandmother to several generations of people who had grown up in the neighborhood. She was loved and respected by everyone, especially those of Raymond's age, who could remember her as a much younger woman when she and her husband Benjamin owned the barbershop at the corner of the street just down from Raymond's garage. Benjamin died many years ago and Ms. Sally was now stooped and with totally white hair. Still, she didn't hesitate to lecture and correct children when she considered their behavior inappropriate. Many times *she had chewed on Raymond* as a young boy and then as a young man. Whenever possible, she had been the conscience of the neighborhood which now seemed to be lost amid all the problems that plagued Dunning. Drugs, robberies, and even murders were now common place and tore a hole in the heart of the community. Still, Ms. Sally never gave up trying to keep young people on a straight path, even if it didn't always last.

Coming into view of the white-steepled church, Raymond noticed three police cars sitting in the parking lot and a fourth at the entrance. There was yellow crime tape stretched in front of the church and across the parking lot. Seeing this, fear rose up inside Raymond, which after a few seconds, gave way to confusion. All kinds of thoughts raced through his mind and then he said aloud, "Oh Lord, what has happened, what has happened?"

Turning into the parking lot, Raymond was met by one of the young policemen standing guard. As he approached the truck, the black officer recognized Raymond as one of the church leaders and waved him ahead. Raymond threw up his hand in thanks. Applying brakes and turning off the engine, Raymond got out of his truck and quickly walked to the side door of the church. This was the same entrance that Doris had used earlier this morning. Pushing the door open he saw another policeman standing in the hallway immediately outside the sanctuary, at which time he also noticed Doris coming up the hallway from Reverend Johnson's office. Raymond could sense a strange excitement radiating from Doris as she reached him. She smiled and hugged his neck as if she had not seen him for a long time; actually, she had seen him just the night before in this same church.

"Raymond, you're not going to believe it! God be praised, you won't believe it!" Doris burst out with excitement.

"Won't believe what?" Raymond was now totally confused. But, before he could say anything else, Reverend Johnson spoke up from his office doorway and headed toward Raymond.

"Raymond, I'm glad you're here."

"Preacher, what's all this? What in the world is going on?" Raymond was reaching the point now that he wanted answers and wanted them quickly.

"Raymond, I can't explain." Thomas Johnson's voice was now low and controlled. "The best I can do is simply to show you. Come this way."

The Reverend took Raymond's arm and ushered him to the door of the sanctuary. Hesitantly, Raymond walked to the door as the young policeman slowly opened it, cautious of what might be found inside. The young cop, who could not have been thirty years old, was a big man, with blue eyes and red hair. He just smiled at Raymond, knowing what was about to happen. Raymond was about to say something else until he glanced upward. At that moment he stepped back, almost backing out of the room, struck by the same emotions as all the others who had already witnessed this scene. He felt amazement, joy, excitement, fear, disbelief, and the inability to express any of these emotions. Raymond was completely at a loss for any words. He simply stood there and stared upward in utter disbelief.

For several minutes he stood not moving or saying anything. It was only when Reverend Johnson took his arm again and guided him back into the hallway that he was jolted back to reality. Being guided to the pastor's study, Raymond sat down. His legs felt wobbly. Doris had remained at the sanctuary door with the young cop, so now it was just Raymond and Reverend Johnson in the office. A long silence followed before Johnson spoke.

"Don't ask. I can't explain it. I don't know why they're here anymore than you do. Maybe they have a mission or who knows, maybe they are returning from some action for God." He continued, "All I know is they're here, and Dunning and St.

Michael's are about to witness more people than this small town could ever begin to imagine. For this reason, we must plan and organize how all this busyness should be handled."

Raymond slowly nodded, saying nothing. Finally, when he did speak, he asked, "Who must we call?" Seemingly thinking aloud, he then added, "We have to call everybody!"

As this unbelievable event unfolding in Dunning began to dawn on him, his excitement took over. A huge smile spread across Raymond's face.

"I've called the Bishop, the police, you, and tried calling the mayor, but he wasn't in," Thomas reported. "I have a feeling it won't be long before the media and *everyone who is anyone* is going to be here at St. Michael's."

"For starters, we're gonna need more police, lots of 'em ….!" For the first time since he had walked into the church, Raymond laughed. "Yes sir, praise God! We're gonna need lots of police. Now, let's start making some more calls."

4

Allan Smith walked into the court house. He was late; but, having spent a good hour over breakfast with Pete Rossling, the Chairman of the Downtown Development Commission, he felt good about the ongoing renovations underway in the old downtown area of the city, the result of receiving a Federal Grant for Renovations and Preservation. What better way to bring visitors to Dunning! Having already experienced a full day of success, what more could he ask for?

Walking into his mayoral suite, Allan's administrative assistant, Lucy Whiddon, glanced up from her computer. "Good morning, Mr. Mayor, you've already had two important calls." Without waiting for a greeting, she continued, "Chief Tyler has called twice and said obviously you had left your cell phone off again! Also, a Reverend Thomas Johnson from St. Michael's Church called and needs for you to call back immediately."

"Shoot! I surely do have my phone off, Lucy." Allan smiled, "Who do I need to call first?"

"If it were me, I'd call the Chief. He sounded pretty excited," she said matter-of-factly.

Walking into his office, Allan smith sat down at his desk, checked his phone list, and dialed Chief Tyler's number. "Bill, this is Allan, I'm sorry that I didn't get your call. I forgot to turn my phone on again. What can I help you with?"

"You haven't heard then?" he asked. From the sound of Bill Tyler's phone he was in his car.

"Haven't heard what, Bill? Is there an emergency that I don't know about?" asked Allan in a more serious tone.

"You haven't gotten a call about events going on over at St. Michael's Church on Everwine?"

"No, what events are you talking about?" asked the mayor, reacting to the seriousness in the chief's voice. "Lucy said the Reverend at the church had called my office, but I haven't been in touch with him yet."

"We've had a call asking for police presence at the church. It appears some kind of *apparitions* or *beings* have been caught sight of in the church," replied the Chief.

"What do you mean by *apparitions* or *beings*? You're referring to something like ghosts?" questioned the mayor.

"Actually, more like *angels*," answered the Chief pensively.

At this point in the phone call, there was a really long pause. For a moment Chief Tyler thought their connection had been broken. Then the mayor cleared his throat. *"Angels?"*

"Yep, that's what I said! *Angels*, at St. Michael's!"

"You headed there now, Bill?" quizzed Mayor Smith.

"Yep, but it will be a couple of minutes before I can get there, I'm across town."

"I'll meet you there. I know some sort of hoax is going on and I want it stopped. Do you have officers there now, Chief?" asked the mayor.

"Yes sir, I do. Should have two or three cars there by now."

"Good, I'll see you shortly." The conversation ended and Allan Smith got up and headed for the door.

Passing through the outer office, Lucy asked, "Gonna be out for a while, Mr. Mayor?"

Over his shoulder Allan answered, "Don't know. It depends on what kind of *angels* I find."

While he was heading to the parking lot, Lucy sat with a puzzled look on her face. *Angels? What's he talking about?*

Chad's car stopped at the entrance to the parking lot of St. Michael's. "What's with all the cops?" he muttered to himself. There were three cars and two policemen at the entrance to the parking lot. *And what's with all this crime tape,* he wondered. Behind him two more cop cars pulled up alongside the curb.

Seeing the WTLA logo on his car, one of the policemen motioned him into the parking lot without question. Glancing in his car's rearview mirror, Chad saw the arriving policemen get out of their cars and join the two standing at the entrance. Still talking to himself, Chad said, "Must be pretty big to merit all this."

At that moment another familiar car turned into the parking lot. This car made Chad groan and mutter, "No, not WDDR already!" But to his disappointment, it was. He recognized the driver. It was Cynthia Davis. "This is just great. Now, I have to deal with the 'Ice Queen of WDDR'."

Shaking his head, he climbed out of his car. It was barely nine o'clock and already hot. Walking toward the sidewalk, Cynthia got out of her car and moved around to the sidewalk, too.

"Chad Simmons, what a wonderful surprise." Cynthia greeted him with a cool smile and mock politeness. "I didn't realize you were out this early. It isn't even noon."

"So kind of you to notice, Cynthia, or is it Ms. Davis?"

Even now with the obvious coolness of their meeting, Chad couldn't help but feel that weird connection he got every time he was near her. It made him angry to think that this young woman with such a patronizing attitude made him feel funny, almost giddy. After all, they had nothing in common except both being reporters, working for rival television stations. The fact that she always looked good enough to be on CNN or in the *Sports Illustrated* swimsuit edition, and he looked like a cheap private investigator, didn't help explain it either. He just knew that he felt funny when he was near her. Once, they had an encounter at Flannigan's, a night spot in Dunning, when he and friends ran into Cynthia and her group. Since that meeting she had given him the cold shoulder. Having had too much to drink that evening, Cynthia had come on to Chad rather strongly. For reasons he could not explain, he backed away instead of taking advantage of her. Chad was sure she had not forgotten their brief encounter. He certainly had not! Was she angry because he didn't take her home or because he saw a side of her that she did not want him to see?

"Ms. Davis will do nicely," she replied somewhat coolly.

Cynthia straightened her jacket and touched her hair as she approached. *Now, why did I do that? Why would I care what he thought about the way I looked?* She thought, *after all, he is Chad Simmons.. Give me a break!*

Chad spoke again, "What's this about? I got word that something was going on here that might be a story maker."

"I have no idea either, just a call saying the same thing," added Cynthia.

They walked together up the sidewalk and to the side entrance of the church, her heels making a sharp, clicking sound on the concrete. Chad opened the door and smiled as Cynthia entered into the building. She did not acknowledge his gentlemanly gesture with even a "thank you."

Inside, it was wonderfully cool and quiet. They noticed a young policeman up the hallway standing by the closed door to the sanctuary. He immediately moved in their direction to meet them. Chad was first to speak to the young cop. "What's going on, Officer?" Been a break in or some kind of vandalism here?"

"You will need to speak with Reverend Johnson. His office is just down the hall. He'll explain," said the young man, pointing in the direction opposite of where the two reporters had entered the building.

Chad and Cynthia looked questioningly at each other as they walked down the dimly lit hallway toward the lighted office at the end. Reaching the office, they heard two voices speaking at the same time. However, upon going through the doorway, they discovered the voices were two men talking simultaneously on their cell phones. Neither of them noticed either Chad or Cynthia in the doorway. Chad rapped on the door frame making their presence known, but both men, even after looking up briefly, continued talking on their phones. Thomas Johnson motioned them into the office just as the two men finished their calls.

"I'm Chad Simmons with WTLA and this is . . . ." Cynthia interrupted him.

"I'm Cynthia Davis with WDDR. What is the reason we're here, Reverend? Is this a case regarding a break in or vandalism?"

"Have a seat, please," directed the minister motioning to two chairs across from his desk. After a couple of moments of thoughtful silence, Thomas Johnson spoke. "This is possibly the greatest story either of you will ever cover. It's not going to be solely a national, but perhaps, an international story. It is going to draw thousands, if not hundreds of thousands, of people to our little church and to Dunning."

Chad and Cynthia, who had started taking notes, stopped with his words and glanced at each other, neither saying anything. Thomas Johnson continued. "An event has taken place here, the likes of which has not been seen in the last two thousand years or so."

Breaking the silence, Chad asked, "Reverend Johnson, what sort of event are we talking about?"

Smiling timidly at Chad, Thomas Johnson continued, "You wouldn't believe it if I told you." Then, getting up from his chair, he added, "Come with me and I'll show you."

Raymond Dickens who had been sitting quietly throughout the conversation chuckled to himself, shook his head, and began dialing the phone once again.

Completely puzzled, Chad and Cynthia rose from their chairs and followed Reverend Johnson out the door and down the hallway. While walking, no one spoke. When they neared the double doors to the sanctuary, the young officer was still standing there quietly. Thomas Johnson leaned in close to the young officer and asked in a low voice, "Has there been any change?"

"No sir, they're still there just like they've been all morning."

Again, Chad looked at Cynthia. Her glance back at him reflected what he was thinking. *What is going on here?* Yet, neither of them spoke a word.

The young officer slowly and quietly opened the door. Chad and Cynthia peered inside; they saw nothing but a silent sanctuary with a pale light streaming through its tall windows. The altar with only candles, a cross, and a large open Bible placed on an oak podium, was quiet and appeared undisturbed. Chad, just about to ask Reverend Johnson what they should be looking for or at, noticed the preacher silently looking upward. That's when Chad saw the *angels*.

Both he and Cynthia looked up precisely at the same time, and as they did, each caught their breaths. Both were just as spellbound as those who had seen the visions earlier.

Out of fear, disbelief, or just simple blind emotion, Cynthia grasped Chad's arm and leaned ever so slightly against him when she spotted the figures. Whether for support or just the need to touch something, or someone real, she held onto his arm. While gazing at this unbelievably captivating scene, Chad was warmed completely by her touch. He wanted to react and take her hand in his, but he didn't dare. He simply stood in awe at the gathering of three *angels* quietly resting in the rafters of St. Michael's Church.

Minutes, seeming like hours, passed before anyone moved or said anything. They simply stood, staring upward, taking in this most unbelievable sight. Finally, Thomas Johnson, the first to make a move, closed the door carefully. No one knew the effect noise or any activity might have on these unearthly visitors, and he didn't want to risk disturbing them. The Reverend, Chad, and Cynthia walked back the way they had come and on to the outside. Outside, the bright light and heat was harsh compared to the cool darkness inside the church sanctuary. The small group stood in the shade of one of the large pecan trees that grew all around the church as a slight breeze rustled the leaves above them.

"Do you see why I couldn't explain what this was about?" asked Thomas with a knowing smile he could not suppress seeing the utter bewilderment of the reporters.

Still shaken, Chad and Cynthia both nodded. This was truly going to be the biggest story of their careers. The implications were going to be more earthshaking than anything imaginable.

Here was actual proof that the words of the religious texts of mankind were true, or at least based on truth; and, in this small, obscure St. Michael's Church, one could see either into, or across, a dimension of time, maybe perhaps into another world.

What else it meant was anyone's guess. Why had these heavenly visitors appeared here? Why could they be seen? Why now? So many questions came to mind but with no answers.

"Reverend Johnson, you know we have to share this story, and more than likely, it is going to grow into the biggest story you or I have ever seen," Chad said, apparently moved deeply by what he had just witnessed.

All coming to the realization of the extreme importance of this event, Cynthia added, "Yes, we have to tell this story; but, we must be careful how we communicate it."

"Reverend Johnson, this is your church and I think you need to say how you want it handled," Chad said, looking at Cynthia.

Cynthia looked into Chad's eyes, only now without the previous competitiveness and rivalry that was there previously. Something unexplainable inside her had just changed.

"I agree, Reverend, you decide how and when to report this story to the public," responded Cynthia.

Chad was completely surprised by the transformation he witnessed in Cynthia in just the past few moments, as well as himself, for that matter. No longer did he sense the tension or resentment that previously existed between them.

Pulling out his handkerchief, Thomas Johnson took off his glasses and cleaned them, paused, and took a deep breath. He began to speak, "In order to prevent a panic or some sort of riot, we have to organize the handling of this heavenly appearance very carefully. I must first consult with my Bishop and our conference for guidance pertaining to a news release. To make this miraculous discovery public will mean lots of police and undeniably media from all over the world, but first and foremost, this site must maintain its *Holiness* as a House of God and, as such, we cannot allow it to become a circus. Therefore, I think it will be wise to limit the number of press and cameras in Dunning and in the church." Still addressing Chad and Cynthia, he continued, "And, as you two represent the local media and Dunning's television stations, I want your stations to provide the coverage and cameras in the church. Your stations will share the telling of this unfolding story to those outside of Dunning."

As the Reverend was finishing, two more black and whites turned into the parking lot followed by a large gray sedan. The police cars parked beside the WDDR car and Police Chief Tyler got out of one. Mayor Smith exited the gray car and both men joined the small group standing outside the church. Drawn by commotion in the church's parking lot, several people from the neighborhood gathered across the street from the little white church. Wondering what could possibly have happened at St. Michael's, the group of onlookers stood questioning all the activity. Soon more people joined an already growing group.

"Morning, Reverend," said Mayor Smith shaking hands first with the minister and then the reporters.

"Good timing, Bill," he said to the Chief, "Would someone care to explain all this to me?"

Chad looked first at Thomas and then at Cynthia before saying, "I think Reverend Johnson can best explain it." With those words, Thomas, Chad, and Cynthia all laughed. The shift to a less serious nature was a welcome release after the tension from such an unearthly experience a few minutes earlier. Somewhat perplexed, both the mayor and the chief looked at them.

Facing Chad and Cynthia, Reverend Johnson said, "If you will excuse us for a few minutes, we'll meet you back here shortly."

Turning toward the church the minister led the Police Chief and Mayor Smith into the church.

As they disappeared, Chad turned to Cynthia, "I am still not sure I believe what we just saw. But, you saw them too, right?"

Cynthia nodded again. Looking at Chad she agreed, "Yeah, they were there." After this remark she stood quietly for a few moments apparently deep in thought before finally saying, "This changes everything I've ever believed. To me, this proves God is *here* and that He isn't alone! I'm just not sure I can really grasp all of this right now." She looked at Chad again, her eyes much softer than earlier and now threatening to tear up. "I'm sorry."

"Sorry? You haven't done anything to be sorry for," Chad offered, surprised by her sudden change, almost apologetically himself.

"Yes, I have," explained Cynthia, looking down, but not going any further with her explanation. It was painful remembering how she felt God had once abandoned her in a time of need; how she had prayed what seemed unanswered prayers.

Trying to break a very awkward moment, Chad said, "Look, this has been an unbelievable morning already. When we leave here, whenever that is, let me buy you a drink or lunch or something. Okay?"

Cynthia surprised Chad with a weak smile from under the threatening tears by saying, "Okay. Yes, that would be good."

Though weak, it was a nice warm smile. A smile that made Chad feel strange inside. *Was this the Cynthia Davis that he had worked with previously? Had she been transformed just by the sight of the angels?* He didn't know, but whatever had happened, he liked the change.

Returning back to the reality of these unfolding, unexplainable events, Chad took a deep breath, "Cynthia, it is okay if I call you Cynthia now, right?" he jokingly asked. She replied with a smile.

"We have to get film crews out here now and prepare for this story to break," Chad continued.

"You're absolutely right. We'd better start the wheels turning," Cynthia agreed, knowing that they had to take what they had seen and present it as professionally as possible to their viewing audience locally and across the nation.

At about the same time, Chad and Cynthia pulled out their cell phones and began contacting their respective stations in preparation of perhaps the most astonishing news of the twenty-first century as it unfolded in this small, southeastern town of Dunning, Alabama. By the time Reverend Johnson, Chief Tyler, and Mayor Smith came out of the church, WTLA and WDDR were in a frantic race to get their mobile units to St. Michael's and set up for a noon broadcast. Chad immediately knew from the look on their faces that they had seen the *angels*, too. The mayor and chief stood as bewildered as the rest of them.

"I'm stunned beyond words," began Allan Smith, shaking his head. "This is simply unbelievable."

Bill Tyler added in a low, somewhat emotional voice, "It's amazing!" Coming out from under the shock of the visions, Tyler continued, "But, with no time to waste, we have to get ready to show the world what is happening here at this moment! And, unless we're ready in the next few hours, it will be mass confusion and total gridlock for Dunning."

Subsequently, Allan spoke, "I can see potentially every hotel filled from Tallahassee to Montgomery and every road with bumper-to-bumper traffic by tomorrow."

"Our on-site broadcasting trucks will be here shortly, Mr. Mayor. And, within hours, mobile units will probably start pouring in from all over the country and maybe even a few foreign countries," Chad informed the others.

Cynthia Davis's mobile phone rang at that moment. Reaching into her purse, she retrieved it and answered, "Hello. Yes, Mr. Newton, just as soon as it gets here. Any idea when that will be? Okay, thanks." Turning to the others she said, "Our truck should be here shortly. Also, my boss has notified our network. This means we'll begin seeing action as early as this afternoon."

Mayor Smith, taking all of this in, turned to the Chief, "Bill, I want all the off-duty officers possible to report here. We have to organize this area now before everything in and around this site gets really hectic and out of control."

Bill Tyler headed back to his car and began making arrangements for the rapidly breaking news item. He realized this event could last maybe a short time or infinitely, but it was positively certain, that Dunning was about to be "center stage" in the news everywhere. Mayor Smith walked away from the group and began making calls to city council members and state officials, including the governor's office. Everything was now moving into high gear. Three more police cars pulled up and Chief Tyler walked to the street to meet them. Within a matter of minutes officers began stringing more yellow tape around the parking lot and the entire church property.

In just less than an hour a large WDDR mobile truck drove up and was waved into the parking lot by the officers. As its crew began getting out, WTLA's truck came slowly down the street and also turned into the parking lot. Cynthia walked over to her truck and Chad made his way to his. It was understood from Reverend Johnson that both stations and crews would share the broadcast of news events as they unfolded at St. Michael's. These local news reporters would provide the main coverage of the story.

Having parked the news trucks, crews began moving cameras out in preparation for an interview with the minister.

It was mid-morning. Word was getting around the community that something very unusual was happening at St. Michael's. The small group of people had now grown into a large crowd across the street, and cars filled with gawkers slowly drove past, trying to get a closer look at whatever was going on. All this activity and it was barely ten o'clock in the morning!

After roughly thirty minutes of preparation, Chad stuck his head inside Thomas Johnson's office. "Reverend, if you're ready, we'll film this interview with you," said Chad.

Grabbing his suit coat, Thomas walked outside with Chad. Camera crews were set up and ready to broadcast the most sensational story of the century. Reverend Johnson, Cynthia, and Chad stood together, and on cue from the news director, the first interview regarding the *angels* began.

Chad was the first to speak. "Welcome to St. Michael's in Dunning, Alabama, for a 'breaking special report' with a most unusual news item. We are speaking just now with the Reverend Thomas Johnson relating to a most profound story unfolding in St. Michael's African Methodist Episcopal Church of which Reverend Johnson is the minister."

Cynthia, now speaking, "The story we are bringing to you live is in cooperation with the WTLA and WDDR news departments. Our story involves images that have appeared in the rafters of the sanctuary here at St. Michael's AME Church. These images appear to be supernatural figures or perhaps, more accurately, "celestial beings" in the form of *angels*. Yes, hard to believe, but you heard me correctly, *angels*."

"Reverend Johnson, you have been in the ministry for more than thirty years and here at St. Michael's for the past twenty-five years or so. Is this correct?" Johnson nodded "yes," and Cynthia continued, "Given your theological training and your spiritual beliefs, you would positively identify these being as *angels*, correct?" Johnson nodded again.

Chad continued with his segment of the interview, "Reverend Johnson, would you please tell us when the images were first seen and how they came about to be discovered."

"Yes, they were first discovered this morning when Mrs. Doris Williams, a member of the church came in. She walked into the sanctuary, looked upward to offer a prayer and saw these illuminous figures and came to me immediately. At first she was unnerved but then filled with excitement and joy at discovering such heavenly creatures paying a visit to our sanctuary."

Cynthia interjected, "Reverend, do you have any idea why these beings have appeared here in St. Michael's?"

"No ma'am, I don't have any idea. I want to hope they were in need of a dwelling place for a while and this is God's house. Or perhaps, they are on a mission from God, but I really can't say why they chose St. Michael's and not some other church or holy place. I, like everyone else, have no idea what all of this means."

"Thank you, Reverend Johnson," Chad replied. "At this time we are going to take our cameras inside the sanctuary so our viewers can witness firsthand what we saw earlier. If our cameras will please follow us inside the church, we'll give our viewers a look as well."

Earlier in the day, Doris Williams left the church to take Tyrone home and wait there until his mother could pick him up. She did not believe he needed to be at the church in the middle of all the activity going on. Seeing the crowd on the television screen in front of her, she was satisfied with her decision. Now, as she sat on the couch in her living room watching the story unfold once again, she was so excited she could scarcely breathe. She felt a strange excitement creeping in and could not tear herself away from the television. Just to know she had experienced the *Messengers from God* firsthand early this morning gave Doris a renewed faith in God and all of His Creation. She watched in awe as the Reverend presented to TV audiences what she had been blessed to see in person!

Reverend Johnson opened the door leading the reporters into the church. Cameramen followed closely behind them with their cameras rolling, without lights, as they moved into the dark hallway. Further down the hallway toward the sanctuary they walked, their shoes making no sound at all on the plush carpet.

Chad quietly spoke into his microphone. "Since we are in a *Holy* place, we will respect it as such and will not disturb the reverence of this room. For this reason, we will not use any artificial lighting for fear of disturbing these beings."

"Hopefully, in this dim light our viewers will be able to see the beings," continued Cynthia. "Can we now quietly and cautiously open this door?"

Having spoken and receiving a nod from Reverend Johnson, the officer standing beside Cynthia slowly opened the door, which swung open without a sound. Cameramen panned the room before moving the cameras slowly upward. At that moment, cameras locked onto three figures resting just above the altar where Doris had seen them earlier.

"Oh, wow!" came the faint whisper from one of the operators. Though not clear on camera, they were actually there, and were unmistakably, winged figures. Just as previously discovered by Doris this morning, they took no notice of the people below. It was as if everything, the beings and their surroundings, occupied a different plane of existence. People watching their televisions at that moment must have been spellbound. For the longest time the cameras were held fixed on the scene, as if the church and its heavenly visitors were frozen in time. The camera then faded to a blackout and the group slowly retreated back through the doorway and down the darkened hall into the bright light outside.

Seconds later, cameras came to life again outside the church as Chad, Cynthia, and Reverend Johnson stood before them in the shade of the large pecan trees.

Cynthia spoke, "Now you have seen what many of us have witnessed today. No one can explain why, but the presence of these beings is beginning to gain the attention of everyone far and wide. We will continue bringing you live updates as visitors and inquiries come in from around the nation and the world. Until then, this is Cynthia Davis with WDDR . . . ."

"And Chad Simmons with WTLA reporting live from St. Michael's Church in Dunning, Alabama. Now back to our regular programming."

The interview ended. Reverend Johnson was thanked for his help before returning to his office to deal with continual phone calls. Chad and Cynthia walked over to the news truck where the film crews were unloading more equipment and setting up awnings to protect them from the summer's heat and sun. Awnings would be needed for any evening interviews or transmissions taking place, not to mention unpredictable summer weather in South Alabama.

Standing beside the mobile truck, Joey, a cameraman with WTLA, turned to the team, "Chad, what do you think this means?" Obviously he was shaken by what they had witnessed.

"Joey," Chad answered, putting his hand on Joey's shoulder, "I have no idea. But, I can say this for sure. It reinforces all those times I sat in Sunday school as a child and heard the stories from the Bible about God's angels. But what it means now, I just don't know."

Cynthia spoke up. "I agree, we don't know what it means, but I'd be willing to bet that we are going to have people coming here pretty soon with all the answers. Then, it will really get interesting."

"Yeah, just imagine the show when the right, the left, the Protestants, Catholics, Muslims, Buddhists, Hindus and everyone else with an opinion weighs in!" added Chad. The entire group laughed. They could just imagine the different groups voicing opinions, not to mention all the kooks who would show up as well. Everyone from *dooms day predictors* to *alien chasers* would find their ways to Dunning.

Television crews were putting the finishing touches on their shelters. It was a good idea to get comfortable; there was no way of knowing how long they were going to be there. Plans at the moment called for TV crews to be on duty around the clock, but for now, they were experiencing a kind of lull before the storm. Chad and Cynthia moved out of the way of the busy crews. Walking away, Chad turned to Cynthia, "Hey, you want to get something to eat before this gets really hectic? That is, if you aren't too busy or have something else you need to do." Trying to explain himself further, he added, "Who knows when we'll get another break."

Cynthia stopped and turned toward Chad, seemingly weighing his offer. While not sure of his intentions, Cynthia was hungry and with the situation at hand changing by the hour, she had to agree with Chad in assuming there might not be another break anytime soon.

"Okay," she said. "It is probably going to be a long day."

Chad was aware from their earlier experiences in the sanctuary, the *angels* had affected Cynthia. He had certainly been affected; however, he had no time to ponder what this meant. He'd think about it later, just as he would think more about Cynthia later.

Walking to the parked cars, Chad offered, "We'll take my car. Okay?"

"Fine," replied Cynthia, and while walking around to the passenger side of the car, she paused and with mock seriousness added, "I'm not sure that I should be seen in this car."

Joking back at Cynthia, "If we see anyone you know, you can always duck down and hide," Chad replied.

"That would really go over well, someone catching me lying on the floor of your car!" laughed Cynthia, returning his humor.

Both were laughing as they got in and drove out of the parking lot, a cop flagging them into the street at a break in the steadily growing traffic.

5

B ack in his car, Allan Smith drove toward his office at the court house. He had lots of calls to make and lots of plans to put in place as soon as possible. Just as he turned onto Main Street, his phone rang. In his characteristic Southern drawl, he answered, "Hello, Mayor Smith."

"Allan, this is Governor Wil Bayer. How are you this morning?"

"Governor, I was about to call you just as soon as I reached my office," said Allan. "We certainly have something on hand here."

"So I hear, Allan," laughed the Governor. "Is what I heard true, or is it a little exaggerated?"

"Governor, it is not by any means an exaggeration. I've just left this little AME church, St. Michael's, on the east side of Dunning, and saw them with my own eyes."

The governor cut in, "By *them*, I suppose you mean the *angels*."

"You've heard then, haven't you?"

"Not only have I heard, but saw a clip on TV not ten minutes ago," continued Governor Bayer.

Allan proceeded to explain, "Now, you know why I was planning to call, Governor. Unless I'm mistaken, we are going to need to activate a National Guard unit to help with crowd control here probably in the next day or so. There is no way of knowing how long this is going to last or how long we'll need the security.

Bayer spoke again, "I'll get on it as soon as I hang up the phone. You'll have troops on duty by this evening. Oh, by the way, I'll see you at your office as soon as I can get away. It seems as though this is something I need to see with my own eyes."

"Governor, you couldn't be more correct. When you do, I'm not sure if you'll believe it."

Governor Bayer closed with, "Okay, Allan, see you possibly tomorrow."

"Thanks, again, Governor, for all your help."

Their conversation being over, Allan ended the phone connection as he turned into the parking lot next to the courthouse. Parking in the reserved space labeled "Mayor," he left his car and hurried into the building. Inside it felt much better. The droning of the cooling unit was the only sound he heard until he entered the mayor's office suite.

"Yes, and if you'll please hold for a moment, I'll connect you with Mayor Smith," said Lucy Whiddon. "Thank you." Placing the caller on hold Lucy said, "This is CNN calling! I was just talking to Robert Wood!"

Allan took a deep breath and walked into his office, cleared his throat before touching the blinking red light, and answered, "This Mayor Allan Smith, may I help you?"

"Mayor Smith, this is Robert Wood with CNN. Do you have a few moments to answer some questions for us?"

"I believe so, Mr. Wood," spoke Allan, knowing what was coming.

"CNN would like to inquire about a story presently being aired on CBS and NBC."

"You mean the news about spiritual beings, or *angels*, being discovered, right?" Allan was beginning to feel a little more comfortable with the story now.

"Yes, this is what's being reported," added Wood.

"Well, Mr. Wood, this is exactly what has been seen. But, of course, people aren't going to believe it's anything other than a hoax unless they see the beings for themselves. I was just at the church and have been blessed to see them for myself. If I were CNN, I'd have a truck and crew here as soon as possible; otherwise, you'll miss one of the most incredible stories in modern times."

Allan sat back and smiled to himself, feeling the excitement of being party to this extraordinary breaking story on the other end of the line.

"Are news services already present?" questioned Wood.

"Oh yes, we have our local affiliates CBS and NBC crews already here with their mobile units and are expecting more in the next couple of hours," Allan added. "I wouldn't wait too long to investigate."

"Thank you, Mr. Mayor," replied Wood. "We'll have a crew on the way to Dunning from Atlanta as soon as we can put one together.

Out in the lobby, Lucy continued to answer the phone, which was now ringing every few minutes. This time it was a newspaper calling from Atlanta. She had already received calls from Birmingham, Jacksonville, and as far away as Denver, Colorado. Fortunately for Lucy, Chief Tyler had called after leaving the church and told her about the events. At first she laughed thinking Bill Tyler was joking; however, she soon realized how serious he was when he gave her instructions regarding handling calls she would possibly be getting from all over the country. In preparation for the swarms of people likely descending upon Dunning in a short time, Tyler called as many heads of city departments as he could.

Bill Tyler wasn't the only one calling people regarding this unexplainable incident today. Whoever had gotten word of the sighting had related it to others. Word was spreading quickly like an uncontrollable wildfire from southeastern Alabama to all across the Tri-States region and across the country. Once reaching network television, this story would, in turn, travel rapidly across the oceans to Europe, Asia, and Africa. In just a matter of a few hours the little city of Dunning would be news around the world.

Allan Smith walked out of his office just as Lucy was hanging up the phone. "Lucy, I guess you know the whole story by now. I was hoping to come back and tell you everything myself, but that didn't work out, did it?"

"Actually, Chief Tyler called and filled me in," Lucy answered. "It was hard to believe what he was saying, and at first I thought he was just putting me on. It isn't a joke is it?"

"No, Lucy, it isn't. Honestly, if I had not seen them with my own eyes, I would never have believed it. But, they're there." Raising his hands and shrugging he added, "Don't ask me to explain *why*. I have no idea."

Lucy's phone rang again. "Mayor Smith's office, how may I help you?" Listening for a couple of moments, a strange look came over her face. Lucy said, "I'm sorry, did you say the White House?"

—∿—

48

Traffic was starting to get heavy as Chad drove from the church. It was now 11:15 AM. The sound of the air-conditioner in his car hummed, making the occasional strange noise that he hoped would not result in the death of the struggling machine. Chad thought, *thank goodness, at least it is cooling,* which was not always the case. Briefly, he had taken the time to clean out his car of its collection of litter—used cups, papers, and news equipment. At first glance, one might think Chad lived in his car. Thankfully, Cynthia seemed not to notice the hodgepodge of other items he kept handy for his work.

"What sounds good for lunch?" asked Chad.

"Anything is fine, just as long as we eat. I'm absolutely starving," Cynthia said, smiling. She added, "And, as long as it's not in this car!"

Well, she had noticed, Chad thought.

His mind racing to think of something good to eat and quiet where they could talk, Chad finally said, "How about Olive Garden? Maybe it isn't too busy this early."

"That sounds fine. Besides, I love their salads," Cynthia said.

"And their bread sticks," added Chad.

"Sounds like you're as hungry as I am," she teased.

"I guess so. With the excitement of this morning, I haven't had time to eat or think about food until a few minutes ago."

Taking a moment to be serious, looking at Chad, Cynthia asked, "Where is all this going?"

"What do you think it means? We saw *angels.*" She continued, "I've never seen anything like this. While this whole experience excited me, it also frightened me."

"Yeah, me too," said Chad, glancing from the road to Cynthia. "Like you, I don't know where this is going or what to make of it; but, I do know we have to inform as many people as possible about what we've seen."

Turning into the parking lot of the restaurant, Chad found a space close to the entrance. There were a few patrons in the parking area, but it was not yet busy. They were just ahead of the lunch hour. Entering, they were shown to a table along the wall, where it was quiet. A young waiter came to take their order.

"What can I bring you to drink?" he asked, as he readied his pad and pen.

"It's early, but I think I need something a little stronger than iced tea now," said Chad. "Make mine a Bud Lite."

Looking up from the menu, Cynthia said, "I'll have a glass of white wine."

Within minutes the drinks came and Chad said with a grin, "I never drink during the day, but today's special. It's not every day that I *see angels* or *eat lunch with the enemy*."

Cynthia, returning Chad's smile, said, "I'm not sure how to take that."

"Well, in the past, you and I have not always been on the best of terms. It's probably my fault for being such a know-it-all most of the time. I'm sorry." Laughing almost to himself, Chad added, "I promise to try to do better."

Looking at Chad, Cynthia spoke, "It's just as much my fault. I have a knack for rubbing people the wrong way. Maybe it's partly because of trying too hard to be the best reporter I can possibly be. Anyhow, I haven't always been very nice to you. But, on the other hand, you've done a great job of making me angry on several occasions when we happened to be following the same story."

Chad watched Cynthia as she spoke. She really was very pretty, about five-six, with long dark brown hair and brown eyes. It was the eyes that got to him, he decided. Her eyes looked at him intently when he talked, studying every word as if trying to see inside his mind. Sitting here now across the table from

Cynthia, Chad was glad he had not taken advantage of her that night in the bar when she had had too much to drink. Had he done so, this conversation would not be possible. She would never have forgiven him. Hopefully, now he had the chance of eventually showing and telling her how he had felt from the moment they first met. Sitting across from her at this moment, he was finally able to admit to himself how very much he was attracted to her.

In the cool quietness of the restaurant, Chad remembered back to the first time he had met Cynthia. It had been in City Hall three years earlier. Both were there with TV crews covering the resignation of a former member of the City Commission who had been caught taking bribes from a businessman in exchange for a contract with the City to replace water pipes. Chad had noticed the striking young woman who didn't mind asking questions, demanding forthright answers from the commissioner's lawyer rather than his dancing around the questions. Cynthia was relentless in asking pressing questions and proving to those at the meeting that she had thoroughly researched the story. It was after the press conference Chad discovered she was a new reporter with WDDR, as well as new to South Alabama. She was trying to break into television journalism and broadcasting after having worked several years with newspaper reporting in the Midwest. From this first meeting Chad felt an attraction to her. He also felt she did not think too much of Dunning. Still, there was an intrigue about her that plagued him.

He remembered walking up to her and saying, "Hi."

She eyed him with the most intense look before asking, "Have we met?"

That day was etched permanently in his mind. It was early summer and Cynthia wore a green suit, very professional. With her brown eyes, she was gorgeous!

He retorted, "Not officially, but I'm with WTLA News. I guess you could say we're competition. But that doesn't mean we can't be friends," he had added with his best smile.

Cynthia had extended her hand and said, "Nice to meet you, Mr. . . .?"

"Chad. Chad Simmons," he had stammered.

"Well, Chad Simmons, I guess we will be seeing each other from time to time. Goodbye."

With that curt dismissal she turned and was gone.

While her dismissal didn't strike him as very friendly, he chalked it up to her possibly being a *Yankee* and just not accustomed to southern friendliness. He did notice as she moved through the crowd and away from the press conference, she had glanced back over her shoulder at him. True, it had been only a short glance, but nonetheless she had looked directly at him. That could be worth something!

By now their drinks had come, bringing Chad back to the present.

"How did you end up in South Alabama, in Dunning?" he asked.

Taking a sip from her glass, Cynthia placed it back carefully on the table. She had just the slightest of smiles and Chad thought he just briefly caught a glimpse of faraway sadness or maybe even regret in her eyes.

"We don't have long enough," she smiled again, shaking her head.

"I'm very patient," Chad said softly, resting his chin in his hand, encouraging her to go on. He sat quietly waiting for Cynthia to continue.

"Okay, Chad Simmons," Cynthia said, "I ran to Dunning because I was trying to start my life over."

Chad didn't answer. He just sat listening.

"I worked for a large newspaper in Chicago, got noticed, and became a reporter only a couple of years out of college. I come from a small town in southern Illinois, much smaller than Dunning, so Chicago offered excitement I had never known. It was a good job, lots of things always going on. It was there I met John. John was unlike any man I had ever encountered. He was handsome, smart, funny, and had a promising career with banking in Chicago."

Chad sat still listening, saying nothing as Cynthia talked. He found her fascinating, aside from being the most attractive woman he had ever met. He sat simply enjoying the sound of her voice and the story she was starting to unfold to him. It was encouraging to him that she not only was talking to him, but was allowing him to see a glimpse into her past life, a life she had kept guarded from everyone in her few short years in Dunning. Why had her attitude toward him changed now? Maybe, it was because everything had changed since this morning at St. Michael's. Chad knew nothing would ever be the same for him again, not Cynthia, or anyone else who had witnessed seeing the *angels*.

Cynthia continued, "We became very close, spending all of our spare time together. Now, looking back, it still wasn't enough. Work was the center of both our lives. It shouldn't have been, but then we thought our relationship and life would go on forever. We were very much in love and just instinctively knew life would go on, one day we would get married, start a family, and grow old together. Isn't that the natural order when two young people meet and fall in love?"

Chad sat unmoving as she talked on.

Taking a drink from her glass, she continued. "One day John called to say he was sick and wasn't going in to work. I didn't think about it being anything serious until I checked with him the next day and he still wasn't any better. Again, I called to check on him when I got off work and he said he believed he had the flu. At that point I decided to go by his apartment to see about him. When I arrived, he was too sick to come to the door. I let myself in his apartment, found him in bed, unconscious. He looked awful so I called 911." Pausing again and taking a long breath, Cynthia barely whispered, "He died four days later, never regaining consciousness."

There was only silence as Cynthia sat looking at her glass as all the old memories she had repressed for about three years flooded back into the present. Chad sat not knowing what to say and yet wanting to say something comforting. Nothing came. For once in his life, Chad could think of nothing to say! His throat felt tight and he choked with emotion. He slowly moved his hand across the table, placing it on top of Cynthia's. When she looked up, Chad was looking at her, his eyes watering.

"I'm sorry," he said quietly.

Sniffing and with a weak smile, she said, "But, today I feel differently than I have felt in a long time. I feel as I did when I was a little girl, sitting in church with my parents, and instinctively knowing God really does control everything about our lives. There is hope and a future for us after . . .," Cynthia paused and sniffed again, ". . . after all this."

Chad could not have worded the way he felt any better than Cynthia's simple explanation of life and death and life again. The presence of the *angels* at St. Michael's had said everything so simply.

The waiter approached with their food, and Chad reluctantly moved his hand from Cynthia's. Lunch could not have gone better. The food was good; but, best of all, Chad felt the relationship between he and Cynthia had definitely changed. Chad now admitted to himself that he was in love with this young woman across the table from him and had probably been in love with her since their first meeting. There was now a connection between them and as far as any relationship developing further, only time would tell. Today, they had shared a rapturous experience like few people and Chad was pretty confident it would tie them together infinitely.

6

Allan Smith's attention perked up as Lucy listened intently to the person who had just called, her eyes darting from the phone to Allan and back.

"One moment, please, and I'll put you through to Mayor Smith."

Pushing the phone button to transfer, Lucy hung up the receiver. Almost breathless from shear disbelief, she said, "He's an assistant to the President of the United States!" Her voice giving way to her excitement, continued, "It's a Mr. Michael Stern."

Walking to his office, Allan moved around his desk, sat down, and lifted the receiver. "This is Allan Smith, how may I help you?" He tried to sound as if this was just another day at the office, but that was extremely difficult to do.

"Mr. Mayor," began the voice on the other end of the line.

"Yes, may I help you?" Allan asked again.

"I'm Michael Stern, Special Assistant to the President of the United States. I am inquiring about the story that is flooding all the networks today. We thought the best way to find out what is going on is by going straight to the source."

"Mr. Stern, just what would you like to know? I will try to bring you up-to-date as much as possible," replied Allan.

"Well, uh, can you tell me specifically what has been sighted there? Are we talking images, beings, shadows, something that looks like celestial figures? Certainly, not beings?"

"Mr. Stern, that's exactly what we have here, *actual beings*," replied Allan. "We have no idea why or how they appeared here; but, whatever the case, they appear to be *living beings* present in St. Michael's AME Church and, specifically, they look like *angels*, three of them, which is the only explanation I have at present."

There was a nervous laugh on the other end of the line. "You don't mean actual *angels*, do you?" asked Stern, waiting for the punch line of a joke being played on him. No punch line came.

"Yes, Mr. Stern. We really have *angels* here in Dunning; honest to goodness, *angels*, *celestial beings*, if you will. I can't be any more specific than this." Allan explained further.

Again, there was a long pause before Stern said, "Do you have any idea as to the possible implications of these, uh, these appearances?"

"I think I do, Mr. Stern. I imagine we will have more people than we can manage here in Dunning within a couple of days, especially, when the networks show up here for live broadcasts." Continuing, Allan asked, "Mr. Stern, is there something that we need to do in coordination with the government in Washington? After all, I have a hunch we are going to have religious leaders from all over the world in Dunning before too much longer."

Finally, Stern realized he was not dealing with a hoax and this *celestial visit* could potentially turn into a colossal international event, greater than anyone could imagine. There were so many implications that could and would impact the thinking of not only the American society, but other societies in the world. If this report proved accurate, it could be validation of many religious teachings, moving these concepts from "the realm of faith to real, hard scientific proof."

"Mr. Smith, take down this number. This is my own personal cell number. Call me with any new developments. Do you understand? Mr. Smith, call me first."

Allan jotted down the number and hung up. He could tell from Stern's voice that he was taking these incidents very seriously. Apparently, Stern was already convinced this was real and there was no way of knowing how an event of this significance would unfold. UFO's had been sighted and reported to the government many times, but sensing Stern's reaction, Allan was positively sure the government had never dealt with *angels*!

Lucy looked at Allan questioningly as he emerged from his office.

"Lucy, in a couple of days Dunning is about to become the center of the world's attention. Reckon we can deal with it?" Not waiting for an answer, Allan turned and walked back into his office and picked up the phone. He still had many people to call.

Looking out his window, Allan saw several police cars assigned as added security driving past city hall heading toward St. Michael's AME Church. Traffic was especially heavy now, crawling along very slowly, and the police cruisers found it necessary to weave in and out of vehicles before turning onto Everwine Street. Traffic had already been blocked off heading north on Everwine, leaving just one lane open for emergencies and temporarily making it a one-way street for other traffic. Reaching the church parking lot, vehicles were flagged in by two other officers on duty. No other cars were allowed into the parking lot. Policemen stood around the church casually talking but not allowing anyone beyond the yellow tape and into the church yard.

In addition to vehicular traffic in front of the church, on the opposite side of the street, a large crowd of people from the neighborhood had replaced the small group from earlier. They stood looking and talking, all trying to hear the latest information. By now it was hard to believe that anyone in the area had not heard about the visitors at St. Michael's.

By late afternoon the parking lot at St. Michael's had two mobile trucks from WTLA and WDDR and about a dozen police cars. Parked along the street in front of the church were more black and whites. It was now very hot and humid. Thankfully, both the street and the church yard were shaded by large pecan trees; otherwise, it would have been almost impossible for anyone to stand outside for any length of time.

While people stood watching events unfold, the sound of heavy rumbling traffic could be heard coming down the street. The crowd watched as a large, mobile news truck, much larger than the trucks already at the church, pulled up to the drive of St. Michael's. Big letters on its sides identified the truck as belonging to CNN. The truck was waved into the parking lot along with the other trucks. CNN technicians got out and began unloading equipment and talking with crews from the other networks. From beneath a shade tree, a camera crew set up and began filming the outside of the church and the continually growing crowd across the street. The way people were lined up, it could have been mistaken for a parade; however, this crowd was standing quietly and waiting for any information to come from the little church. The angry, hot sun was moving slowly into the West, leaving Dunning baking in the early summer heat. Even with late afternoon approaching, the heat remained oppressive.

—— w ——

Half a world away, lights shone brightly across the low skyline of the city of Riyadh. Muhammad Ibn Harassi sat in front of the television in his living room. By satellite he was watching the international news from CNN. He enjoyed keeping up with the latest news from around the world, especially American news which he always found interesting. So many viewpoints could be expressed without getting into a difficult situation if one person's views happened to be different from another's. Americans were able to discuss, debate, and argue, all while being on air. Not everyone always agreed, but differences in views were allowed and this kind of openness was refreshing to Harassi.

Harassi's life was not always so easy. As Assistant to the Press Secretary of the King, he must be very careful about what he said or did and with whom. While the King was a very well educated, sophisticated man, the society, of which both were a part was very conservative and traditional, to say the least. One must always be aware of the views and opinions of those who were not quite so tolerant and may have had tremendous influence in government or society. Then, too, always present were the religious police of whom citizens must be constantly aware.

Harassi graduated several years back from Lincoln College at Oxford University in England with a degree in International Affairs. His life away from the desert kingdom had widened his understanding of people and their differing ideas. He enjoyed school life at Oxford; a western education in a western culture, plus all the aspects of a large modern city like London, not far from Oxford. He often found himself slipping back and forth between the two cultures, both of which he had become a part. However, not everyone shared that same attitude. For many it was: *just right or wrong and no in-between.* Just that simple! Life was not that uncomplicated for Muhammad.

He sat watching the newscaster on screen in a dark blue suit with a red striped tie, teeth too white to be natural, as he continued with the news of the day.

> *Today, in Dunning, Alabama, a small city in the southeastern part of the United States, a strange scene has taken place in a small protestant church. Eyewitness accounts say that figures reported as angels have been seen inhabiting the church. News services are presently on the scene following these events. We take you now to Dunning for extended coverage.*

Following this introductory statement, the picture moved to video footage of a scene filmed inside St. Michael's. It was footage taken earlier with Cynthia and Chad when the story first broke. As the camera panned upward, the footage clearly revealed that it had captured images of what appeared to be *angels* resting in the rafters. Muhammad sat frozen to the screen of the television. He thought, *certainly this has to be some sort of trick, a computer graphics manipulation most likely!*

However, as Muhammad looked more closely at the images on the screen, his first impression sent a chill through his body. The large, winged figures certainly looked real! He sat following the coverage for several minutes including interviews with two reporters, at which moment the network cut to a discussion with the commentator and an analyst. Confirming the footage had all the merits of being real, the analyst added that a full investigation would follow before it would be fully authenticated.

When the newscast moved to international events and the fire storms in southern Greece, a direct result of hot, dry weather with no rainfall, Muhammad picked up the remote and turned off the power. Sitting there in an eerie sort of quiet, he replayed in his mind what he had just viewed and pondered what he should do. Should he call Ishmael Hadi, the King's Press Secretary, also his boss? He could speak frankly with Ishmael. They knew each other well and had grown up as childhood friends. Each respected the abilities of the other. While still indecisive about his next step, the phone rang. After waiting for a couple of seconds, he answered it. "Hello. Yes, Ishmael, I was just about to call you."

The two men exchanged a few pleasantries, and then Ishmael Hadi laughed and said, "I was watching television, a news program on CNN International. There was an unusual and somewhat interesting story about the appearance of *angels* in a town in Alabama in the southern sector of the United States. I was calling to see if you could find out any details about the story. You have friends with CNN in Atlanta, don't you?"

"This is really ironic. Ishmael, that's why I was about to call you. I was watching the same program and I wanted to discuss it with you. You have already answered my question."

"Your friend," Ishmael questioned, "Who is he?"

"Tom Weatherman. Tom is a producer with the Middle East Office. I can call him and see what he knows."

"Muhammad, for the time being, I think it is better that we keep this between the two of us. If it turns out to be true. . ." Ishmael stopped. "Well, we'll cross that bridge later."

"I will call my friend as soon as he is in his office. That should be about nine o'clock Eastern Standard Time. Then, I will phone you."

"Thanks, Muhammad. Goodbye."

"Goodbye, Ishmael."

The television report and the conversation with Ishmael made Muhammad wonder: *Suppose this incident is exactly as it appears. Suppose God's angels have been seen in this little church in Alabama. What did it all mean? Had God sent them? Did it mean...???*

There were too many questions for now. He would wait to see what happens. Muhammad got up, turned the lamp off, and went to bed. *"Angels,"* he said aloud as he walked from the room. *"Angels!"*

Back in Dunning, Raymond Dickens had called everyone he could possibly think of to tell them this unbelievable story. He had begun by calling his wife, Edna, at home. At first, she did not believe him, until she saw the news clip on television. Then she, like others, was beside herself with excitement. By the time Raymond had completed his telephoning, the story was being broadcast on all of the news services. Leaving the church, he went home. Even at home he continued receiving calls until finally he left the residence phone off the hook and turned off his cell phone. Just before temporarily isolating himself from outside communication, Raymond had received a call from Reverend Johnson. The Reverend asked Raymond to be back at the church by two o'clock that afternoon when Bishop Brown was expected in Dunning. The Bishop had requested to be at the church to assist in any way possible. Johnson also told Raymond he had spoken with Mayor Smith once again regarding handling such huge crowds of people streaming in to the vicinity of the church and possibly, making the sanctuary more accessible for those who wanted to see the *angels*. A decision was reached whereby the City would erect a kind of temporary canopy running from the parking lot and down the sidewalk to shield people from the intolerable sun, heat, and possibly afternoon showers. With crews working overnight, the canopy could be completed fairly quickly.

Television coverage continued with local interviews and film footage from inside the church. Over and over these clips were shown, interrupted only by live broadcasts with updates from outside the church by local channels, WDDR and WTLA, and now CNN, CBS, NBC, ABC, and FOX. All afternoon news trucks had been arriving, surrounding the little, white framed church on Everwine Street. The street became so busy police closed it entirely to all except emergency and special vehicles. The sidewalk across the street from the church was completely filled with curious onlookers. People of every description could be seen in the crowd. Many consisted of church members or people who lived in surrounding neighborhoods. Others came from across town. Still others had driven to Dunning from surrounding towns, some from as far away as Montgomery, Tallahassee, Marianna, and Panama City. They all wanted to see the *angels*, persistently asking, "When are we going to be allowed to see the *angels?*"

Such was the scene when Chad and Cynthia returned from lunch. As they turned onto Everwine, they found the street blocked by police barriers. Fortunately for them, the WTLA markings all over the car gained them a wave on through the barrier. The cops standing on duty looked hot in the afternoon heat. Chad and Cynthia were amazed at how large the crowd had grown in just the space of a couple of hours. They turned into the parking lot now filled with news trucks and equipment. News crews buzzed all around. Access from the parking lot to the church was now blocked off by a police barrier. It was amazing how much had happened in the brief time they had been gone.

As Chad and Cynthia got out of the car, several reporters with their cameramen, mikes labeled CNN, ABC, and CBS, approached them. Totally surprised by the bombardment of questions, Chad glanced at Cynthia, both realizing at the same time, they were being questioned because they had been the first to see and report the *angels* to the world. In effect, they had been elevated to a semblance of celebrity status because of their reporting!

"Mr. Simmons, can you tell us exactly what you think the *presence* in the church *is* that you may have witnessed?" questioned a young man with CBS.

Chad paused for a moment, "It's not what I think I saw. It is the same thing that everyone watching television saw. I saw *angels*! There are *angels* in the rafters of this church. Why they are there or why they are visible, I can't tell you. What I can say is they are *there*!"

"Do you think this appearance may be a kind of prophecy?" asked a very attentive young woman wearing glasses from ABC. "Is it a sign from God?"

Chad held up his hand and smiled, "Wait, I just saw them. I can't explain them, and I don't know who can, if anyone. I certainly wouldn't offer any sort of analysis. After all, I'm just a reporter like you. You should pose those questions to someone who is better versed on the prophecy topic."

"Miss Davis, would you comment on the *angels* as you saw them?" questioned the young man with CBS.

Cynthia looked at the reporter and then at Chad before answering. "I really can't add any more to what Mr. Simmons has said. They're there and we have no idea why."

With this exchange of words, the reporters thanked them and turned facing their cameras to reiterate Chad's and Cynthia's comments before signing off with the promise of more information later. Chad and Cynthia stood gazing at the little church which was beginning to look more like a major crime scene than a house of worship with all the tape, barriers, and police. They looked across the street at the crowds of people now stretching completely out of sight. It was astounding how this scene had changed since this morning and, with Monday afternoon slipping by, it didn't appear the little church was getting back to normal anytime soon.

Thomas Johnson sat in his office. His day had been a whirlwind of phone calls. He had received calls from ministers all over the Tri-States area of Alabama, Georgia, and Florida; in addition to calls from newspapers, television stations, members of his congregation, and even a call from someone claiming to be a low level assistant to the Pope! All had the same question: "Were there really *angels* in his church?" Glancing at his watch, he noted it was almost two o'clock. Bishop Brown was scheduled to be at St. Michael's momentarily. In an effort to accommodate the large numbers of people who were steadily descending upon the town hoping to catch a glimpse of the visions, Reverend Johnson had been in touch with Mayor Smith. At about ten past two, a police car, followed by another dark Ford turned into the parking lot of St. Michael's. Cynthia and Chad were standing there as the cars drove in and parked. Both the mayor and police chief exited from the police car. Two very distinguished-looking black men got out of the other car. Together, the four men approached Chad and Cynthia.

"I see you two have become associated with some other members of the media," joked Allan Smith.

"Yes, it's getting pretty busy around here now," Chad responded.

Addressing Chad and Cynthia and shaking hands all around, the Mayor said, "This is the Bishop for the Southeast Alabama African Methodist Episcopal Church, Doctor Derrick Brown, and his Assistant, Jeffrey Smoots."

Dr. Brown was a short, dark man with white hair. He wore black-rimmed glasses and a dark suit with the white collar associated with the clergy. On first impression, Dr. Brown showed his true nature as a warm, engaging man, easy to talk to, and with a great sense of humor. He demonstrated one who truly possessed the warm, loving spirit of God. He had been a minister for many of his seventy-eight years, living and working his way from one small rural church to another, always mindful of his task as a loving father to his congregations. Dr. Brown's hard work and dedication led him to being appointed five years ago to his present position of Bishop.

"A pleasure to meet you," said Chad as he and Cynthia smiled and nodded, exchanging warm handshakes with the bishop and his assistant.

"The pleasure is mine," said Dr. Brown. "And, I understand we have a wonderful sight here at St. Michael's."

"That we do, Sir," Allan replied, motioning toward the church.

By this time, reporters across the parking lot noticed the activity and quickly closed in around the group. Cameras were rolling as they tried asking questions. The mayor was able to fend off the questions with a simple, "We'll answer all of your questions shortly."

The group walked toward the church while reporters and their cameras were stopped at the side entrance, still trying to push for information. Unable to go any farther, due to the police tape and about half a dozen police officers, the reporters waited not so patiently outside.

Reverend Johnson emerged through the door as the small group reached the side entrance to the church. "Dr. Brown, I am truly happy that you came so quickly."

"I'd have been here sooner, but as usual, several things came up that had to be addressed before I could get away," the bishop responded.

"No matter, Bishop, you are here now and you must see this miracle!"

Greetings out of the way, the group moved inside. The mayor, Chad, Cynthia, and Reverend Johnson all knew what was about to happen. Bishop Brown could feel his excitement beginning to rise. He sensed that contagious feeling from the others, a feeling of fear and excitement that spreads through a crowd when confronted by something unexplainable. Walking from the bright daylight into the dark hallway, it took a couple of moments for their eyes to adjust. It was dark, cool, and eerily quiet. In front of them at the door, leading into the sanctuary, stood the around-the-clock guard of the police force. With a nod from the Reverend, the young officer slowly opened the door giving a clear view of the entire room. The room was just as before, completely quiet with nothing out of place. Looking upward into the wooden rafters, the bishop saw what the others had seen earlier. The *angels* were there, unbelievable and majestic in appearance. They sat as if *the fabric of time* had been torn, leaving a gap between the two dimensions of earth and heaven, completely oblivious to all the excitement going on beneath them. Bishop Brown stood in absolute, unmitigated, amazement. Nothing in his seventy-eighty years even remotely compared to this moment! He gazed spellbound, almost unable to comprehend what he was seeing. At first he tried to rationalize the vision, but could not. It was a *tear in time,* exposing an unknown dimension visible for the first time since Jesus appeared to earthly beings after his crucifixion and resurrection. It was as if he could see the *angels,* but they could not see him.

Bishop Brown looked at Reverend Johnson still lost in total amazement and disbelief. Thomas Johnson looked at him, smiled and nodded. The bishop looked at the others standing with him. Everyone present was emotionally and spiritually overcome by the vision in the sanctuary. They simply stood there looking up into the rafters; and, as they did, tears rolled down Bishop Brown's cheeks, visibly coming to rest on his starched white shirt. After an indeterminate amount of time, they reverently backed into the hallway and closed the doors.

On the return to Reverend Johnson's office, no one uttered a word. Once inside, Johnson was the first to speak, "They are *angels*, aren't they, Bishop?"

Sinking into a chair, Bishop Brown looked at the preacher, "Oh, they are most definitely *angels!* God be praised!"

He sat for a couple of moments before speaking again. "Could we please have prayer?" Without a word, all closed their eyes and bowed their heads as Bishop Brown prayed.

> *Father, O Great and Glorious Father, You have sent a remarkable vision to our church today. While we don't understand, we thank You for allowing us this glimpse into Your Kingdom. If it be Your Will, may we use this vision as an example of Your power and love for Your children so that others may see Your work in Your world. In Your Son, Jesus Christ's, Holy Name, we pray.*
>
> *Amen.*

Following the prayer, the hush continued as they all contemplated the past few amazing minutes. Speaking in a low, still somewhat emotional voice, oblivious to the others, Bishop Brown said to no one in particular, "This is truly a miracle. A real miracle!"

Looking around at the others in the room, he returned to them from his own thoughts. "As soon as possible, Thomas, we have to make this available for everyone to see. This will convey God's presence in such a way as no one has seen in two thousand years.

Reverend Johnson nodded. Then Mayor Allan Smith spoke, "Bishop, we have begun plans already for doing just that. This evening, plans are to construct a covered area in the parking lot. It will help protect those waiting to go inside from the sun and the heat. To supervise the potentially large crowds that are certainly going to be drawn here, we are bringing in National Guard troops and additional police. Visitation in the church will begin as soon as possible."

"Mr. Mayor, have you received inquiries from either state or national governmental agencies regarding the *angels*?" Chad asked.

"Actually, Mr. Simmons, we have been in contact with both governments," began Mayor Smith. "I imagine we will soon begin receiving visitors not only from these agencies, but from some foreign groups as well."

Chief Tyler spoke up here. "That's the reason speed is of utmost importance in getting preparations going here. Who knows the kinds of numbers we're expecting."

"Would you want to make a prediction on such numbers, Chief Tyler?" Cynthia asked.

"No, I wouldn't even attempt a guess. Whatever the case, we must be prepared for any situation."

Allan Smith offered a possibility. "Suppose we have ten thousand people in Dunning by Saturday, or one hundred thousand by next week? I can imagine buses rolling in here from all over the country, not to mention visitors from foreign countries. After all, we're talking about a MIRACLE FROM GOD visible to anyone! It's not like we are predicting that Elvis is going to perform!"

"Actually, that would be a miracle if he performed, Mayor," joked Chad with a slight smile, which brought a round of laughter from the others.

Proceedings effected by the *angels* were now beginning to happen quickly. As the meeting in Reverend Johnson's office reached closure, Chad and Cynthia walked out of the church, leaving the others to discuss organizing for an inevitable rush that would surely affect the mundane life in this sleepy southern city,

7

A s they walked into the bright afternoon sun, Chad and Cynthia noticed the crowd growing even bigger. As far as one could see, people filled the opposite side of the street from the white framed church. Outside their mobile units, Chad and Cynthia noted the parking lot was now filled with police cars, news crews of every major television network, and local television stations from all over the Southeast. Obviously, the story at St. Michael's in Dunning was developing into a major newsworthy event of national interest. Chad's phone rang, "Chad Simmons," he answered. It was Jim Stuart, his boss.

"Chad, I've been talking with Sam Newton at WDDR. We've decided to continue the entire story of the *angels* in conjunction with both stations. You and Cynthia Davis will continue to broadcast together. We'll give live updates for the major networks throughout the day for as long as this story continues to progress. Besides, the City of Dunning has already decided that all the networks will broadcast through your reporting."

After a brief pause, Chad said, "Wow!" This meant he and Cynthia were about to become really known, maybe even nationally known. They would be the direct link between the *angels* and television viewers around the nation and possibly the world.

Throughout his conversation with Stuart, he had been standing next to Cynthia. She was watching and listening intently as the conversation continued. Other members of the television crews were listening as well, also in anticipation of further developments. Stuart continued, "You'll broadcast live at the end of the five o'clock news, providing the lead story for the evening's national news on all networks at five-thirty. You two get ready for that live broadcast. I'll get back with you afterwards."

With Stuart's final instruction, the conversation ended. Everyone still looking at Chad was waiting to hear what had just been said. Before having a chance to explain, Cynthia's phone rang. It was obvious from her conversation that she was speaking with her boss, Sam Newton. The crew continued waiting attentively until she said, "Yes, I understand. Bye."

"I have a feeling that you just heard the same thing I heard," Chad said.

"If you mean that WDDR and WTLA are working as a team and will broadcast together, headlining national news, then yes!" answered Cynthia. The TV crews standing with them let out a cheer!

"Okay, guys, you've heard our instructions. Let's get busy setting up for a five-thirty spot with the big boys," directed Chad with an air of confidence. He pulled up a chair under the awning of the WTLA truck and sat down. Glancing over at Cynthia, he patted the chair beside him. "Might as well get comfortable so we can get to work."

Cynthia smiled shaking her head, "Yes, it looks as if this is going to be a long afternoon."

She sat down beside Chad and in doing so her shoulder brushed his. He felt that same strange little spark of electricity he felt earlier as he looked at her dark hair and could smell the slight scent of her perfume so close to him. It felt good working with her. It felt good being so close to her and seeing how quickly their relationship had changed with the surprising, yet brief, events of the day. Chad felt as if on this day his life was about to change forever. Not only was he coming to terms with feelings for Cynthia that he had refused to accept previously, but he now felt a peace about life after having seen the *angels*. The hard, callous view of life Chad had developed from years of reporting tragic events seemed to be replaced with feelings of hope. Were the *angels* responsible?

As they began talking about the broadcast, Cynthia took notes. Chad intuitively believed she felt something for him, too, with her sitting so closely and making no attempt to move. At times she leaned even closer to reach for a pen and touched his arm while talking. While doing so, she pretended not to notice; but, Chad knew it was intentional and he was delighted by it. He could feel electricity between them, which he had never felt with anyone else. Obviously, something was here, something bringing them together. Maybe it was the *angels* after all. Strangely, the events of the day had brought out hidden feelings shared by both. Chad couldn't help thinking about their lunch earlier and how he felt after hearing Cynthia's story. His opinion of her changed as he thought about the sadness she had carried for so long. He had truly been changed by all the events transpiring around them. He knew he would never be the same again. But, how could anyone who had seen *God's Holy angels* NOT be changed?

Chad and Cynthia worked through the hot afternoon under the shade of the awning while large fans circulated the muggy air. Much of their work involved coordinating with the other news teams to provide a television feed to them. As now programmed, Chad and Cynthia would first broadcast live across the nation; they would then be followed by the network journalists from each of the various stations. At five o'clock in the afternoon programming really went into high gear with all teams hustling to make sure they were ready for a monumental broadcast. The cameras were set up all facing the front of St. Michael's Church. Thankfully, the huge trees provided some relief from the heat, as well as the air from the fans. However, despite the mugginess, Cynthia had repaired her makeup and looked cool, even if she wasn't. Chad changed his shirt and tie but did not bother with a coat.

Five thirty approaching, everyone made ready. A small monitor was showing the local news broadcast from the studio of WTLA, another one showing WDDR's. The local news opening with only a brief mention of the sightings at St. Michael's, adding that an expanded segment would be given with the national news at 5:30, following local weather and sports. WTLA, a CBS affiliate, ended with a program reminder of the local story, then cut to the networks.

Jeff Glor, News Anchor with CBS, opened the evening news program with top stories of the day, laying groundwork for their main story.

"Tonight, we bring you an unbelievable story from the small southeastern Alabama city of Dunning. Early this morning in this small, quiet town, a staff member of St. Michael's AME Church arrived to discover visitors hanging out in the church's sanctuary. These visitors are not the typical visitors to one's church that comes to mind. These appear to be *angels!* Yes, I said *"angels"*. These celestial beings appear to have taken up residence, for the moment anyway, in the sanctuary of this small church. Several people have already witnessed these figures and throughout the day, news programs have been airing videos taken by the crews of CBS affiliate, WTLA and NBC affiliate, WDDR."

"In conjunction with these two local stations, we are now going live to Dunning, outside of St. Michael's, for an update from local correspondents Chad Simmons of WTLA and Cynthia Davis of WDDR. Chad, Cynthia, can you hear me?"

With a nod and a signal from the technician, the broadcast from Dunning began with Chad.

"Yes, Jeff, we hear you. It's just as you stated. This amazing story begins with figures we are calling *angels,* who have been seen in the sanctuary of St. Michael's."

"Twice today, Jeff, Chad and I, as well as several other people including church and local officials, have witnessed these beings," Cynthia interjected. "The figures appear to be in a 'state of rest' taking no interest whatsoever in people watching them."

Again, Chad spoke, "They don't seem to see us, as if they are on a different plane and it's only we who see them."

Jeff returned with, "This is really amazing! Can we see the film footage shot inside the sanctuary again?" For a brief moment the film played again for the nation, showing the same scene from earlier in the day, and just as before, the beings were clearly visible.

After the film ran, Glor continued, "What do local authorities and church officials say about these figures?"

Trying to answer as accurately as possible, Chad said, "Jeff, local church and city officials have no explanation for any of this. It seems they were seen quite by accident when a member of the church entered the sanctuary early this morning."

Cynthia added, "These *angels* have in no way acknowledged their presence nor attempted to make contact with anyone. They just appear to be in a kind of tranquil state."

"This is really quite incredible!" Glor continued, "And it certainly poses some profound questions about faith and God."

"Yes, if this phenomenon proves to be as it seems, then religious beliefs will surely be affected by these unbelievable appearances," continued Chad. "We will simply have to wait and see what will be the final outcome. We plan to speak with church officials tomorrow in our continuation of this story."

"Thank you, again, Chad Simmons and Cynthia Davis, for this extraordinary report. We will certainly continue following this story very closely as it unfolds. With this story from our local reporters Cynthia Davis and Chad Simmons, we close this segment."

Scenes around the church and of the nearby city streets showed the growing numbers of people and traffic in the city of Dunning. As the report ended and Jeff Glor moved on to another story, the camera crews ended their transmissions, and both Chad and Cynthia put down their microphones.

"Nice job," said Josh, the on-site producer, to Cynthia and Chad as they got up from the desk and walked back to their mobile units parked side by side in the now full parking lot, looking more like a tail-gating party at a college football game than a Sunday morning worship service. Satellite trucks, vans, cars, cameramen, reporters, and police vehicles filled every available square inch of space. The hum of generators added to the sound of voices of reporters each giving their spin on the *angelic* events.

Looking back over her shoulder, Cynthia replied, "Yes, thanks, Josh!"

Following the end of the news report, city crews began immediately moving trucks and equipment into place in order to begin construction of the temporary, covered shelter for the large number of visitors expected to descend upon Dunning for a glimpse of the heavenly visitors. Crews planned to work all night to have the walkway completed by morning, thereby, enabling the church to open its doors for closely supervised tours of the sanctuary. If the heavenly visitors were disturbed or even aware of the noise and commotion outside, they gave no hint. They simply remained in a resting state above the rafters of St. Michaels. Those in charge of scheduling decided no further reports, other than a rebroadcast of earlier information, would be necessary until Tuesday. Grateful for this brief respite, Chad, Cynthia, and most of the crews were able to shut down and try to get some rest, leaving only maintenance crews on site. At this point, no one knew what Tuesday might bring.

Walking to his WTLA car, in the fading early evening light, Chad opened the door to get in. He glimpsed Cynthia approaching her car. Pausing, he tried to think of something to say. He was really not ready to go home and he wanted to be with Cynthia. He wanted to hear what she had to say about the day's events; he wanted to watch her as she talked. It was crazy, but he just wanted to be near her.

"You did a great job before America this afternoon," began Chad, leaning on his open door.

Approaching, she smiled, her face revealing the stress of the day. "Thanks, you didn't do too badly yourself."

"I'm tired out from this long day, but thought I'd go get something to eat and have a drink before going home. You interested?" Trying to be passive about it, Chad held his breath, fearing she was going to say no.

"I'm really tired, Chad. It has been a long day and this heat has drained me." Even as she said this she could see a trace of disappointment in the well-concealed smile he presented.

"Just thought you might want something before going home; but you're right, it has been a long day."

Cynthia stood looking at Chad as he tried to make it sound as if it were no big deal. She sensed that it was a big deal to him, and despite the fact that she was very tired, she wanted to be with him also. She had discovered earlier he was not the pompous bore he appeared to be in a crowd. He was thoughtful and caring. He had sat through lunch and listened to her tell about her life. He sat and listened, offering no judgment. For the first time in a long time, she felt a connection to someone. Strangely, she hardly knew him, but in one day things had changed so much. She had told this relative stranger her personal secrets and she felt the need to talk about the unbelievable events that had come to pass. And, she wanted to talk about them with Chad.

"You know, I am hungry and the drink sounds nice. Where do you wanna go?" asked Cynthia as she opened her car door.

"Great," said Chad with a smile that spread across his entire face. *He really does have a beautiful smile and is quite good looking,* thought Cynthia. It made her feel better to see him smile with his boyish openness.

"Meet you at the King's Tavern?"

"Sounds like a plan," answered Cynthia.

"Okay, I'll be there in a couple of minutes," Chad replied, climbing into his car. *Anticipation of spending more time with Cynthia, dispelled his earlier disappointment.*

Joseph Turbon sat staring at the television in his cheap motel room. He had been watching the story of the *angels* in this one-horse town unfold all day. The story and the images of the *angels* convinced Joseph that he had been right. He was now sure his reading and his interpretations of the scripture in the Bible were correct. *The end was near!* Didn't this sudden appearance of the *angels* prove it?

Joseph Turbon was thirty-eight years old. Having fallen from one job to another since he was a teenager; he had never found his place in life. Joseph had married and now had three children. Even with a family, he had not found stability. Finally, Joseph discovered God in a small church near his home and embraced religion with his whole being. Unfortunately, he began to fall outside the teachings in his small, non-denominational church and left it after an angry confrontation with the minister over Joseph's view of God's plan for the world and its inhabitants. It was then he moved to rural Slobee, Arkansas, and began his own church with his own style of preaching, which, in part, was based on an angry message about the vengeance of God. For several years Turbon preached the "end of time" and the "return of God" to take his people home. In the *Born Again Church of the Setting Sun,* Joseph Turbon preached to a small congregation regarding his vision of God and the last days. In this rural setting of Slobee, he felt his message often got lost among people who did not understand or appreciate his leadership through God's word. But, now, things were changing. With the appearance of the *angels,* he just had to go to Dunning to assume his role in this final "end of the ages."

In a sense, the events happening in Dunning were a vindication of Turbon's hard work and his wife and children abandoning him because he refused to support them. The only money he earned was the paltry sum he received passing the plate in his church services. His extended family even turned away from him, convinced he was mentally unbalanced and was, without a doubt, indisputably radical in his views. Joseph was convinced that God was directing him to "usher in" the earth's final days. Partly because of his radicalism and extreme views outside of the norm, he had been alone for the past three years except for just a small and dwindling following in his church. Packing his meager belongings into his faded blue 1985 Chevy truck after hearing about the *angels,* he was on his way South to Dunning, Alabama, by eight o'clock that night. Driving all night, Joseph arrived by midmorning.

Turbon wasn't the only evangelical minister seeing his interpretations of the "end times" taking place with the visions appearing in St. Michael's. By morning, several ministers including some nationally-known televangelists were making preparations to travel to Dunning. The presence of such prophetic ministers could possibly serve as a spring board for other such extremists interpreting the *angels* as being a sign from God that "The Church Age" was ending. Each came with his own mission as to how preparations should be made for the END according to each one's own interpretation of the Bible. William Renfro was one such evangelist moving into action.

Speaking out on his televised *Southwest Evangelical Ministries* from Austin, Texas, he called for a day of repentance and preparation for the beginning of the "end times." According to Renfro, the last trumpet was getting ready to sound. With national attention given to the images in St. Michael's, churches around the national began offering varying views as to what these sightings meant. St. Michael's continued receiving phone calls from all around the country, so many, in fact, Thomas Johnson finally gave up trying to answer all the calls and let the phone ring.

At seven-fifteen PM, after a very long and exciting day, Thomas walked from his office, back down the hallway to the sanctuary. The policeman on duty at the door had changed again since Thomas last walked through the hallway. He quietly spoke to the young officer.

"I appreciate the work that all of you are doing for us, Officer," as he squinted to read the name plate in the dark hall, "Williams," he added.

"That's okay, Reverend, it's an honor to stand here," the young officer replied.

"Have you looked inside at our visitors?" Johnson questioned.

"Yes sir. When I first came on duty, Officer Kimbell had me go take a look."

"What do you think, young man?" questioned the minister.

"Reverend, my dad is a minister, like you. All my life, I grew up believing, so I really wasn't surprised. Maybe inspired, or amazed, would better explain the feelings I had when I saw them." Shaking his head he added, "I've always believed in *angels*, Sir, but never thought I'd see one in this lifetime."

Reverend Johnson smiled at the young man. *This was just another example of faith*, he thought. *This is what faith is all about, accepting, but not trying to explain too closely why you believe something because it's too big for you. Until now this is kind of the way we have always viewed God and heaven, not truly understanding the how and why about God, but believing that God is always here. But now, all of a sudden, we can see a glimpse of God through this tear in time, or whatever one might call it. Thomas did not understand and he certainly wasn't going to try to explain something he did not understand. God was much too great and complex to try to comprehend, much less explain.*

"Let's have another look in there, Officer Williams," said Thomas.

The young officer opened the door and they both looked upward into the rafters. As earlier, nothing had changed. There they were! Both men stood, marveling at the sight. While Thomas had been in to look at this scene several times already, he still was unable to fully accept the magnificence of the sight. Once again, he stood with the young officer, gazing upward and just as before, he could not help but be awed by the images above him. Here was truly an image of God!

Afterwards, Thomas Johnson and Officer Williams walked out of the little church. No security would stay in the building at night, only around it. After wishing all of the officers around him a good evening, Thomas walked to his car, unnoticed by the reporters who had settled in for the evening, and drove home, leaving the now silent church to the *angels*!

As night closed in and the sun slid behind the trees, lights started coming on inside the houses along Everwine Street. The police presence remained discretely outside and around the church property. The number of people watching from across the street decreased somewhat, but a faithful few remained even as activity around the church diminished. Television trucks from all of the networks were parked side by side filling up the parking lot, with the exception of reserved parking. Lights were burning in and around the trucks, but all that could be heard in the growing darkness was the hum of the generators for the mobile units. The little church was now completely dark except for a pale, unworldly light coming through the stained glass window of the sanctuary and reflecting on the trees outside.

It had been an amazing day! The most amazing day Dunning, Alabama, had ever seen, or would probably ever see again!

Thomas Johnson drove to his house on nearby Wenting Street. Turning into the driveway, he felt the tiredness of the day hanging heavily on him. Getting out of his car, he walked with his coat over his arm, up the back steps, to the kitchen door, and inside.

"Elizabeth, I'm home."

"Okay, honey," was his wife's reply from the living room.

Walking through the kitchen he hardly noticed dinner was on the stove. Moving into the living room where Elizabeth sat watching television, Thomas laid his coat on the back of the couch. On the screen was a special news bulletin about the *angels*. Elizabeth looked up as Thomas leaned down and kissed his wife on the forehead. Standing there behind the couch, he put one hand on her shoulder and she placed a hand on his.

"This is so unbelievable," Elizabeth began, barely above a whisper. "When you called earlier, I didn't know what to think."

"I know. It sounds so crazy," Thomas said, looking at the pictures from his church on the TV screen. "Tomorrow, you will have to see for yourself."

"Thomas, why have they appeared in our church?" questioned Elizabeth, voicing the same question that seemed to be on everyone's mind.

"I have no idea, Elizabeth. I wonder why we can even see them at all. I have no explanation for any of this."

Elizabeth knew her husband very well. He was not the type of minister who tried to read in between the lines as to what he felt God wanted him to say. He never viewed himself as a "mover or shaker" in the church, just simply a servant of God, who felt that it was his task to enlighten people about God and his Son, Jesus, the Holy Spirit, and eternal salvation. He put into practice God's message of love, compassion, forgiveness, and help for the needy. Thomas never tried to put words into God's mouth.

Elizabeth saw Thomas as a quiet, simple, caring man. If he was happy with his little church and trying to do his part to battle against the evils of society in his community, to spread the love of God, that was enough for her. She was proud of him. Honest and humble, he sought no call to a larger church with more prestige or money. In addition to his service as a minister, Thomas Johnson was also a serious religious scholar. From boyhood he had read and studied all he could. His interests included history and science, as well as theology. Deciding on a career as a young man, Thomas had been pulled between following the ministry and his love of astronomy.

Even after his decision to choose to follow God's direction and going into the ministry, he still enjoyed the study of astronomy. The vastness of the universe and the wonderment of God never failed to inspire or awe Thomas. He often shook his head in disbelief at all the anger and narrow-mindedness of people who sought to impress their own views of God upon others. Thomas believed the God he prayed to daily and sought for constant guidance was so much bigger than just this little planet that he and the rest of mankind resided on. He was careful when trying to express his view of God to his congregation. After all, God was creator of the universe and not just earth. Oftentimes, people failed to understand that man must look beyond this tiny speck in His creation. If God created all of this, then, how could He be concerned with just the earth? Thomas had no patience with the petty arguments that had existed between religious groups throughout history and on into modern times.

"What will happen tomorrow?" asked Elizabeth.

"Tomorrow we will start allowing people into the church to see the *angels*," said Thomas, still looking at the TV screen. "We'll go down early so you can see them."

Elizabeth stood up and said, "Come on honey, I'll get your dinner." As they walked into the kitchen, Elizabeth added, "I'm not sure I am ready to see them. Not yet."

Chad pulled into one of the few open parking spaces in the parking lot in front of the King's Tavern. Turning his ignition key to the off position, he waited for Cynthia to arrive. It was dark, but the dark and the quiet felt good. He sat, putting his head back against the headrest, enjoying the coolness of the car's air-conditioning before it faded into the summer evening's heat. As he waited in silence, Cynthia's headlights appeared in his rearview mirror and her car pulled up beside his. He smiled to himself, thinking how happy he was at that very moment. Even tired and drained from the day's amazing events, he was happy. The fact that his relationship with Cynthia had changed was one of the reasons. But, seeing the *angels* in the chapel had taken away any cynical attitude Chad had developed over the years of working with people who most often disappointed him. He had seen it all—corrupt politicians, petty criminals, sad domestic and family disputes, business people who didn't mind cheating their customers to make a dollar! His cynicism now seemed replaced with a sense of hope, *hope* in the future and *hope* in people.

Chad quickly got out of his car to open Cynthia's door.

"Hello, again," Chad said as he waited for Cynthia to exit her car.

Getting out quickly, she answered with a tired smile, "Hi."

Walking into the building, the cool air from the overhead fan felt refreshing compared to the heat of the early evening. Summer's heat and humidity in South Alabama could be horrendous.

Inside, they were seated in a large, wrap-around booth which could actually accommodate a larger party. A young, red-haired woman smiled as she seated them, recognizing them from television. *It is nice to be recognized as a celebrity of sorts,* thought Chad as they settled into the booth.

The restaurant had been there for many years and in keeping with its theme, was decorated in a dark paneling with wrought iron lighting fixtures displaying gas lights. Paintings of the English countryside decorated the dark room. The décor gave the room a cozy, relaxed atmosphere and the quiet booth provided an ambiance that could not have been more perfect.

"May I get you something from the bar?" a young waiter inquired.

"You surely can. I'll have a draft beer, thanks, and the lady will have. . . ." said Chad, pausing as he looked at Cynthia for her to complete the order.

"I'll have a glass of white wine, please," she added.

As the waiter turned away to get their drinks, Chad said, "Well, it has been a day. The most unbelievable day ever!"

Smiling and nodding her head in agreement, Cynthia said, "You're absolutely right. There's no other way to put it. I'm still not sure that I totally comprehend all that has transpired today. And, I can't believe that you and I were seen across the country on every television network! Can you believe that?" she added with a burst of excitement.

While sitting there other parties continually entered the room.

"Looks like we were just ahead of the crowd," remarked Chad, observing a group now drifting in. "Hey, isn't that Robert Wood, with CNN?" he continued.

"It is! And, look who's with him!" declared Cynthia. "It's Bob Silver with ABC News!"

"So it is. Wonder who else we'll see in here?" mumbled Chad.

By this time, their drinks had arrived and the waiter had taken their order. Chad was just beginning to tell Cynthia how much he had enjoyed working with her when they were abruptly interrupted.

"Excuse me, I'm Robert Wood, and I saw your broadcast on television this morning."

"Thanks," replied Chad looking up. "We certainly know who you are, Mr. Wood. I'm Chad Simmons and this is Cynthia Davis."

"Thanks, and I know who you are. You did a great job this morning with the story." Pausing, and showing a somewhat mischievous smile, Robert Wood added, "And, it looks as if you two will have the exclusive role in bringing this story "live" to all of America. To be perfectly honest, I guess we are all a little jealous of that." Then, he added lightheartedly, "But, those are the breaks in this business."

"Please sit with us, Mr. Wood," said Chad, motioning him to sit, as he slid around closer to Cynthia.

Both Chad and Cynthia were flattered that Wood had come over to their table and had recognized them from their reports. Chad liked Wood immediately. He was not a self-serving *prima donna,* but a genuine, down-to-earth guy. He had been in the news business for years and was as professional as they come. Chad remembered Wood's reporting when he was a teenager and now he was sitting at their table!

"May I butt in, please?" Their party was interrupted by another voice.

It was Bob Silver now standing beside their table.

Wood rolled his eyes in mock agitation as he slid over to make room for Silver.

Extending his hand, first to Cynthia and then to Chad, he said, "I'm Bob Silver."

"I'm sure they know who you are, Bob," joked Wood. "They guessed I had to bring you along, since you have no friends or crew who'd go out with you!" Wood's good-natured barb drew laughter from the others.

After a few general comments about Dunning and the uncomfortable weather of South Alabama, Silver took on a more serious tone.

"You know," posed Silver, "This story has the potential of being the biggest story that any of us have ever been, or will be, a party to. A story like this would have been nothing more than just a human interest story in the past, but with all the national attention and news coverage, and the fact we have live coverage of these........these *angelic* visitors, all the mumbo-jumbo stuff goes out the window. We have to address the *reality* of these *angels,* not just from a religious perspective, but from the fact that here they *are!*" Silver addressed the group.

"Exactly," said Wood. "The obvious question is not only why they are here, but subsequently, what impacts will this have on the religious views and beliefs of all our societies. Will we go on fighting about who is right and who is wrong?"

Chad shrugged before saying, "I'm not equipped to answer those questions. In fact, just thinking about all this makes my head ache."

They all nodded in agreement.

"What else can be said? I saw them; Cynthia saw them. They are real," added Chad.

"By tomorrow these *angels* will become even more of an enigma when people are allowed to visit St. Michael's," Cynthia observed.

The group continued talking through dinner after Wood and Silver accepted the invitation to join Chad and Cynthia at their table. It turned out to be a memorable evening for both Chad and Cynthia, dining with two of the best known reporters in America. The night could not have gone better with each feeling they had arrived and were now a part of a national news reporting league, not just small-town television. Truly, they had been thrown from small-town America into the national news spotlight and facing the realization of never being the same again. The evening flew by with abundant conversation. As it grew later and the activity in the restaurant began to slow, Wood and Silver stood to leave.

"Thanks for sharing your evening with us," said Wood.

"It was all our pleasure," Chad replied as Cynthia smiled in agreement.

"I'm sure that we'll have a lot to talk about in the coming days," added Silver as they exchanged parting handshakes.

After Wood and Silver left the restaurant, Chad and Cynthia sat alone in the booth. It was now quiet with only a few late diners left.

"This has been a pretty amazing day," Chad said, looking at Cynthia. The dim light with the glow of the candle on the table made her even more beautiful. Her dark eyes reflected the light from the candle. Chad did not want the moment to come to an end. He didn't want it to ever end.

"I wonder what will happen tomorrow." Cynthia said quizzically. Looking down, she seemed lost in thought before looking at Chad again. "You know, for a very long time I have been fooling myself. Now, I don't feel that way. I feel different, almost as if I were reborn this morning. I feel that life has purpose again and that we are a part of a plan that is so much bigger than any of us can ever begin to imagine."

Chad studied Cynthia before speaking. "I think you're right. In reality, we have so little control over our lives. Things happen that we are never able to explain, nor do we understand how they happen. Like today, the *angels,* and now, the two of us sitting here talking like this."

Looking around the quiet room, Chad finally murmured, "I guess we'd better go. Looks like we've just about closed this place down." He could see that Cynthia was drained from the long day and knew that tomorrow would be just as long and busy as this day had been.

"Yeah, I guess so," nodded Cynthia. "I'm very tired."

Paying the bill with his credit card, they walked from the building toward their cars. Chad walked Cynthia to her car and waited as she unlocked it.

"Thanks for the evening. I really enjoyed it," said Cynthia. "And thanks for listening to me earlier today when I unloaded my previous life on you."

"No, don't thank me. I should be thanking you. I felt……very privileged for you to talk about yourself with me."

Chad continued, "Besides, I think today's events have forever changed both of us."

"Good night, Chad," said Cynthia, opening her car door.

Before getting into her car, she suddenly learned over and kissed him lightly on the cheek. After getting into the car, closing the door, and turning the ignition key, Cynthia put down the window and with a serious and thoughtful look said, "Thanks." Putting her car into gear, she drove out of the parking lot.

"Good night," Chad said aloud to no one in particular. He stood there and watched the tail lights of her car disappear. That simple, "thank you for listening kiss" lingered on Chad's face as he got into his car and floated rather than drove home.

Across town, residents along Everwine Street peered out their windows upon hearing noisy rumbling trucks. The sounds they were hearing on the darkened street belonged to that of a convoy of Alabama National Guard trucks rumbling into town bringing the promised support for Dunning.

8

Tuesday morning dawned just as hot as Monday had been. Chad got up early anticipating another busy day and after his usual shower and shave, put on his best looking shirt and tie. He wolfed down a bowl of cereal, along with two cups of coffee, while watching the news on the television in his apartment. WTLA morning news was showing clips from yesterday's broadcast by Cynthia and him. When the camera switched to a live feed from the mobile unit at St. Michael's, Chad stopped eating and stared as the camera panned from the front of the small church down the street. He was astounded by the staggering crowd that had already formed in front of the church so early in the morning. The crowd extended as far as one could see. Not only was a large police presence there, but they were joined by national guardsmen who stood along the street and churchyard as well. It was barely seven o'clock AM.

His phone ringing drew Chad away from the television. Putting down his cereal bowl, he answered the phone, "Hello, this is Chad."

"Chad, it's me, Cynthia."

She didn't have to tell him who she was; he could never forget her voice.

Smiling into the phone, Chad said, "Hi. You're up early."

A laugh from her made him smile again.

"Actually, I've been up since five. Is your TV on?"

"As a matter of fact, yes. Have you seen the crowd at the church this morning?" Chad asked.

"Yes, and have you seen CNN this morning?" Cynthia questioned.

"Our story and interview is the lead story on the morning news. One of the news anchors hinted that the President may even come to Dunning to see the *angels*. Can you believe it?"

"I have a sneaky feeling that he is just one of the many dignitaries that is going to show up in Dunning," Chad quipped; then asked, "When do you plan to drive to the church?"

"I was thinking about leaving in just a few minutes. What about you?" Cynthia questioned.

"Same here. I'll meet you there in half an hour, if you like," said Chad. "Better make that forty-five minutes to an hour. There's no telling how long it will take to get through all the traffic, which I can only imagine is going to be terribly congested."

"Good, I'll see you there shortly. Bye," she said before hanging up.

Chad ended the connection and stood for a moment holding the receiver of the phone. A pleasant warmth spread all over him just hearing her voice on the phone. Hanging up the phone, he smiled again. He felt like he was sixteen again when talking to Cynthia. It was astonishing how today this woman could make him feel so alive and just a few days ago she would barely give him the time of day. He simply could not get enough of just hearing her voice.

In the process of Chad getting his coat and looking for his keys and cell phone, the scene across town was really livening up at St. Michael's. Not only were the crowds of people enormous, there were also small groups of people at various places holding signs, some of which read, THE END IS NEAR and GOD WILL PUNISH. A scuffle had taken place as a man tried to set up a small public address system across from the church to preach to the people waiting in line. This self-appointed preacher put up a struggle with the cops and had been arrested and removed screaming that *"God had sent him to precede God's appearance."*

Unfortunately, the *angels* at St. Michael's brought out not only just the curious who wanted to know what was going on, but fanatics as well, who truly believed that God was directing them and those who followed them to carry out His plan. One such fanatic was Joseph Turbon.

Arriving in Dunning, Turbon experienced no difficulty finding St. Michael's Church. All a person had to do was follow the crowds of people who continually gathered in the vicinity of the church. No parking was to be found anywhere near Everwine Street and Turbon was forced to park many blocks from the church. Parking his old truck, he got out and followed the crowd of people who, like himself, wanted to see this reported miracle. He was only able to get close enough to see the steeple of the little white church because of so many people already there. Turbon stood in the crowd for several hours before deciding to leave and come back later.

Chad turned his WTLA car into the line of cars in front of the police road block and waited a couple of minutes. As cars were turned aside one after the other, forbidden to travel down Everwine, he finally approached one of the policemen at the road block. Fortunately, the young officer recognized the car and Chad.

"Morning," he said to Chad.

"Hi, looks kind of busy here," responded Chad.

"Beats anything I've ever seen," said the young cop. "You can pass through, but watch for people darting across the street. They built a shelter last night for those waiting to see the *angels*. Took them all night, but the city got it finished. Maybe it will at least help prevent heat strokes as people wait to get into the church."

"You got that right," Chad smiled to the officer. "What is it, about eighty-five degrees already, and it's barely eight o'clock?"

"Something like that," said the officer motioning Chad through.

Chad shook his head in amazement at the mass of people filling the sidewalk, waiting to get a chance to get close to the church. It was truly unbelievable. Thanks to his very visibly marked WTLA car, he had no trouble getting down the street and into the parking lot at St. Michael's. As the young officer said, a covered walkway had appeared overnight. It was simply made of tall wooden posts and metal roofing with yellow police tape serving as a barrier to help prevent line breakers. The walkway extended at least two blocks alongside the parking lot of the church and was filled with people already. Policemen and national guardsmen lined up by the covering in an effort to keep order among the people. At the walkway's beginning, people waited patiently in the long line.

Driving to the church, Chad received a call from Jim Stuart telling him that he and Cynthia would carry a live broadcast on all networks as soon as the church was opened to the public. He was also informed that the line of people waiting to see the *angels* would be tightly monitored; no one would be allowed to stop or enter the sanctuary, just slowly and silently walk past, viewing the *angels* from the open double doorway. This would enable a slow, but continuous flow of people all day and into the evening.

As Chad parked and got out of his car, he noticed Cynthia's car already there. She was sitting under an awning beside the WDDR mobile truck with a portable air conditioner blowing. Approaching the awning, she smiled and motioned for him to come and sit in the cool breeze of the air conditioner. Her smile brought an instant smile from him.

"Ready to begin again?" asked Cynthia.

"Sure. It looks as if this is going to be quite a day," said Chad, glancing back at the crowd.

"Before we open the church for "silent tours," which, by the way, is what the tours are being called, Reverend Johnson and Mayor Smith are going to accompany the first tour of reporters. Our friends, Wood and Silver, are on this tour," said Cynthia. "Bob called a little while ago to confirm it."

"Great idea! There is no way that you or I could explain what we saw in that sanctuary, Cynthia. But, as people begin to see these images, it's going to have a tremendous impact," replied Chad.

"Morning!" came a voice from across the parking lot. Looking up, Cynthia and Chad saw Bob Silver and Robert Wood walking toward them looking unquestionably the part of national reporters with their spotlessly neat appearances.

"Everyone ready to go?" asked Chad.

"You bet," said Wood, flashing his movie star smile.

The four of them walked toward the church, ahead of the growing group of reporters from not only the United States, but from several locations outside the country. Approaching the group, the Mayor was just about to introduce the Reverend

Johnson and Doris Williams to the reporters. Cameras were recording live feeds as he began the introductions.

"Good morning! We are presently directing the news media through St. Michael's ahead of the public tours so that our television reporters may witness firsthand what we have been talking about and better enable them to relate to viewers what we are seeing here. We have with us Reverend Thomas Johnson and Mrs. Doris Williams who were the first to see the angels. Also with us are Chief of Police, Bill Tyler, and our local television news team, Cynthia Davis and Chad Simmons, who first reported the news about these visitors."

"Ladies and gentlemen, without further delay, let's continue inside."

As the cameras continued to filming from the outside, the collection of news media was moving toward the side door of the church. A quiet tension fell over the group as they entered the darkened hallway from the bright sunlight outside. Just as the day before, the church was kept dark and quiet. The sound of shuffling feet on the carpet and the low hum of the air conditioner were the only sounds that disturbed the quiet in the little church.

The group walked toward the doors of the sanctuary, stopping briefly for eyes to adjust to the darkness of the inside. Chad noticed that the hall was lined with a row of policemen standing quietly on duty, as well as the two who were placed at the open doors of the sanctuary. Theater rope barriers blocked the entrance into the sanctuary. WTLA and WDDR cameras were positioned one pointing down the hall, and one pointing upward into the sanctuary rafters.

Doris Williams and Reverend Johnson led the group as they slowly moved down the hallway. They were followed by the Mayor, the Chief, Chad, Cynthia, and a few other reporters and news personnel making up the first group. Standing in the doorway again and looking upward, Chad and Cynthia saw the unmistakable images of the *angels* as brilliant as ever and perhaps even more shimmery. They were in the same position as the day before. Gazing upward, Chad could sense Cynthia beside him. He felt her hand reach to take hold of his and squeeze it tightly. The sight of the *angels* and her touch created a feeling of electricity in Chad like nothing he had ever felt before. He was hoping Cynthia felt the sensation too! Reporters walking into the doorway were struck with the same awe and utter disbelief that had affected the others the day before. They stood frozen, simply unable to make sense of what they were seeing. Moving away from the sanctuary, there was no sound at all from the group, only the padded sound of feet on the carpet and the droning of the AC unit.

From the sanctuary, down the hallway and out the door, they walked. The camera crews were waiting outside. They captured the faces of the reporters as they came into the daylight. People watching television across the nation must have been enthralled by their faces. Some looked bewildered, others shaken, and still others had tears in their eyes. One woman had broken down and was crying quietly, comforted by one her fellow reporters. Obviously, all had witnessed something that went beyond each one's understanding. The scene could not have been more dramatic if it had been staged for television.

As they moved away from the door and around to the parked mobile television units, the police began to direct those waiting in line toward the little church. Slowly the line of people began to snake its way along under the covered walkway toward the sanctuary of the church. The line stretched from the parking lot, down the sidewalk, and out of sight. There were hundreds of people waiting to see the reported visions of St. Michael's. Television cameras captured everything. People everywhere viewed the images of the church, the lines of people, the police, and the guardsmen. The scene outside St. Michael's was beginning to look surreal, almost like a story from long ago about God and his involvement with mankind through the stories of the Bible.

The first group of reporters having access to the sanctuary moved around the satellite trucks with their equipment and generators, going to their various locations to report with each one's respective networks. Wood and Silver stayed with Chad and Cynthia. After the other reporters had gone, Robert Wood looked at Chad and Cynthia and then at Bob Silver and commented, "I'm not sure what I just saw. I can't even begin trying to explain it; but, I do believe that none of us will ever again be a part of anything of this magnitude."

Obviously, Wood had been shaken by what he'd seen.

"Didn't we tell you that you had to see it for yourselves?" Chad reminded Wood.

"Yeah, but . . ." Wood's voice trailed off for lack of words to express his thoughts.

Bob Silver then spoke up. "Whatever we witnessed, it is our journalistic duty to try to convey it to our audiences. As Robert said, this is the biggest story of our careers and probably our lifetime. Who knows maybe even since ancient times!"

"I understand now," said Robert. "Not until I saw it for myself. But, now I understand. Come on guys, let's get to work and make sure this story is the biggest that has ever been."

Wood and Silver walked away to their own individual units to make live broadcasts as the others were doing. Their departure left Chad and Cynthia alone. Cynthia turned to Chad, "Okay, I guess you and I need to go and do our live spots now. The Mayor is scheduled to be here to speak with us before interviewing with the other stations."

They walked to the awning between the mobile trucks of WTLA and WDDR. Sitting in two directors' chairs, they began making preparations for a live broadcast complete with film footage of this most recent tour and live shots of people making their pilgrimages through the church to see the *angels*. The cameraman held up his hand to signal the beginning of the broadcast. Counting down with his fingers, he pointed to them.

"Good morning from Dunning, Alabama. I'm Cynthia Davis."

"And I'm Chad Simmons."

Cynthia continued, "This morning at St. Michael's AME Church visitors were allowed for the first time to see firsthand the *divine beings* earlier witnessed and reported in this small church. As you can see on your television screens, the throngs of people coming to see the *angels* are tremendous."

Then Chad spoke, "The line to enter the church extends as far as one can see. Within days Dunning is expecting to have hundreds, maybe thousands of visitors. From what we are told, all hotels within a hundred mile radius are completely booked. Sources tell us the city is opening facilities usually reserved as hurricane accommodations to provide sleeping for many of these visitors, if needed."

The camera focused on Cynthia again. "We have with us this morning the Mayor of Dunning, Mr. Allan Smith."

Smith, who had come to the interview only moments earlier, positioned himself into the view of the camera, sitting next to Cynthia.

"Mr. Mayor, thank you for speaking with us this morning. I'm sure you have been overwhelmed with interviews by all of the media."

"Thank you for having me, Cynthia," began Allan. "Yes, it is proving to be a busy morning. Crowd control and traffic jams downtown and around the city are a major problem and it has been necessary to put police officers at most prime intersections to manage the traffic. Dunning has never before had to deal with anything like this. As you can see, we have quite a large unit of the Alabama National Guard assisting the local Dunning Police Department, and I might add that there is also a large Alabama State Trooper contingency in and around Dunning as well."

"Mr. Mayor," Chad interjected, "In addition to crowd control and traffic, has the city made any preparations for dealing with health or heat-related emergencies?"

"Yes, we have, Chad. Working overnight, the city crews constructed a covered walkway to protect people from the heat and sun. Many people making their way to see the *angels* of Dunning are not prepared for 95 to 98-degree temperatures with relative high humidity readings. Not being familiar with this type of weather, there is always the risk of sun or heat stroke and we are prepared to deal with any such emergency. We have fire and rescue units standing by."

Cynthia spoke again, "If the camera will now turn and face the street, you will see several ambulances and EMTs standing by for such possibilities."

Across the street a row of white ambulances, marked with blue and orange stripes, was parked with attendants standing outside in a group, talking with policemen. Everything appeared calm and orderly.

Mayor Smith continued, "We hope we have everything covered, but there is always the unseen likelihood of an unexpected emergency."

"Mr. Mayor, it certainly looks as if Dunning has planned well to deal with all that is going on at present," added Cynthia.

"I certainly hope so, but we will just have to wait and see what the following days bring," continued the Mayor.

Cynthia, ending her interview with the Mayor, "Thank you for speaking with us today and we will speak with you again as our story further develops.

—⁓—

At CNN Headquarters in Atlanta, the phone rang in Tom Weatherman's office. Looking up from studying the papers in front of him, Tom answered the phone.

"Yes, this is Tom," he answered, pausing to concentrate on the call. "Of course, Muhammad, it's very good to hear from you. How is the Kingdom of Saudi Arabia?"

For a few moments Tom Weatherman and Muhammad Harassi exchanged pleasantries and answered questions about each other and what each had been doing. It had been almost six months since Weatherman had heard from Harassi. They first become acquainted during the days of the Gulf War when Saddam Hussein had launched his attacks and threatened Saudi Arabia. They discovered they had similar interests and had become close friends during those days of the Gulf War.

Following the war, Weatherman made several trips to Saudi Arabia and had produced a number of documentaries on Harassi's desert kingdom. The documentaries all treated Saudi Arabia with an air of fair optimism and Harassi's kingdom had not been depicted negatively in any way. Weatherman had been very careful not to offend, while at the same time painting an accurate picture of this conservative nation, influenced strongly by its historical Islamic beliefs. An understanding and mutual respect had developed between the two men. On several occasions they collaborated with each other on projects relating to their work.

Finally, Weatherman asked the question, "Muhammad, how can I help you?" which opened the door to Muhammad's call.

"Actually, I saw the CNN report last night on the very interesting and perplexing article about the *"angel sightings"* being reported in your state of Alabama." Muhammad continued, "It appears that it has become a major story in the United States and across Europe. Do you validate this story as authentic, or is it some sort of hoax just to gain publicity?"

"Muhammad," Weatherman began, "From all appearances, it is an accurate story. I'm planning to fly to Dunning in the next couple of days to see for myself. In fact, as we speak, Robert Wood is broadcasting from Dunning after his recent tour through the church where the sightings have taken place. From his reports, he is convinced that the *angels* are real. Muhammad, highly respected members of the community have also validated the authenticity of these beings. I'm quite certain the *angels*, or whatever you choose to call them, must be real from everything I hear from all the people who have actually witnessed the *angels.*"

"Tom, what would be the chances of your waiting until I can get to Atlanta and going with you to see these *angels*?" Muhammad asked.

"How soon can you be here?" Tom replied.

"I can leave today and be in Atlanta in the morning," answered Muhammad.

"Sounds good." I'll arrange flights for us and wait for your call when you arrive." Tom added, "Call from the airport and I'll meet you there."

Tom and Muhammad exchanged goodbyes and hung up.

Once the call was over, Tom Weatherman sat for a few minutes thinking about their conversation. He wondered why Muhammad had expressed such an interest in this story of the *angels*. The subject of religion had to be handled carefully, especially when the views about religion in a conservative nation were so explosive. While the same *God* was worshiped by Jews,

Christians, and Muslims, there were distinct differences in each group's own doctrine with regard to *God*.

Could there possibly be a chance of a shift in the understanding of God between the opposing beliefs of Islam and Christianity because of this story in Dunning? Could this appearance of the unearthly beings initiate a chance to bridge a divide that had existed for over a thousand years? There seemed to be more questions than answers for Tom. He would have to wait to hear from Muhammad regarding his reactions to the *angels* as the story continued to develop.

Muhammad dialed the number of Ismael Hadi. The phone rang twice.

"Ismael, this is Muhammad. I just completed a conversation with Tom Weatherman of CNN in America. He tells me that from all appearances, the sightings of the *angels* are real. He is traveling to the church site in Dunning, Alabama, to see for himself. Fortunately, he said that he would wait for me to travel with him. By doing so, I should be able to see for myself and come back with information that might be important in deciphering all of this. With Tom, I should not draw attention."

"Good, Muhammad," said Ismael. "If these sightings are real, it could pose some very serious questions, questions we will have to examine. Go ahead, make reservations, and leave as soon as possible, Muhammad. I will talk with you as soon as you have any information and are able to call me. Thank you. Go with *Allah*."

Hanging up the phone, Ismael looked out the window; much of the bright light of the afternoon was muted by retractable blinds covering the windows. However, it was still evident the city was busy and noisy by the sound of cars. It could have been a city anywhere in the world except for the figures walking outside, women covered from head to foot in long dark robes accompanied by men in western dress, or others in traditional long white robes. Many questions came to mind now, questions that Ismael did not want to entertain until he heard from Muhammad. Sitting back in his chair, he said to himself, "We'll have to wait to see what *Allah* gives us."

9

Following his interview, Allan Smith walked to his car and prepared to return to City Hall. Promptly, he received a call on his cell phone from his secretary, Lucy, who relayed a message to call Michael Stern as soon as possible. Wondering to himself what this was about, he got into his car, switched on the ignition, and turned the air-conditioning control on high before locating and calling the number that Stern had given him the previous day.

"Michael Stern," was the answer on the other end of the line.

"Mr. Stern, this is Allan Smith. I have just received your message. I'm sorry that I missed your call earlier. How may I be of assistance?"

"Yes, Mayor Smith, I was just watching you on television. Things are looking pretty busy down there," said Stern.

"Absolutely. I could safely say that I've never seen anything like this in my entire life. The crowds are growing steadily."

Pausing briefly, Stern then said, "Listen, Mayor Smith, the reason I called is that the President has had a number of calls from representatives of various governments wanting information about the church sightings. Since we have only the news at present to field these calls, the President thought it best that we send someone in this department to see these images. I'm planning to come to Dunning tomorrow afternoon just as soon as I can get there. Can I count on your help to participate in this endeavor without any undue attention? We don't want to make this trip into a major event, so discretion would be best at this time."

Allan answered, "I'll have someone waiting for you at the airport when you arrive, Mr. Stern. Have your office call my office with the details of your arrival as soon as you have completed your final plans. You may be certain this will all be kept completely quiet. Are there any other plans that I may assist you in making?"

"Thanks, but it will be a very quick trip there and back to D.C. The President is eager to see what this is all about."

Allan added, "Everything will be ready for your arrival tomorrow afternoon. I look forward to meeting with you."

"Great, and thanks for your help," Stern replied. "As I said, I appreciate your keeping this undisclosed for the time being. Goodbye."

"Goodbye," said Allan, disconnecting the call. Pulling out of the parking lot and turning onto Everwine, the mayor made his way back toward City Hall. While driving, he could not get over the huge crowds; either waiting to see the *angels* or standing across the street simply watching all that was going on. People of every age and in every imaginable walk of life were there to see this unbelievable sight.

Smith's mind was racing. *What was this really all about? Would Dunning ever be the same again?* It scared him to think about the impact this appearance of heavenly visitors could possibly have on their quiet town. *Would it turn Dunning into a New Jerusalem or Mecca? Only time would tell.*

Allan Smith was distracted from his thoughts by a commotion on the street. A scuffle had broken out between two men who were waiting in line. A tall, red-faced man became angry when a younger man tried to cut in front of him. The heat, plus the crowds, equaled a great potential for trouble, whether it was just differences in opinion as to the purpose of the visitors, or just the fact that nerves were easily frayed. Fortunately, a large police and National Guard contingency stopped the confrontation before it escalated into a real fight.

This is a prime example of what great potential there is for trouble when religious differences become involved, thought Allan. Picking up his phone again, he dialed his office.

"Lucy, get up with Chief Tyler and have him meet me when I get to the office. Yes, it's about Michael Stern. He is going to be in Dunning tomorrow afternoon and we need to have someone pick him up at the airport and bring him to my office when he arrives. And it has to be top secret."

He listened to Lucy for a moment then said, "What kind of visitor? He's there? Now?"

As usual, Lucy was thinking ahead, preparing him for a potentially delicate guest. She was already making plans for a smooth operation with the President's assistant as she dealt with this surprise visitor. It was people like Lucy who made his job easier and made him look good. He was glad that he had someone of her efficiency who was able to anticipate problems before they even happened. Lucy was an expert at multitasking and he would go so far as to say maybe even mind-reading.

Reaching city hall and entering the building, Allan walked to the elevator and went up to his second floor office. Pushing through the dark, wood-paneled door labeled **Mayor Allan**

Smith, he saw Lucy at her desk and a man sitting in a chair outside his office dressed in a dark suit, wearing expensive shoes, and a styled haircut that screamed "detail man." Before he could speak, the man was on his feet and offering his hand to Allan. His wrist sported an expensive watch and on his hand, a large diamond ring.

"Mayor Smith, I'm Reverend William Renfro."

Taking the extended hand Allan said, "It's a pleasure to meet you, Mr. Renfro. How can I assist you?"

"Mayor Smith, I'm sure you have seen our broadcasts on the SEM Network. I represent *Southwest Evangelical Ministries* in Austin, Texas, which is a very large organization of non-denominational churches across the Southwest and Midwestern United States," Renfro began, introducing himself.

"I think I'm familiar with your organization, Reverend Renfro," said Allan as he glanced over at Lucy, working at her desk. Lucy, cut a glance their way and rolled her eyes, acknowledging the direction in which the conversation was about to move. She, like Allan, could see something coming as Reverend Renfro moved forward with his pitch.

"Representing such a large following of citizens in the United States, I thought it would be proper to ask for your permission to set up a booth and on-site cameras just outside of St. Michael's Church. I also thought it would be proper to ask for a tour through the church with my cameras following the end of the public tours this evening."

There it was! Renfro was asking for a privileged role at St. Michael's. Allan knew if he granted his request, he would be in trouble with every other religious group that came to Dunning. Besides, St. Michael's was Thomas Johnson's church; furthermore, he didn't like Renfro's looks or his attitude with respect to seeking special privileges. There was something about this Renfro character that made Allan want to get up and go wash his hands.

"Reverend, as much as I would like to say *yes*," Allan started very diplomatically, "I have to say *no*." Without waiting for Renfro to object, Smith continued. "If I allowed you that privilege, then I would have to do the same for any and all groups who came to me, and that is simply impossible."

"But, don't you see, your allowing us to have close contact with this occurrence simply gives credence to the work of our ministry and our belief that God's kingdom is at hand?" argued Renfro. His voice detected that slight irritation of being told "no." He wasn't accustomed to that. Renfro continued, "Isn't there something that we can do to resolve this issue? Our organization is willing to pay for the privilege and the opportunity."

Allan now was becoming a little agitated with Renfro's slightly veiled attempt to buy special favor. Suppressing his desire to speak openly and bluntly with this man, Allan simply said, "I'm sorry. It just isn't possible. If there was anything else that I could do, I would be happy to try to make it work."

"Thank you, no. We really need to play a role in this miracle, but you don't seem to understand the importance of our request," Renfro replied.

Standing there for a few moments, neither man spoke.

Finally, Renfro spoke again. "Then, that's your last word on it, I suppose?"

"Yes sir, that's my last word," said Allan.

Extending his hand again to Allan, Renfro said, "Thank you. Goodbye." And, with a final nod, he was gone.

The door shut and Allan turned to Lucy. She looked at him and again rolled her eyes and turned back to her work. Allan didn't believe for one second this was the last he would hear from the Reverend Renfro.

Walking to his office, Allan heard Lucy's phone ring. "Mayor Smith's office, how may I help you? Yes sir, let me put you through."

Allan's extension rang. "Mayor, it's me. Lucy said I needed to call you as soon as possible. What's up?"

Allan instantly recognized the voice of Chief Bill Tyler. Sitting down behind his desk, Allan continued, "Hi, Bill. I've got another job for you. Tomorrow afternoon Special Assistant to the President, Michael Stern, is flying down to Dunning from Washington. It will be a short trip, just here and back again. I need someone to meet him at the airport and bring him to my office. Can you have someone ready to meet him?"

Tyler answered, "Sure. I should be able to meet him myself, unless something happens that I haven't planned for."

"Good, then bring him to my office as soon as he gets in," said Allan.

"Anything else at the moment?" questioned the Chief.

"Yes, Bill, we need to keep this visit from Stern completely quiet. And, let me say that you've done a great job with everything surrounding the *angels* at St. Michael's. Just thought I'd let you know."

"Thanks Mayor. It's been anything but dull. But, you know, I still find it hard to believe that they are actually here. I mean, why are they here, and why can we even see them?"

"I can't answer that Bill. It's like you said, they're here, period. Say, if you're not too tied up when Stern arrives, could you try to be here?"

"Okay. Talk with you later," said Bill, disconnecting the call.

Allan hung up his phone as well and leaned back in his chair. "Could it get any bigger?" he wondered aloud.

The phone rang again. "Mr. Mayor, it's the Governor on the line," said Lucy.

"Thanks Lucy, I'll take it." Answering with his most official greeting, "Governor Bayer, how are you, Sir?"

"Fine, Allan. And you?"

"Considering all the excitement here, pretty well. How may I help you Governor?"

"I'm planning to be in Dunning by the middle of the afternoon tomorrow. Could I possibly meet you at your office?"

Allan smiled to himself. "Actually, your timing is perfect, Sir. I'm expecting the Special Assistant to the President of the United States at about that time. It would be great if you could be in my office while he is here."

"I'm not surprised, Allan. You have a world-wide interest story developing very quickly." The Governor continued, "Oh, by the way, I had a call just a few moments ago from a Reverend William Renfro."

"Why am I not surprised?" responded Allan, with guarded sarcasm.

The Governor laughed. "I guess you're finding out there are other people who want a part of the action."

"Exactly, sir," laughed Allan.

"Well, I told him I had nothing to do with the *angels* in Dunning and that didn't seem to make him very happy." replied the Governor.

"I can imagine it didn't, Sir" Allan went on.

"Anything that I can do?" questioned Bayer.

"Thank you, Sir, but you've helped a lot already with the Guard, State Troopers, and our friend Reverend Renfro."

"Good enough, I'll be at your office around three then," responded the Governor.

"Thanks again, Governor, see you at three," added Allan.

Hanging up the phone Allan again thought about Renfro's visit, "You weasel, you tried to pull rank on me and go to the top. Now, there is no way that I'll let you take your agenda on the property. I'd let the King of the Dark Planet in first!" Allan muttered to no one in particular.

By mid-morning at St. Michael's, the line extended its way from the side door of the church, through the covered walkway, down the street, and out of sight. Crowds of people stood across the street watching the comings and goings of law enforcement and news crews just as they had for two days now. Cameras panned the whole scene for network television. Surprisingly, in the heat and bright sunshine, there had been only a few medical emergencies. Still, plenty of medical care was available, if needed. Mayor Smith and his staff had planned sufficiently in the short time they were allowed. One might have thought the President was coming, judging from the number of police and National Guardsmen present.

Following the morning broadcast and interviews, Cynthia and Chad were very busy. Between interviews of their own, they dealt with details for the evening news, which was to be broadcast from their mobile site using St. Michael's as a backdrop. Both Cynthia and Chad interviewed people standing in line providing human interest stories which would be broadcast in conjunction with their news reporting. There had been talk that the networks were making plans to have their prime time network news programs broadcast from Dunning.

As each newscaster walked along with a cameraman in tow, making intermittent stops for interviews, Chad kept his eyes on Cynthia. He watched her every move with enjoyment. Even in the heat she looked professional and gorgeous. Her slender form in heels and a suit moved along with ease and her bright smile contrasted beautifully with her long dark hair. Once, as he moved along the line watching Cynthia, she glanced in his direction and caught him looking at her. Embarrassed, he quickly turned away knowing she had seen him.

Stopping beside an old man in jeans, a plaid short-sleeved shirt, with his head shielded from the sun by a University of Georgia baseball cap, Chad quizzed, "Hi, I'm Chad Simmons with WTLA. May I ask you a couple of questions?"

The old fellow looked up at him, smiled and nodded saying in a low voice, "Sure. I ain't never been on TV before."

"Would you tell us your name?" asked Chad, putting the microphone in front of the older gentleman.

"Jim Bevis."

"And, where are you from, Jim?"

"I'm from just down the road a piece. Over in Blakely," replied the man.

"Jim, what is your reason for coming here today? After all, it's not the most comfortable place to be on a Tuesday morning." Chad wiped his brow with his hand. The late morning was humid and sticky.

"I guess I just wanted to see them *angels* or see if they was really here." Jim continued, "Been a church goer all my life. Read about 'em, but never thought I'd see one, least not this side of heaven."

"Thanks, Jim, for talking with us," said Chad as he moved on down the line of people.

Next, he stopped beside a young man, tall, slender, with sandy blond hair. He stood quietly by himself, saying nothing to anyone around him.

"Hi, may I talk with you for a couple of moments?" Chad said to the young man.

The young man nodded with a faint smile.

"Would you tell us your name?" continued Chad.

"My name's Thomas Smith."

"Thomas, where are you from?" Chad questioned.

"I live over near Miller's Crossroads, just off Highway Two," the young man replied.

"What is your reason for coming here today, Thomas?" The tall young man paused for a moment before thoughtfully replying. "I guess I came here to...... maybe see a glimpse of the other side."

"Why is that important to you?" asked Chad.

Looking down and then in the direction of the church Thomas continued, "My Momma died last year. Cancer. She wasn't but forty-five." With eyes misting, he continued, "I wanted to see something about where she is. Maybe get some sort of good feeling from it."

His answer caught Chad by surprise. Not knowing exactly how to respond to this, Chad touched the young man on the shoulder and said, "I have a feeling you will, Thomas."

On down the line he walked, talking with people along the way. Chad encountered varied answers to his questions from the multitudes standing in line, of which several involved touching stories such as the one Thomas had told. But, in speaking and listening to with them, Chad reached the conclusion that many of these people were here trying to come to grips with personal life encounters and tragedies and, maybe, the hope of reconciling them with beliefs they had developed throughout their lives.

One particularly interesting story came from a young woman, short with dark hair and dark eyes. When Chad asked her why she was here, she told him that she had never believed in God, an afterlife, or heaven! As he encouraged her to explain then her presence here, she added, "While I've never thought there was anything after this life, a kind of empty feeling is here inside, that nags, what if there is? Maybe I've been wrong. I want to know."

And so it went for almost an hour.

When Chad finally decided to end the interviews, he looked around for Cynthia, who was nowhere in sight. Not spotting her anywhere, he felt a twinge of disappointment. He simply had this need in him to be near her. As silly as that sounded, it was the way he felt whenever he was away from her.

"Let's find some shade, Shawn," Chad finally suggested to his cameraman.

Walking back to the parking lot with the many TV trucks and cars, Chad saw Reverend Johnson walking from his car to the back entrance of the church. Entering at this location, the Reverend could go to his office and avoid getting caught up in the line of people slowly moving into St. Michael's from the side door in their quest to see the *angels*. At the second door on the side of the church, the one that opened into the hallway which led from the sanctuary in the direction of the minister's office, people were streaming out of the church. Chad observed these people and tried to read their reactions from seeing the *angels*.

He was certainly not surprised by the varied reactions. As policemen directed them back down to the street and off the grounds of the church; some were crying, others talking quietly, still others just excited, while some simply walked away, lost in their own thoughts and questions. Chad watched for a few moments before turning toward the WTLA mobile site.

Walking in between the trucks, vans, cars, and awnings of the many news teams, Chad headed for the WTLA truck. Since it was beside the WDDR mobile unit, he hoped that Cynthia would be there. He felt both stupid and angry at himself for not being able to control his thoughts and the fact that most of his thoughts had to do with Cynthia. The emotions he felt for her were just too much to push into the back of his mind for very long. These emotions eased their way back too easily. Once he admitted to himself how he felt about Cynthia, she was always there. Even if she never felt as he did, it didn't matter. He was honest with himself for whatever it was worth.

"Where is she? What is she doing? Oh well!" Chad said to himself at his inability to alter these thoughts.

"You were pretty busy out there." Chad heard her voice.

Looking up, Chad saw Cynthia sitting under the awning of the WDDR mobile unit, a fan blowing to keep the heat at bay. There in the director's chair with the breeze of the fan blowing her dark hair, Chad forgot about the heat and uncomfortable weather of South Alabama momentarily.

"You look busy yourself," he replied with a smile brought on by hers. *She completely fascinates me*, he almost said aloud.

Pulling up a seat beside her, he felt the breeze from the fan, accompanied by the scent of her perfume. They were both wonderful.

"Can it get any busier or any hotter?" He complained, wiping his forehead again.

"It can and will, I'll bet," said Cynthia as she leaned over and picked up a water bottle from the low table in front of her.

Chad's phone rang. Glancing at the screen, he saw that it was Jim Stuart calling.

"Hi, Jim, what's going on back in that cool studio?" Chad asked as he winked at Cynthia. Her smile back at him was contagious he decided. "Tomorrow? Are you sure about this, or is this something just being considered?"

Listening intently, his eyes darting around, Chad said, "When will they begin setting up? Okay. Thanks, Jim. Bye."

Putting his phone away, he looked back at Cynthia, who was looking at him questioningly. It was obvious that she wanted to know what had just been said, but wasn't going to ask.

"It was my boss, Jim Stuart," Chad began, "Tomorrow evening the CBS News is going to broadcast from Dunning with Jeff Glor. And, you can bet that means NBC, ABC, Fox, and the others won't be far behind!"

"Didn't I tell you it would get busier?" challenged Cynthia with a smile.

"But, get this," Chad said, baiting Cynthia as he dragged out his announcement.

"What? What else did he say?" Cynthia asked, knowing that he was teasing her now.

Smiling, Chad leaned back in his chair and continued. "You and I are going to be with Jeff Glor as co-anchors. And, CBS and NBC are going to share the program along with Lester Holt!"

Jumping up and grabbing Chad's arm, an excited Cynthia burst out, "No! You're just telling me that!"

"For real," laughed Chad. "I promise."

10

Reverend Johnson closed the outside door and walked straight to his office. The past two days had been the busiest of his entire career in the ministry. Even at home the phone rang continually day and night. Calls were coming in from churches all over the country, every imaginable news or religious organization, and just plain curiosity seekers. As he sat down in the chair behind his desk with his head in his hands, the phone rang yet again. Against the promise he had made to himself not to answer the phone, Thomas picked up the receiver. Answering with, "Reverend Johnson," he listened intently, trying to make out the voice on the other end of the line.

"Who is this?" he said, sitting up straight in his chair. The phone went dead. For a moment Thomas sat thinking about the call. Snapping back to the reality of the moment, he quickly thumbed through his emergency numbers, picked up the phone receiver, and began punching numbers on the key pad.

When the voice of Lucy Whiddon answered, Thomas Johnson said, "This is Reverend Johnson at St. Michael's. Is Mayor Smith available?"

"Just a moment, please," Lucy professionally replied.

"Reverend Johnson, how may I help you this morning?" Allan Smith answered.

"Mayor," began the audibly shaken voice of Thomas Johnson, "I just received a threat."

"A threat? What kind of threat, Reverend?"

Thomas took a deep breath and continued, "A man called just a few minutes ago telling me this appearance of the *angels* in St. Michael's is God's plan, or more specifically, as he put it, 'a sign of the times,' an event of prophetic significance that points to the END TIMES. This man went on to say that God had spoken to him and he had specifically received instructions from God to bring on punishment to a sinful world filled with false prophets and false teachings. He said he was in Dunning to carry out his assignment. He claimed to be a "prophet" sent by God."

"Reverend, could this possibly be some sort of sick joke?" questioned Allan.

Thomas answered, "He surely didn't sound like it. His voice sounded really serious, almost resigned to carry out some sort of frenzied, fanatical plan."

Allan thought: *If it wasn't enough just dealing with the logistics of this whole thing with unexplained angels, now we have a nut thinking he is God's agent to carry out punishment or a possible terrorist attack!*

Allan asked, "Did this person give any indication as who he might have been, or for whom he might be working?"

"None! We've never had any sort of threat against St. Michael's, or me, for that matter," continued Thomas.

"Okay. I'll get in touch with the Police Chief. We'll double the police presence and have all of our personnel on the lookout for any sort of suspicious or odd behavior," said Allan. He then added, "What is going to make this doubly hard is we can expect some pretty odd behavior going on in Dunning without the risk of threats."

"Yes," said Thomas Johnson, "I'm afraid that you're right. It's sad to think that someone would take something as beautiful as the presence of the *angels* and twist it to meet their selfish goals."

"But, isn't that what people have done for hundreds, if not thousands, of years," continued Allan, "Tried to make their own selfish will, God's will?"

Letting out a troubled sigh, Reverend Johnson answered, "Yes, I'm afraid that you're probably right."

Changing the direction of the conversation, he added, "Thank you for the help. I hope it's just as you suggested, a sick joke. But it sounds more like a sick mind!"

Allan hoped so too, but he couldn't count on it. There were too many people in Dunning to simply blow off a crackpot threat and forget about it. Consideration for the safety of high-ranking officials, such as the President of the United States, had to be taken into account as well.

Allan ended the conversation with, "Call me immediately if you hear any more or have any suspicions about who this caller might be."

"I will, Mayor. Thank you. Goodbye."

Allan sat back. Running his hand through his hair, he thought: *Yeah, this is all we need.*

He reached for his phone to call Bill Tyler. The Chief must be informed about this latest development so that he can make any necessary preparations should such a threat become a reality.

The flight from Riyadh to Atlanta was uneventful. Muhammad Harassi was able to fly directly into Hartsfield-Jackson International Airport, arriving on a Wednesday morning flight. Thanks to his diplomatic immunity, Muhammad cleared Customs easily and proceeded to call Tom Weatherman.

"Tom, this is Muhammad."

"Muhammad, good to hear from you, how was your flight over?" inquired Weatherman.

"It couldn't have been smoother," returned Muhammad.

Tom continued, "I have the tickets for flights from Atlanta to Dunning. It will save us a four hour drive. I hope you didn't mind my making those arrangements?"

"No, not at all, Tom," Muhammad said. "After the flight, a long drive by auto would not be the most pleasant of things."

"Good. I'll meet you at the Delta Desk, South Terminal at ten."

Hanging up his office phone, Tom stood and prepared to leave the CNN Headquarters. He called his wife, Jan, to tell her that he should be back late evening unless returning flights were canceled, which could be likely flying into a smaller airport. Just to be prepared, he had packed an overnight bag. The drive to the airport was uneventful excluding the bumper-to-bumper, eighty-mile-per-hour, white-knuckled traffic that always plagued Atlanta. Parking in a sea of cars in the airport parking lot, Tom got out of his car and walked into the terminal. He immediately spotted Muhammad sitting beside the wall in front of the Delta Desk.

Seeing Tom enter, Muhammad stood smiling and walked to meet him. Shaking hands they exchanged hellos and a bit of small talk while walking to the desk to retrieve their boarding passes, Muhammad towing his small bag. The airport was busy as usual. Heading toward security, they talked about families and events going on in each of their countries. Removing shoes and sending personal belongings through the X-ray machine, they passed into the gate area for flights.

Their flight wasn't scheduled to leave for another couple of hours and having already passed through security, Tom asked, "Muhammad, how about something to eat before we leave?"

"That actually sounds good. The food aboard these flights always leaves something to be desired," laughed Muhammad.

Walking up to one of the self-serve eateries, they selected sandwiches and drinks before finding a seat. As usual the airport was crowded with travelers. There wasn't a better place anywhere to "people watch" than in an airport. People of every age and description moved about on their way to varied sections of the country and beyond. As usual there were many young soldiers wearing familiar military fatigues and carrying large bags off to unselfishly defend the U.S.

As they sat to begin their meal, Tom came to the main topic of Muhammad's visit.

"I'm sure you have heard as much as I have about the *angels* that seem to have inhabited this small church in Dunning," began Tom.

"Yes, unless something has transpired since I last had the opportunity to watch a news program," Muhammad answered. He then added, "What do you make of this, Tom?"

Chewing thoughtfully, Tom looked at Muhammad for a moment. "I don't know that I can truly explain it, but, based on the reports, it appears that…….." Here he paused and smiled rather sheepishly. "It appears that these images really are something from another dimension. For lack of a better description, let's say they look like *angels*."

Muhammad was intrigued by the prospect that *angels* were actually there, but what did it mean if they were in this insignificant little church? Why had they not chosen Mecca, the Mosque at the Dome of the Rock, or, for that matter, even St. Peter's Basilica in Rome?

Answers would, of course, have to wait until they got to Dunning. They finished their meal, talking about events and threats of terrorism in both Saudi Arabia and the U.S. They decided it would be better to visit the church before proposing other possible theories or explanations.

The usually quiet flight to Dunning on the small Delta commuter plane was filled with conversation centering on the *angels* of Dunning, which everyone wanted to see themselves, and there was no shortage of explanations as to why they had appeared. Everything from *'the end of time'* to *'a rip in the fabric of the universe'* was explored in many animated conversations.

Behind Tom and Muhammad sat an elderly lady with a man in a khaki suit.

"There must be some sort of hoax playing out in Dunning. I just cannot imagine the Lord allowing this sort of hallowed appearance *there* of all places. A little church across the tracks can't possibly be where the Lord would allow such a vision to take place, if it is indeed real," observed the elderly lady. She continued, "I've lived in Dunning all my life and this can't really be happening."

Nodding sympathetically, the man in the khaki suit said, "It does sound strange, and who knows what it really means."

Tom Weatherman leaning over to Muhammad said in a quiet voice just above a whisper, "See what I mean? Everyone is talking about the visitors."

Muhammad shook his head. "And, apparently everyone has his or her own opinion about the appearance of such."

In what seemed only a few minutes, the small commuter plane circled and prepared for a landing.

Muhammad looked out of the small window at the farmland spread out beneath him. Dotting the countryside below were woods and fields laid out in patterns of various crops and a sprinkling of small ponds scattered about the fields. The airport approached a single runway and prepared to land.

It is really not a very large airport, Muhammad thought. The plane touched down with screeching tires on the runway and taxied to the terminal. Exiting the plane by portable stairs, they were immediately overwhelmed with the heat and humidity of South Alabama. Walking across the hot pavement and into the terminal building, the roar of the jet engine was replaced by an intercom announcing the plane's arrival and the time for the next departing flight to Atlanta. Glancing around the terminal, Tom saw Robert Wood approaching them.

Extending his hand to Tom he asked, "Good flight?"

"Not bad. Only takes minutes from Atlanta. Up, then down, and you're here," replied Tom.

Turning to Muhammad, Tom said, "Robert, I would like you to meet my friend, Muhammad Harassi. He is with the Saudi Arabia Office of Information. However, just for now, we don't need to advertise it."

"Very happy to meet you," said Wood, extending his hand to Muhammad.

"Any changes, Robert?" asked Tom, referring to the sightings, while retrieving and loading their small bags into the trunk of the car.

"Nothing with the *angels*," began Wood, but then quickly added, "It's the town that's changing. Already thousands of people have descended upon Dunning, and the crowds seem to be growing larger by the hour."

Have you seen them yourself, the *angels*, I mean?" asked Muhammad as they settled into Robert Wood's car.

"Yes, I have," responded Robert.

Expecting more of an answer than he received, Muhammad waited a couple of moments. When Wood said nothing more, Muhammad persisted, "Robert, what do you believe they are?" He was trying not to sound too inquisitive, but his interest was so great that it was difficult to disguise it by the tone in his voice. Again, he waited for Wood to answer.

Turning the ignition switch and starting the engine, Wood looked over at Muhammad, *"Angels.* I think they're *angels."*

Pulling out from the parking space, Wood drove the three of them from the airport toward town, moving with the flow of an ever-increasing number of cars making their way into Dunning. At every signal light, there were traffic issues accompanied by long waits. Police and guardsmen directed traffic which was moving a snail's pace. Approaching the center of town, the snail's pace gave way to a slow crawl. What should have taken fifteen minutes took almost an hour and a half.

Reaching Everwine Street, they encountered a police roadblock. Just official cars and news vehicles were allowed through; no traffic. Wood stopped his CNN marked car at the roadblock, letting his window down, and presenting his CNN identification to the policeman on duty. Looking at the card with Wood's picture on it and then back at Wood, after few moments the young black officer handed it back to him and motioned them on through to Everwine.

Muhammad and Tom were amazed at the huge number of people lining the sidewalks which stretched all the way down the street and disappeared from sight. Tom Weatherman could think of no other event that had drawn such a huge throng of people so quickly. There were thousands of people lined up to get a chance to see the visitors. Muhammad shook his head in disbelief as they drove slowly following the crowd toward the little white church. Reaching the church parking lot, again Wood presented his CNN identification card before being passed through into the parking lot filled with trucks, cars, and portable studios.

Parking the car, they got out and walked toward a large CNN truck. Now, slightly after two in the afternoon, the heat was bearing down on them. Robert Wood led them into the shade of the CNN awning. After introductions and seating themselves, Robert reached into a large ice chest and produced bottled water for each of them. Handing his friend a bottle, he quipped, "As hot as in Saudi?"

Shaking his head and smiling, Muhammad returned the joke, "No, this is cool compared to home."

All laughed at the heat joke. However, sitting in the shade of the awning with an outdoor air conditioner blowing on them, they almost felt cool. Almost!

"Is there a chance we can get a look at the visitors this evening?" proposed Tom, wiping his forehead as he swallowed a drink of cold water.

"I think it might be arranged as everything settles down for the evening," answered Robert. Then, with a note of anticipation, he added. "I hear that we might have an important visitor coming in this afternoon from Washington. Just a rumor, mind you, but I hear he's an Assistant to the President."

"That really should be interesting," commented Tom looking at Muhammad who nodded in agreement.

"Until then, it's probably best if we sit tight and wait for this chaos to quiet somewhat. I'll make a few calls to try to find out what is in the works. Maybe we can slip into that tour if we play our cards right."

Weatherman stood up and said, "I'll be back in a couple of minutes. I think I may be able to call a couple of people now to find out what is going on." He stood and walked away from the group toward the front of the truck, where he reached for his cell phone and began punching numbers.

The phone in Allan Smith's office rang and Lucy's voice chimed through the open door, "Mr. Mayor, its Chief Tyler."

Picking up the desk phone Allan said, "Bill, I'm glad you called. We've got a problem." Without waiting for Bill to answer, Allan continued. "I've had a call from Reverend Johnson. Seems he's received a threat from someone claiming to be an agent of God—this "kook" says he is on a mission from God, Who has instructed him to punish us."

With a grunt followed by a couple of moments of silence, the Chief of Police said, "Does Johnson have any idea who this person might be?"

"No, the Reverend said he doesn't have a clue! But, you know there is always someone willing to push some hidden agenda when an occurrence of this magnitude is taking place."

"Okay Mayor, I'll put more officers around the church and try to get more guardsmen there as well." *What Tyler really wanted to say was that he would put more police and guardsmen there to prevent this nut from trying anything stupid!*

While waiting at the airport for Stern and his Assistant, Police Chief Tyler had missed Wood's and Harassi's arrival by minutes. Then, only a short time later, he caught sight of a small twin-engine jet land and taxi to a stop not far from the terminal gate. He knew instinctively that one of the two men leaving the plane and walking to the terminal had to be Stern. He was right. He walked over to the two men and, introducing himself, said he would be giving them a ride into the city. It was at this point, Tyler phoned Mayor Smith.

"Just letting you know, I'm leaving the airport now. I have Mr. Stern and his assistant with me and we should be in your office in about an hour. That is, if the traffic doesn't get any worse."

Glancing at his watch, Allan noted the time. "Sounds great. I'll see you here in an hour. Bye."

Before he had time to consider other options for dealing with this threat, Smith's phone rang again.

"Mayor, it's the Governor again," said Lucy.

"Thanks, Lucy, put him through," Allan directed.

"Allan," the familiar voice of Governor Bayer spoke on the other end of the line.

"Hello, Governor Bayer. How may I help you?"

"I'm about two blocks from your office and I'll see you shortly. Have there been any updates or news of which I've not been made aware?" the Governor continued.

"No, Sir. Not at the moment. Did you have any trouble getting into the city?" asked Allan.

"Actually, yes. It took longer than I anticipated. There must be hundreds of cars trying to get into Dunning," commented Governor Bayer.

"I believe it will only get worse," predicted Allan, continuing, "Governor, your timing couldn't be better. Chief of Police Tyler just called informing me that the President's Assistant, Michael Stern, and his Assistant are at the airport with him and they are leaving as we speak."

"Good, I'll be in your office shortly," Bayer replied.

Allan hung up the phone again and sat back. He quietly meditated over the events that had transpired in the last couple of days. Not only had there been this unbelievable miracle in Dunning, but in just a few minutes the Governor of the State of Alabama and a representative of the President of the United States would both be in his office!

As expected, within ten minutes Governor Bayer walked into the Mayor's office. He was greeted by Lucy who led him to Allan's office. Rising from his chair, Allan extended his hand and said with his welcoming southern charm, "Governor, it's so good to see you again."

Governor Bayer returned the smile and the handshake adding "It's good to see you too, Mr. Mayor."

He offered the governor a seat in one of the leather wing-back chairs across from his desk. Allan then seated himself and waited for the Governor to speak.

"Allan, this really is most unbelievable. I'll bet there are more cars on the streets of Dunning right now than in Montgomery or Birmingham during rush hour! Maybe even more than in New York City!

Allan leaned back nodding his head in agreement. He then stated, "I am open to any suggestions you may have to keeping our city running in an orderly fashion, to some degree, of course, as more curious people venture into Dunning."

"It seems to me, Allan, that you have everything pretty well under control. But I have a feeling that if the President comes, and it appears that he might, we will need even more security!" Have you considered, too, the possibility of attracting any foreign visitors?" continued Bayer.

"Foreign visitors?" Allan looked at the Governor.

Bayer went on, "I think there is a possibility as this occurrence continues growing we will see a multitude of dignitaries and visitors from around the world. Who's to say, even the Pope might want to come to Dunning to see the *angels*—not to mention representatives of other religious factions such as Jews, Buddhists, or Muslims. See my point?"

"I haven't thought much about that," replied Allan. "But I guess it's a possibility."

"I think it's very good possibility," added Bayer.

Lucy entered the office with a tray, coffee pot, and cups.

"Thanks Lucy," smiled Allan. "Governor, I don't know what I would do without this lady. She's the one who runs this office and keeps me going in the right direction."

Laughing at Allan's words, Bayer added, "I know exactly what you mean. I have the same situation in my office, only her name is Linda."

Obviously pleased at the flattery, Lucy poured the two cups of coffee, and asked, "Cream or sugar, Sir?"

"Just a little cream, please, Lucy."

For the next hour and fifteen minutes or so, Mayor Smith and Governor Bayer talked as they waited for Michael Stern to reach City Hall. They discussed additional security measures which might be needed if dignitaries such as the President, or even similar world leaders, did pay a visit to Dunning. Next, they moved to the problem of housing and medical care for the thousands who would not be able to find hotels. It was at this point in the conversation that Allan told the Governor about the threat that Reverend Johnson had received. The time went by quickly.

At three-thirty-five the phone rang. Allan thought perhaps it was Bill Tyler calling to tell him they were near, but it wasn't. Lucy spoke into the phone.

"Mr. Mayor, this is a 'Tom Weatherman' with CNN News. May I put him through to you?"

"Yes, Lucy, I will speak with him."

Holding his hand over the speaker, Allan mouthed, "C N N."

Governor Bayer nodded as Allan began to speak, "Allan Smith, how may I help you?"

"Mr. Mayor. I'm Tom Weatherman with CNN News. How are you this afternoon?"

Noting the obvious state of chaos, the Mayor replied, "It's been a busy couple of days as I'm sure you and your team are aware."

"Yes, and I don't see it slowing down in the near future, either," added Tom.

Without any further pleasantries, Tom went to the point of his call. "Mr. Mayor, I have with me a very important representative from the Kingdom of Saudi Arabia, a 'Mr. Muhammad Harassi'. As you can imagine, because of sensitive religious and political implications, this visit is not to be made public at this particular time. I think you see the point."

Tom continued, "I was hoping that this evening after the church closes its tours for the night, that it might be possible for Mr. Harassi to see the *angels* for himself so that he can impart this knowledge to his government. Mr. Mayor, I believe this whole series of events has the potential of possibly changing relationships between nations and perhaps altering religious thinking as we know it today."

Allan listened intently as Weatherman spoke. Governor Bayer watched Allan and wasn't missing a thing. As the Governor sat studying the face of the Mayor and listening to Allan's end of the conversation he knew the discussion was about something important.

"Mr. Weatherman, maybe we can arrange something. Could you and your party come to City Hall this afternoon? We possibly have several critical events unfolding."

Weatherman answered, "Yes, we can be there. What time is good to meet with you?"

"How soon can you be here?" Allan asked.

Glancing at his watch, Tom said, "We should be able to be there, if traffic permits, in about twenty minutes. At present we are at our CNN site in the parking lot of St. Michael's."

"Tell you what," said Allan, "I'll have a police car bring you and your guest here. It will take less time. An officer will be in contact with you shortly."

"Mr. Mayor, this is important, and I really appreciate your arranging this meeting," replied Weatherman. "We look forward to seeing you shortly. Goodbye."

"Goodbye," replied Allan, as he hung up the phone.

Looking back to the Governor, Allan leaned back in his chair. "Events are really getting interesting now."

Governor Bayer, looking puzzled, asked, "What does *interesting* mean, exactly?"

Sitting up straight in his chair and with a slight smile, Mayor Smith began relating to the Governor his conversation with Tom Weatherman, "It appears that not only are we about to have a visit from a representative of the President of the United States, but also a secret emissary from the King of Saudi Arabia."

Returning the same smile, as he straightened up in his seat, Bayer chuckled and said, "Yes, Allan, I have to say that *interesting* may be an understatement."

Alan buzzed Lucy to make the arrangements for the group from CNN.

At four-ten in the afternoon, the door to the Mayor's office opened and Police Chief Bill Tyler entered, accompanied by a short, slender man with dark hair, wearing glasses, Michael

Stern. Stern was followed by a tall man with blond, close-cut hair who looked more like a body guard than an assistant. Lucy led them into the Mayor's office. As they entered, Allan and the Governor stood and shook hands with both new visitors. Chief Tyler was the first to speak,

"Mr. Stern, this is Mayor Allan Smith and our esteemed Governor of Alabama, Wil Bayer. Governor, Mayor Smith, I would like to introduce you to Mr. Michael Stern, Special Assistant to the President of the United States."

Stern said, "Thank you for making this meeting possible, especially with the state of confusion you are dealing with at present." Turning to the tall man with him, he added, "This is my Assistant, Steve Howell."

Howell did not speak, but only smiled slightly and shook hands with the two men.

Allan then spoke, "I hope you had a good flight from Washington. Did you experience any problems?"

"Other than the traffic getting here, it wasn't bad." Stern continued, "Any new developments with the ....," he paused, "visitors?"

"No," Allan answered, "that is unchanged, but a new wrinkle in events has occurred."

"Wrinkle? What kind of wrinkle?" Stern questioned.

"Mr. Stern, in a couple of minutes we are expecting another visitor."

Allan went on to explain the call he had received earlier in the day from Tom Weatherman of CNN News regarding his guest. At this point in the conversation, Governor Bayer shared his thoughts with the group pertaining to the relevance of this first meeting with a foreign leader. All agreed with his thoughts on the matter that such a meeting could potentially have a major impact on international relations. Stern pounced on this new development with a renewed interest.

"Is there a room where I could make a private call?" Stern asked.

"Certainly," replied Allan, standing and directing Stern to the conference room that adjoined his office. Stern and Howell went into the room and closed the door behind them.

Governor Bayer said, "Yep, this does appear to give the whole situation a new wrinkle. Otherwise, he would not have needed to speak to someone so quickly about this, possibly the President."

Almost immediately Lucy opened the Mayor's office door and slipped in quietly, closing the door behind her. She walked over to Allan, leaning in close and murmuring quietly, "Mr. Mayor, your other guests have arrived. Do you want me to show them in?"

Allan thought for a moment then said, "Lucy, tell them we will see them in just a moment. We have an issue we must deal with first."

Lucy nodded and walked out of the office, closing the door.

Five, then ten minutes passed. Allan, Governor Bayer, and Chief Tyler sat waiting for Stern to return to the room. Then, after about fifteen minutes, the conference room door opened and Stern and Howell reentered the office.

"I'm sorry for the interruption, but the information you just passed on to us did require a conference with Washington," said Stern. "The President advised that we meet with the individual to whom you referred, but it must be kept completely quiet for the time being. I hope this is agreeable with you." Stern's tone indicated he was making more of a statement than a request.

"Certainly, our meeting will be kept completely confidential, Mr. Stern," said Bayer. "We are committed to complying with our President's wishes."

"Thanks, your cooperation is imperative and I might add appreciated," replied Stern.

Allan nodded his head and changed the conversation, "Mr. Stern, our distinguished visitor has arrived. Would you like to meet with him now?"

"Yes, absolutely." said Stern.

Allan buzzed Lucy. "Lucy, would you please bring our guests in now."

The door opened with Lucy standing by the door. Three men entered the office. Again, as introductions were made, Tom Weatherman, Robert Wood, and Muhammad Harassi shook hands with each person in the room. Once introductions were complete, Allan Smith began the conversation.

"Mr. Harassi, we are honored to have you visit Dunning. We understand this trip needs to be treated with utmost delicacy. It is both fortunate and ironic, that you are here today, as well as Mr. Stern, who is representing the President of the United States."

Michael Stern then added, "We both are interested in the events that have been unfolding here in Dunning and neither of us, nor any of our representatives, have been present thus far to witness the phenomenon seen by so many people in St. Michael's Church. You, like me, I'm sure, have seen the film footage and live broadcasts on television. We are all curious as to what this strange occurrence is about and want to see for ourselves. I hope this unplanned meeting will be acceptable to you and your government."

After listening to Stern, Harassi spoke. "Thank you for agreeing to keep this confidential for the present. Should this meeting become public before we can ascertain the validity of such an unprecedented appearance of these visions, or *angels*, we cannot cause any undue embarrassment to my government. I think you can see how our meeting becoming public could work against both our nations, especially if extremists and ultra-conservatives were to get wind of this."

Stern replied, "Absolutely. Your visit will be handled with complete discretion."

"Now back to the visions. Has everyone seen these *angels* with the exception of Mr. Harassi, Mr. Howell, and me?" questioned Stern.

"Everyone, I think, except for me, as I have just arrived from Atlanta with Muhammad today," said Weatherman.

"I haven't been to St. Michael's either," added Governor Bayer.

Stern then asked, "When will it be possible for us to go to the church, Mr. Smith?"

Allan, turned to Bill Tyler, "Chief, what do you propose?"

Tyler, clearing his throat, answered, "Mr. Stern, we have set a schedule of visitation for the public from eight o'clock in the morning until seven in the evening. At seven we close the church to the public. However, as of last night, we discovered people staying in line all night so they would be at the church when it opens first thing in the morning. Our best bet would be to travel to the church in a police van or other marked vehicle. With so many official cars coming and going, we won't as likely be noticed as unusual or out of the ordinary. Our best time to go would probably be between ten and eleven in the evening."

Everyone thought for a few moments about what Chief Tyler said and agreed his suggestion would be the best time to visit to St. Michael's.

As the group began to make plans for the visit, Allan picked up his phone. "Lucy, would you please call William Buren to see if he will make sure our reserved rooms are ready at the *Holiday Inn*." Then adding, "Thanks Lucy," knowing that it would be done.

William Buren, Hotel Manager, always kept several rooms in reserve for circumstantial emergencies such as this. These rooms were separate from the rest of the hotel and perfect for high-profile personage. Being always prepared for unforeseen situations, the city paid well to ensure rooms were always available.

Hanging up the phone, Allan instructed Bill Tyler to make sure the group would be transported to the *Holiday Inn* and made comfortable. He also instructed Tyler to have dinner delivered to their rooms from the *Steak and Ale Restaurant* down the highway. It would be almost impossible to go anywhere for dinner due to all the people in Dunning; thereby, "take-out" offered the best option, for both expediency and confidentiality.

11

By midafternoon, the weather was extremely uncomfortable, even for a summer afternoon in South Alabama, but a huge crowd of people still waited at St. Michael's as the line steadily snaked its way into the little white church. The covering constructed by the city was a blessing. Surprisingly, there had only been a few calls for medical assistance from EMTs on standby along Everwine Street. A passing cloud blocking out the sun for even a time would have been a blessing! Rain had been forecast for the evening, but still at four o'clock, there were no visible clouds.

After doing a couple of TV spots for their respective stations, Chad and Cynthia now began putting on finishing touches for the five o'clock local news. Watching from the parking lot, it seemed somewhat strange to see news teams readying themselves for their evening broadcasts from the church yard. The two local stations were the only ones with permitted access to the church and affiliating networks had to work in conjunction with WTLA and WDDR.

Preparations complete, Chad walked across to Cynthia's awning. "Hi. Say, I was thinking, how about letting me cook dinner for you this evening? Besides, it will be impossible to find a restaurant in Dunning that isn't completely full," he offered.

Cynthia looked up from her papers. With mock seriousness she said, "I didn't know you could cook. Or, can you really?" Tapping her pencil on the table, she added, "Or perhaps, this is just an excuse to get me to come over to prepare a meal for you."

Unable to keep her serious demeanor any longer, Cynthia laughed at Chad who wasn't buying this serious bit anyway, and began to smile. Cynthia couldn't help thinking in the middle of her act *Chad had the prettiest smile and perfect, white teeth.*

Holding up both hands in surrender, Chad shook his head, "Honestly, I can cook. Growing up with two brothers and no sisters, my mother insisted we all learn to care for ourselves and the house. This meant cooking, cleaning, washing, and even ironing clothes. Mom was a real drill sergeant."

"Well, you'd never know it to look inside your car," added Cynthia, enjoying the good- natured exchange.

"Say 'yes', and I promise it will be a pleasant surprise." Holding up one hand as if giving an oath, Chad said again, "I promise."

Chad hoped that she would say 'yes' and, he thought perhaps she would, but always present was the fear she would say something like, *"It's the night to wash my hair, which usually means no thanks, I already have plans."*

After a pause of maybe ten seconds, but seemingly much longer, Cynthia said, "Okay. Okay, Chad, but I'm not cooking!"

"Great. How about eightish, then? My apartment, 1213 Building D, Oxford Village Apartments."

"Okay," said Cynthia jotting down the numbers on a pad on the table. "That's just south of town on Highway 231, isn't it?"

"Absolutely," said Chad. "See you about eight then?"

"Eight," said Cynthia.

The sound of thunder could be heard in the distance. Even so, there was no sign of rain anywhere near the city. Only a dark cloud on the horizon and a slight breeze starting up gave any hint of a possible change in the weather. But for now, it remained hot and humid. The crowd of people in line to get inside the church stretched as far as the eye could see. Across the street the crowd of bystanders was just as large—standing and watching people, watching cops, watching guardsmen, watching the little framed church, hoping that just maybe, something would happen. *The feeling of excitement permeated the air as so many people waited and wondered why this happened in Dunning? Why are these angels here? How long will they stay here? Is all this just the beginning of something no one yet understood?*

With afternoon fading into early evening and bad weather threatening, gradually people began to move away from the church; still making plans for coming back the next day. Only those dedicated souls remained who waited under the awning across from the parking lot, and were determined to be first in the church the following morning. The sound of distant thunder was no deterrent to them.

Darkness approached. The scene slowed down and mobile TV units began turning on their lights, giving the parking lot the appearance of a campground surrounded by lights and awnings. Even with a reduction in the number of people on the street, the police and guard presence did not diminish. If anything, the number was beefed-up to cope with the increasing numbers of people and the potential for trouble.

By eight o'clock a breeze from the west picked up and skies in that direction were displaying distant flashes of lightning in the dark clouds. These signs offered the hope of possible rain.

Completing his own mobile unit segment with WTLA News, Chad left the church. He rushed toward home, stopping by the market quickly to get a couple of steaks, some potatoes, and fresh asparagus. Reaching his apartment, Chad put charcoal in the grill on his balcony and lit it before preparing for his dinner guest.

He wanted everything to be perfect. He put candles on the table and set out his Fiesta Ware, went into his bathroom and showered quickly, preparing for Cynthia's arrival. Now, feeling refreshed by the shower, he moved to the sink. Looking into the mirror, Chad studied his reflection as he applied shaving cream to his face and began to shave. *Not bad for a guy well past thirty,* he thought. Smiling at his image, he could barely contain the excitement that he was feeling. Cynthia was coming to his place. Why did he feel as if he were sixteen again and had never had a woman over before? Yet, there it was again, the feeling in the pit of his stomach he felt whenever he was near her. If he had not been so excited, he would have been angry at himself for allowing such uncontrolled feelings to rule his actions. At eight-ten the doorbell rang. Chad looked around the room once again before going to the door. He looked through the door's peep-hole before opening it and saw the image of dark hair that could only be Cynthia's. Taking a deep breath, Chad practiced a smile.

"Hi. I see you found me," he said, opening the door.

"Did you think I couldn't?" laughed Cynthia. "Do I need to remind you this is Dunning, not Chicago?"

"True," shrugged Chad. "Come in."

Walking into the room Cynthia was pleasantly surprised. The apartment looked nothing like she had imagined. There were no stacks of papers, cups or plates sitting around. It was very neat and clean. Stylish. A low, brown leather couch sat with an iron and glass coffee table in front of it. The beige carpeting was clean and freshly vacuumed. An end table sat beside the couch with a comfortable looking chair angled across the corner. Framed pictures hung on the wall. A watercolor in a gold frame hung behind another chair with a floor lamp beside it. A small Persian carpet lay under the coffee table. Cynthia noticed two framed pictures sitting on the end table: one with a middle aged couple sitting together and the other of three boys, teenagers. Across the room, beside the sliding glass doors to the balcony, was a table set for two.

"Whose apartment is this? Who did you bribe to use their place?" Cynthia questioned in animated surprise.

"Don't be cruel," said Chad. "Just say you are completely and utterly astonished and that you had no idea what a talented decorator I was." Her reaction was to roll her eyes and shake her head.

Cynthia looked at the rows of books lining the wooden bookshelf in the living room, which consisted of classics, as well as modern novels, and a variety of historical accounts. The varied collection of books surprised her. Then she noticed the music that was playing quietly in the background. It was a CD with the music of Tchaikovsky. This wasn't the Chad Simmons that she thought she knew. Upon seeing all this, she was even more intrigued than before. Chad wasn't the careless playboy type reporter he wanted people to think he was. She was struck with a new awareness that there was much more to him, more that she wanted to get to know.

"A glass of wine from my personal cellar, Madam?" Chad offered, holding up a glass from the kitchen while looking through the pass-through just above the counter which divided the two rooms.

"Yes. Thanks," said Cynthia as she continued to look around the living room. "Is this a picture of your parents?" she questioned, glancing at the pictures on the table.

"Yep, and the other one is me and my two brothers, Jeff and Drew."

"Tell me about them. Do they live close by?" continued Cynthia.

"Let's see." Chad paused for a moment as he worked to uncork the bottle of red wine. "Mom and Dad live at Panama City Beach, just down the road. My mom is a retired teacher and my dad is a retired engineer and now a government contractor with the Navy. They bought a condo and retired there a couple of years ago."

Still working with the bottle, "Jeff is an accountant and lives with his wife, Beth, and their two children in Atlanta. Drew," he paused searching for words, "Drew was in the Army, a career officer. He was killed in Iraq five years ago." Becoming hoarse with surprising emotion, Chad continued, "His death almost killed Mom. Dad still won't talk about it, even though it's been five years. Some things just don't fade easily."

Surprised, Cynthia looked at Chad. He continued to be something far different from what she had always seen. This Chad made her feel privileged to get a glimpse of the real and completely different Chad. To her, he was nothing at all like he had previously appeared. He was altogether a different person.

"I'm sorry, Chad," Cynthia began. "I didn't mean to pry. I had no idea," her voice trailing off.

"It's okay," Chad shrugged, pouring two glasses of wine. "We can't change the past, can we? We can only live in the here and now."

Neither said anything for a couple of awkward moments.

"Say," he changed the subject. "Are you excited about tomorrow and working with the big boys on national TV?"

"Of course! Aren't you?" Cynthia responded as she took a sip from her glass. The blunder about Chad's brother was still nagging at her.

"Yeah, I guess so. I mean, who wouldn't?" said Chad.

"But?" continued Cynthia, waiting for him to complete his thought.

"But, somehow a lot of the things that I used to see as important don't seem so important now. I suppose after seeing the *angels*, I've rethought a lot of things," said Chad, "a lot of things that still seem impossible to understand, as the *angels* for example, and things like heaven and an afterlife. I am beginning to see things differently. I feel more optimistic about people and see goodness, even with all the bad in the world. I think the *angels* have brought life itself into focus for me along with the realness and the power of God."

Listening, while walking to the sliding glass door to the balcony, Cynthia looked out across the roofs of the apartment complex and the darkening sky. As evening was approaching, an occasional flash of lightning lit up the western sky. Almost to herself, Cynthia spoke. "I know what you mean. I sometimes feel as if my life is irrelevant insanity, as if none of what I do is important. Why do we go on with all of this? This world is only just a part of our existence. But, exactly what is on the other side, I don't know."

The wind had begun to pick up moving the branches of the small water oak standing behind the building back and forth, its leaves rustling. Cynthia slid open the door. She could feel the wind. While it was still warm, the wind carried with it the hint of rain and the possibility of a coming storm. Walking out onto the balcony, the breeze blew her hair back; Chad stood watching her from the doorway. "She is so beautiful," he muttered quietly to himself. "How is it that she might ever find me interesting?"

He shook his head and moved through the doorway. Standing behind Cynthia, Chad said quietly, "I think we may have some rain soon."

She turned facing Chad, "I think you may be right." She turned again, facing west and toward the coming weather. Chad reached out his hand and touched hers. Without looking, Cynthia took his hand in hers. She did it without thinking, as naturally as if she were in an old relationship that had been going on for years. For the longest time they stood there, saying nothing, not moving, simply watching the darkening sky and the flashes of the lightning.

Completely enthralled by the atmosphere of the moment and totally captivated by Cynthia, Chad reluctantly broke the silence. "I think the charcoals are about ready," he said, and releasing Cynthia's hand, walked back into the apartment's small kitchen. Checking the oven to see if the potatoes were ready, Chad then took the steaks and asparagus out of the refrigerator and headed to the grill.

Cynthia stood watching him, wine glass in hand. "I owe you an apology."

"Yes?" questioned Chad, carefully placing the food on the grill, steaks sizzling as they touched the hot grill.

"I find out that not only do you cook better than me, but you keep house like my mother, and you read, and listen to good music!" Cynthia continued. "Is there anything you can't do?"

With mock seriousness, Chad appeared to be deep in thought for a moment before adding, "Yes, I can't sing."

They both laughed.

Dinner could not have gone better. The food was delicious, the setting and music perfect. Cynthia looked radiant in the soft candlelight. Chad had never been happier. Just sitting across from her and being with her made him wish this evening would never end.

After finishing dinner, Chad said, "Now, for dessert."

"No, absolutely not!" argued Cynthia shaking her head. "I couldn't eat another thing!"

Smiling back at her Chad said, "That's good, otherwise, I was going to break out the Oreos and milk!" Again, they both laughed. The whole evening felt magical.

"Let's find somewhere more comfortable to sit," said Chad standing up.

Cynthia rose and followed him to the couch. Chad sat down after she did, being careful not to sit too closely. He didn't want to make her feel uncomfortable by invading her space. Why this bothered him was anyone's guess. Sitting one cushion away seemed proper.

Why is it that I have always been so comfortable with women, but with her I'm at a loss for words and feel like a teenager? Why can't I just be myself? What he really wanted to do was to reach over and touch her, to move close beside her and take her in his arms. He wanted to kiss her so very badly, to tell her that he loved her.

Yet, he sat and did nothing. They each sat for a few moments, waiting for the other to say something. Finally, Chad stood up and walked to his bookshelf. Looking through the shelves, he pulled out an old leather-bound book. "Here's something I want you to see."

Cynthia looked with interest as he walked to the couch and sat closer to her this time.

Opening the book, she saw photos of long ago Dunning. Recognizing the building that was now the headquarters of WTLA, Cynthia exclaimed, "So, your station's offices was once a hotel!"

She looked through the many old photos in the book. She found it thoroughly fascinating to see the many faces of people, now gone; but the places still there, even though changed with time. Everything always changed! Regardless of what one wanted, nothing ever remained the same. Not places, not people.

Sitting closely, Cynthia could smell the clean scent of the soap with which Chad had showered. She liked the way they sat closer as they looked through at the pages of the book. It made her feel safe and warm. It brought back feelings of belonging with someone, feelings that she thought were gone forever. It made her want to sit even closer, to touch him and have him touch her.

Finally, looking up from the book and pushing those thoughts away, Cynthia said, "I should be going, tomorrow is another busy day for both of us."

Chad not only wanted her to stay the night, he didn't want her ever to leave. As she stood, he stood also. A feeling of helplessness came over Chad. Had she been one of the women Chad saw in his nights of partying, he would have let things play out as they might. But, with Cynthia, he felt differently. He wanted her to stay, but only because she wanted to stay. Taking her purse from the chair by the door, Cynthia turned to thank Chad for the wonderful evening. He had truly surprised her.

Lingering by the door, about to leave, she knew her feelings for Chad were much more than that of a casual friendship or just a working relationship. The truth was she cared for Chad. She cared for him more than she had previously allowed herself to admit. Cynthia had not experienced what she was feeling now, since Chicago. Looking into his eyes at that moment, she knew she never wanted to leave.

"Thanks for the wonderful evening," she said, leaning forward to give him a kiss as he leaned in toward her. As their lips touched, an electrical current passed through them both. What had been intended as a light *thank you* kiss for dinner turned into a kiss that flooded each of them with intense emotion. It was a kiss filled with warm, passionate affection, and a reassurance their evening was not destined to end at this point. Cynthia felt her purse drop to the floor as she put her arms around his neck and moved closer to Chad in the kiss. He felt like a small animal being captured by a large snake. He felt powerless to do anything. He felt electricity like he had never felt. It was reminiscent of the first time he kissed a girl in the tenth grade outside of the gym following a high school dance. Gwen Knight was the girl. Only this time it was much more impassioned and he wasn't afraid that her mom would come around the corner and catch them.

Chad moved closer into Cynthia's embrace as she moved even closer toward him. It was as if they melted into one, standing at the door. They kissed passionately holding each other close for the longest time. Finally, Chad leaned back, their eyes intent on each other. Without a word, Chad took her hand and they walked from the door, down the hall, into his bedroom. Distant thunder rumbled again as the wind rose outside and rain began to pelt angrily against the glass doors. Finally rain had come to Dunning!

12

The arrival at the hotel was uneventful. The City having its "prearrangement program" of keeping rooms on standby for unforeseen situations had been a good move on the part of Allan Smith's leadership. Another room was not to be found in any of the surrounding towns of either Northwest Florida or Southwest Georgia. The group waited inside the city cars as Chief Tyler went to the desk and secured room keys. Stern and Howell had a room, Wood, Weatherman and Harassi another, and the Governor and his assistant, William Roland, another. A fourth room was given to the two state troopers who had accompanied the Governor. Chief Tyler told the group of men that dinner would be brought in an unmarked van at seven and another unmarked van belonging to the city would pick them up at ten o'clock. In the meantime, there was little to do except relax in the cool motel rooms and wait for the situation to quiet down at St. Michael's.

Entering room 417, Robert Wood leaned over the air-conditioning unit to make certain the temperature was set on "high." It was. As Weatherman and Harassi came into the room putting down their bags, Wood looked out through the window before drawing the shades to keep out the sunlight as the sun now just above the horizon made its descent low into the west. He could see the busy highway from the window. The moving traffic was bumper-to-bumper, the kind of traffic one expects to see when people flee north trying to escape a hurricane on the coast, only now it was going both directions.

Dropping into one of the chairs, Wood pushed the "on" button of the TV's remote control. As the television came on, he moved through the stations searching for CNN. He located the channel just as a camera was panning the scene in front of St. Michael's. Though late in the afternoon, he saw huge crowds still lining both sides of the street. Shaking his head he said aloud, "Just look at this! It's amazing!"

Both Weatherman and Harassi stopped and looked at the screen. Tom spoke first, "I cannot wait to see this myself."

Also, looking at the screen, with his eyes fixed on the images, Muhammad echoed Tom's comments, saying, "Neither can I stand to wait." His voice held a hint of uncertainty in it. *What does it mean?* He thought to himself. *What does it mean?*

The three men relaxing, tried to watch the television; instead, they sat talking about the *angels*, the town of Dunning, and how neither of them had ever seen so much excitement over anything else, including war and natural disaster. Occasionally, they glanced at their watches. The late afternoon seemed never-ending.

Next door in 418, Michael Stern lay propped up on one of the beds, his shoes on the floor, his coat and tie placed neatly over the chair beside the bed. Steve Howell sat at the small table reading from one of the folders he had brought with him, his large brief case on the floor beside him.

Stern took his phone from his case and keyed in his home phone number. Within a couple of moments, he spoke. "Melinda. Hi, it's me. No, I'm not at the office and it doesn't look as though I'll be home for dinner, either."

Listening to the voice on the other end of the line, he answered, "Actually, I'm in Dunning." Pausing briefly, he added, "Yes, Dunning, Alabama. Right again. The place where the *angels* have been seen."

"Hon, I don't know. No. I promise. Yes, when I get home, I'll tell you all about it. Okay. Bye."

As he broke the connection, Steve Howell looked up from his work. He smiled as Stern shrugged and without a word looked back at what he was doing.

Stern readjusted himself; leaning back against the pillows propped against his back and closed his eyes. "Can you believe we're here in South Alabama, waiting for dark so that we can go see some *angels*?"

Howell again smiled. "It's as unbelievable as seeing Congress work together!" he concluded, then continued looking at the papers spread on the small table.

After a couple of moments Steve stopped and looked at Stern. "Mike, do you believe the President is going to come here, to Dunning?"

Stern spoke without opening his eyes. "Steve, I honestly don't know. I guess it depends on what we see and report back to the President. From what we've seen and heard through the media, there is something here. I don't know what it is, but there's something that is certainly out of the ordinary!"

Steven Howell had known Michael Stern since college. They had gone through Boston College and then on to law school together, both gaining their credentials after passing the bar. Michael had always been interested in politics, unlike Steve, who thought most politicians were self-serving crooks and wanted no part in it. Michael had become involved with the campaign of Senator Stuart Wallace of Massachusetts when he ran for the Presidency. He had won, thanks mainly to his promises to reestablish American leadership in the world, and to help the nation regain its self-image following a disastrous scandal involving the former president, John Shoulman, over bribe-taking from lobbyists while serving in Congress.

Michael had gained Wallace's attention by his organizational skills and sound advice on national issues. As the campaign continued, Stern was given a bigger role, consultant to Wallace. Upon winning the election, Wallace named Stern as one of his personal assistants. Michael Stern, in turn, called upon Steven Howell to be his assistant, knowing beforehand Steven's attention to detail and his complete honesty. Steven never missed anything. Michael had long known Steven would be perfect for the job because he was not a 'yes' man and would always give honest advice, even if it wasn't what one wanted to hear, a mistake made by many politicians after getting elected. The majority of politicians are not interested in hearing views that do not agree with their own personal agendas. Michael learned early on having only one voice offering advice was never good. In many cases there could be two rights and no wrongs. It was a question of which side one wanted to make angry. It was too easy to isolate oneself from the true nature of circumstances centered on politics of any nature.

It had been quite an undertaking for Michael getting Steve to take the job. He first had to convince him he would never ask him to do anything that was contrary to his values or conscience. It had been a hard sell; but, in the end, Steve said 'yes' when Michael convinced him that by taking this job he could possibly make government cleaner and less influenced by the many lobbyists who prowled the halls of Congress with pockets full of cash. In some ways Steve was like a conscience.

When the door shut to 419, Governor Bayer pulled off his coat, sat down on the bed, kicked off his shoes and loosened his tie while he instructed, "Bill, call the office and let them know we'll be here until late evening. Tell them it might even be morning before we get back to Montgomery."

Bill Roland, the governor's assistant, nodded, "Yes sir. Do you need me to call the mansion and inform Mrs. Bayer about your plans?"

"No thank you, Bill. I'll call her a little later when she has had time to get home. I think her plate was pretty full today."

Bill began making the call. As he did, Wil Bayer dosed off to sleep listening to the drone of the air-conditioning and Bill Roland's voice in the cool room where they waited for their chance to see the *angels*.

At seven-thirty there was a knock on the door of Room 417. Answering the knock, Robert Wood opened the door to a young delivery man carrying two large plastic bags with the *Steak and Ale* logo on the side. Taking the bags, Wood tipped the young man and closed the door. Wood, Weatherman, and Harassi sat down at the small round table, pulling out the Styrofoam boxes with their dinners, and began eating the steak, salad, and baked potatoes. While eating, conversation went back to their approaching mission to view the *angels*. Weatherman and Harassi felt their excitement build as they talked. Wood understood completely. He had been there. He had seen the *angels*. He wasn't sure exactly how to explain what he had seen, but still, he had seen them. There wasn't anything he could do to prepare Weatherman and Harassi for what they were about to experience. He didn't try. He simply tried to answer their questions as well as he could.

Similar scenes were taking place in the other rooms as everyone ate and tried to imagine what they would find at St. Michael's. Now it was just a matter of eating and waiting until they could go to the little church with as little notice as possible. Sitting and talking after eating, the continual rumble of thunder in the west accompanied their conversation.

Still, just sitting and watching TV, along with only small talk, seemed to slow down the time. The hours of waiting, seemed endless. A loud clap of thunder signaled rain that could now be heard falling on the roof and the concrete outside. It would be a welcome relief from the heat of the summer evening and would, perhaps, send home the massive congregation of people waiting to get a glimpse of the *angels*. Harassi got up and walked to the window. Parting the blinds he looked outside. Against the darkening sky, the rain was coming down in sheets. The parking lot resembled a river as the water rushing across it carried away the dust and the heat of the day. Another roll of thunder could be heard in the distance.

"You certainly don't see weather like this at home," he said aloud, as he closed the blinds and turned back to the others.

The rain continued falling as they waited for ten o'clock. At five minutes before ten, a knock on the door of 419 was answered by Bill Roland. It was Dunning's Chief of Police, Bill Tyler.

"Hi. Time to leave," said Chief Tyler as he stood dripping in the doorway. "Is the Governor ready to go?"

Bill Roland stood back from the doorway, "Come in, Chief. Looks like it's really wet out there."

"Thanks. I think I will. I do believe the rain has set in for a while," Tyler said, removing his cap with a stream of water running from it. Water also ran off the yellow police raincoat he wore, leaving small wet spots on the carpet. Behind him thunder sounded again. A long, low roll carried across from the west as distant flashes reached across the dark sky. The steadily falling rain, reflected by the light of the street lamps on the dark pavement, was clearly visible. Governor Bayer walked out of the bathroom drying his face after washing the "sleep" from his eyes.

"Say, we may have some weather this evening, Chief?" Bayer asked putting on his tie in front of the mirror.

"Yes sir, I believe so. But, at least with this weather, the crowd has thinned out dramatically over on Everwine, and it should keep all the news people under shelter."

"That's good," said Bayer. "With our special guests, we don't need anyone being suspicious and asking questions."

Putting on his coat, he and Roland moved toward the door.

"Better take these umbrellas. It's raining pretty hard out there now," Tyler said producing two black umbrellas.

"Thanks. I hate the thought of having to drive back to Montgomery soaked," chuckled Bayer.

As they walked out of the room, Bayer could see the rain coming down in the headlights of the van parked in front of the room. Inside he could see the dark figures of people already seated as the windshield wipers fought a losing battle to maintain a clear view. Quickly moving around in front of the van, Chief Tyler opened the side door. Bayer and Roland got in quickly. Inside were the other members of the group, Weatherman, Wood, Harassi, Stern, and Howell. Getting into the front passenger seat beside the driver, Tyler looked back at the group. "Everyone ready? Missing anyone?"

From the back Weatherman answered, "I think this is it, Chief. We're ready when you are." The van backed up, its red and white lights shining through the sheets of rain as it exited the motel parking lot toward the main highway. Traffic had thinned considerably, but there were still cars splashing through the standing water on the wet roadway. Turning onto the bypass the van traveled due north until it turned east into town driving through the old part of Dunning. This part of the city dated back to the late 1800s. Most of the buildings were dark now with only the street lamps to make out the darkened fronts of the silent buildings. As the van's driver drove down the street, the men inside sat silently looking at the rain falling over Dunning, each lost in his own thoughts, and wondering with some apprehension, what they were actually going to find once inside the church.

Because of the rain, the traffic was almost gone from downtown now and as they reached the roadblock at Everwine, there was virtually no traffic. Two police cars sat in the street in front of the barricade blocking traffic onto the street. As the van slowly pulled to a stop in front of the barricade, an officer wearing a yellow raincoat and cap cover walked around to the van while two other cops, sitting in the comfort of their dry black and white, watched.

"Everything okay?" asked Chief Tyler, leaning across the young policeman driving the van, to speak to the officer outside.

"Chief Tyler, it's all quiet from here. This rain has driven everyone inside." Looking up and down Everwine Street, the officer added, "You should have the church all to yourselves."

"That's good. You men just keep an eye on things." As an afterthought, Tyler added, "I guess we still have the guard presence down there."

"Yes sir," replied the officer, "they just changed the sentries about fifteen minutes ago. Plus, several of our cars are at the church, and it appears there is not much activity at the news portables. Guess they've tried to find dry spots inside their trucks."

"Guess so. Okay, thanks," added Tyler.

Running up the window, the van moved around the police blockade and down Everwine. In the steady rain, dark shapes emerged that were actually houses along the street. The only hint of people inhabiting the houses came from the soft glow of lights shining through some of the windows and curtains along Everwine Street.

The van rolled down the silent street to the sound of splashing puddles and turned into the parking lot of St. Michael's. Through rain-spotted windows, no one was able to see outside into the dark night. The long, covered walkway along the street was unoccupied, thanks to the wind, blowing rain, and lightning that had driven everyone inside in search of drier surroundings.

Looking closer, as their eyes adjusted to the dark, the men could pick out National Guardsmen standing in the rain dressed in rain gear and armed with M-16 rifles. They were stationed around the church and at various locations along the block. As the van stopped a police officer walked from the door on the side of the church to the van. Again, the window went down and Chief Tyler spoke to the young officer.

"Everything quiet here?" he inquired.

Inspecting the van and its occupants, the officer answered, "Yes sir, as quiet as a graveyard."

Chief Tyler turned to the group behind him and said, "Okay, gentlemen let's get out."

The group exited the van opening umbrellas. Rain continued to fall with a steady, heavy rhythm. Tyler led the way from the van to the covered awning. Lowering their umbrellas, the group walked silently and quickly toward the dark church with the sound of the rain beating on the metal roof above their heads. Inside, the front part of the hallway was lit with dim, yellowish lights. Everything was quiet except for the sound of the rain and the low hum of the air-conditioning system. Chief Tyler, leading

159

the way, was met by a police officer and a young officer of the National Guard. Tyler shook hands with both men and quietly spoke to them before returning to the group who after exiting the van had waited just inside the door.

At that moment, Allan Smith came up the hallway with Thomas Johnson. Smith introduced everyone to the Reverend and he shook hands with each.

"Gentlemen, Reverend Johnson is the minister here at St Michael's and he, along with a church member, Doris Williams, were two of the first to see the *angels*."

With the slight smile of someone with a secret and speaking in a low voice, Reverend Johnson said, "Thank you, Mr. Mayor. I guess everyone is ready to view our visitors."

Looking at the men, Allan said, "They are probably beyond ready!" It was evident that they were eager to see the visitors and yet didn't know what to expect. A loud clap of thunder shook the little church. Everyone jumped with it and the excitement that had been building all day.

"This way please, gentlemen," directed Reverend Johnson, as he turned toward the sanctuary doors being guarded by two police officers. Walking slowly toward the doors, Muhammad glanced nervously at Tom Weatherman. Tom took a deep breath and exhaled.

Upon reaching the closed doors and receiving a nod from the Reverend, the officers opened them. No lights were turned on in the sanctuary. It was lighted only by the street lamp shining in through the large stained glass windows, plus a silvery light burning just above the altar. As the group looked upward, they saw them! The silent celestial beings sat or stood just as they had been when viewed previously. They took absolutely no notice of anything going on in the world below them. It was just as if they were tired and resting after some long journey or battle of which the mortals below had no concept. While almost close enough to touch, they were separated by what seemed to be a fourth dimension.

The men in the small group below stood silently, spellbound by the scene they were witnessing and with each one lost in his own private thoughts. From the Governor, to the President's men, to the representative of the King of Saudi Arabia, all simply stood and stared, mesmerized, trying to make reason out of what they were seeing.

Steve Howell crossed himself as he stared upward. Michael Stern simply looked in disbelief. It was Muhammad Harassi who reacted most openly. Upon looking at the figures, Muhammad slowly knelt and bowed his head for a few moments, then looked up again at the figures bathed in soft light. If the figures were aware of the mortals below them, they did not show it.

Thomas Johnson stood with them, allowing each man time to absorb and then comprehend what they were seeing. As many times as he had looked at the scene above, Thomas still found it hard to fathom. For the longest time they all stood there quietly looking at the sacred, unearthly scene above them. When approximately five minutes had passed, Reverend Johnson touched the Mayor's arm and he, in turn, touched the Governor. Slowly they turned and walked out of the room and back down the hallway. Muhammad was the last of the group to leave. Slowly he rose to his feet and walked from the room.

"*God is great!*" he muttered softly to himself. He looked once again at the figures before following the others down the hallway.

Thomas Johnson led them past the pastor's study to a conference room. Inside the smell of coffee filled the room. After everyone was in the room, Thomas turned to the group. "We have coffee and refreshments for anyone who would like some." Without waiting for a reply he added, "Any questions or comments?"

For a few moments it was quiet, and then Michael Stern spoke. "This is incredible, simply incredible! Totally unbelievable! I don't know anything else to say. I have never really been a religious person; I mean, I believe in God, but never really gave much deep thought to religion."

Then with a light chuckle, he shook his head and said, "Yes, I do need some coffee, unless you have something stronger, Reverend!"

The laughter now seemed to break the spell that had been holding everyone. They began to talk, exchanging feelings about what they had seen as each took steaming cups of coffee. The Governor taking a sip from his cup, exclaimed, "This is great. Nothing like a hot cup of coffee on a damp night!"

The others agreed. The coffee seemed to make everyone feel better. Even Reverend Johnson thought it was unusually good and said so.

"Someone sure knows how to make a good cup of coffee," observed Allan, as he sipped from his cup.

"Actually, it's made with water that comes from an old well which has been here since the building of the church," explained Thomas.

As they continued talking, Michael Stern turned to Thomas Johnson, "Reverend, may I use your office to make a call to Washington? It would possibly be quieter in there."

"Certainly, Mr. Stern. Just come with me, please," Reverend Johnson answered as he led Stern back into the hallway and to his office. Stern walked in and Thomas turned to close the door allowing him privacy.

"Reverend?" said Stern rather sheepishly.

Thomas turned to look at Stern. "Yes, Mr. Stern?"

"Those were *angels* we just saw, right?" Stern asked.

It was as if he needed a reassurance before communicating to the President the spiritual scene he had witnessed moments earlier.

Thomas nodded with a kindly smile as he turned facing him before closing the door. "Yes, Mr. Stern, you just witnessed honest-to-goodness *angels* from somewhere in God's Kingdom."

Michael Stern dialed the number of the direct line to the White House. The phone rang once before being answered by a screening operator.

"Yes, Mr. Stern," spoke the voice on the other end of the line.

"Let me speak with the President, please," said Stern.

Again there was a ring as the call was transferred. This time it rang several times before a voice on the other end answered, "Yes, Michael. What have you got?"

President Wallace sat in an overstuffed chair in his bedroom. It had been a long day beginning at the usual six AM. Now it was eleven-forty-five PM and he was very tired. Still he had instructed Michael Stern to call him as soon as he had examined the situation in Dunning.

Stuart Wallace knew that Stern's assessment of the events would be accurate and unbiased. After two days of nothing but stories about the *angels* on national television, Wallace wanted some conclusive answers. His office was already receiving calls and messages from capitals around the world with inquiries regarding the television news stories. While none of them offered to send representatives at this time, it was obvious they were fishing for hard information to clear up the stories that were being shown on television around the world.

"Mr. President," Michael said, pausing to take a breath and still not sure what he was going to say, continued. "I'm calling from the pastor's study in St. Michael's Church. I've just been in the sanctuary with a few select guests." He hesitated trying to choose his words carefully. President Wallace sat patiently waiting for Stern's explanation. He knew that Stern would give him a logical explanation for these visions. He relied on his help to explain to the nation and the rest of the world what was actually being seen in Dunning, Alabama.

"Michael, are you there?" the President asked.

"Yes sir. Sorry. I have just come from seeing the images and," his voice trailed off again. "Mr. President, you have to come here and see these things for yourself. What I saw really were *angels*, as unbelievable as it may sound. *Angels!*"

Wallace sat forward in his chair as if this might help him to hear clearer what Stern had just said.

"Michael, did I hear you correctly?" asked the President.

"Yes sir, you did. I saw what I think were *angels* sitting and standing in the rafters of this little AME church in Dunning. I can't think of any other way to describe what I saw. You know I have never been a churchgoing person, but neither am I an atheist. These figures appear to be legitimate heavenly *angels*."

It was quiet for a couple of seconds. Neither the President nor Stern said anything.

The President finally broke the silence. "Is it possible for you to come back to Washington tonight?"

"Yes sir. I can probably be back in about three hours," said Stern looking at his watch. "But first I must tell you about another interesting development."

"Go ahead, tell me now," coaxed the President.

"An unofficial representative from the King of Saudi Arabia is here also," reported Stern. "It appears that he was sent to scope out the news stories about the *angels*."

"You don't say," said President Wallace, mulling over that last bit of information. "That opens some really interesting avenues.

Is it possible to get this representative to return to Washington with you?"

"I'm not sure Mr. President. He flew in from Atlanta with CNN Executive, Tom Weatherman," Stern added. "I think he would prefer that his presence not be noticed at this time. It could make for a rather sticky situation if it became public that a representative of the ruler of the *holiest place in Islam* was visiting a Christian church to see *angels*."

"That's true," mused the President. "Talk with him and see what he thinks about the situation. See if a delegation might be possible and, if so, who might it include. Tell him your conversation will be kept completely confidential. We certainly don't want to fuel any extremist factions."

"Very good, Mr. President, I'll be leaving for Washington in a short while," advised Stern.

"On second thought, Michael," the President added, "talk with this representative and find out any information you can. Get some rest and I'll see you when you get back in the morning. That should be soon enough."

"Mr. President, I think this is something you really will want to come and see for yourself," continued Stern.

From their conversation and the tone of Stern's voice, Wallace knew instinctively the *angels* spectacle was indeed something far more than a publicity stunt activated by this small town church. With the interests of the many variant religious groups around the world, especially from the Middle East, this incident of the *angels* appeared to be something that could affect world religious beliefs and relations. Wallace knew now beyond a doubt that he must travel south and see the *angels* for himself.

"We'll talk when you get back. Thanks Michael," said the President.

"Yes sir. Good night," said Stern.

"Good night," the President replied.

A knock at the door brought Stern from Washington back to Dunning. He ended the phone connection and opened the door. It was his assistant and friend, Steven Howell.

"You probably need to come in here, Michael," said Steven.

Leaving Reverend Johnson's office, they walked back to the conference room. Upon entering they found the group sitting around the table. Muhammad was speaking as the rest of the group listened.

"Reverend Johnson, How do you explain these *angels* or *"jinn"* here in your church?" asked Muhammad as he directed his question to the Reverend who sat beside him.

"Mr. Harassi, I can't explain them." Taking off his glasses, he cleaned them with his handkerchief. After a short pause, he continued. "As I have told you, they simply appeared here a couple of days ago. Nothing out of the ordinary has happened here to merit this visit."

With a kindly, almost fatherly smile, Thomas added, "There is no explaining God and how He chooses to reveal His Will. Some of us are Christian, some Jew, and some Muslim. We all pray to the same God for his guidance, and his mercy. We pray that we follow in His light and not in darkness. Darkness is life without God. God is bigger than any of us! God is pure goodness and can only be served in goodness. What He does and how He reveals Himself is unknown to us." With a slight laugh he continued, "Maybe our greatest failing is trying to put words into God's mouth. After all, He is God of the Universe, not simply just this little blue sphere we live on."

Muhammad nodded, "I agree, Reverend. I feel a sense of joy and thankfulness having been able to witness this most unbelievable event. Thank you for allowing me to be present.

What impact this will have on our differences in religious beliefs, I don't know," Muhammad added. "We will have to wait and see."

Michael Stern spoke. "Mr. Harassi, when you communicate with your government, will you suggest that your King, or any of your country's religious leadership, come to Dunning?"

Harassi taking a more non-committal stance said, "Mr. Stern, all I can do is report to my government what I have seen and stress the enormous impact that it has had on me. I would like for the King to come and witness this himself, but as to what he will do, I do not know. Mr. Stern, like all of us here tonight, I think I have seen a glimpse of God. Maybe this glimpse into God's Kingdom will alter our world if enough people come and see this extraordinary sight. Maybe it will help to end the wars and evil that is carried on in God's name by many people."

Muhammad was obviously as moved as were the others by the sight of the *angels*. For a few minutes, the group sat quietly saying nothing.

Finally, Reverend Johnson spoke. "Before we leave, would anyone like to see our visitors one last time?"

To answer his question, everyone said "yes." It was likely to be something that would be a part of them for the rest of their lives, something with which nothing else would ever compare. They stood, walked out of the room and back down the hallway to once again gaze at the visitors from some unworldly dimension. Leaving the small church half an hour later, the rain was still continuously falling. It was quiet in the van on the way back to the hotel. Through the dark streets they rode, each man lost in his own thoughts about life, death, angels, and God. Each man eternally touched by the knowledge of something unbelievable across the divide that man believes separates life and death.

13

When Chad awoke, he felt the darkness around him. He heard the sound of rain outside and he felt the warmth of Cynthia's body next to his. She lay closely pressed against him, her breathing slow and regular, and the sound of one in deep sleep. Chad's arm was around her waist and her hand was clasped around his as if to insure that he could not escape. Chad had no intentions of escaping. He never wanted to let go of this moment. Lying close with Cynthia, he wished this moment could go on throughout eternity. Never had he felt so complete, so fulfilled with his life. Cynthia had changed him just as he had been forever changed by the images of the *angels* in St. Michael's. The touch of her hair against his cheek felt like silk as did the smoothness of her body. She stirred briefly seemingly disturbed from some faraway dream. It quickly passed as she again lay still beside him. Chad smiled in the dark. With no one to see or understand, still he smiled with complete fulfilled happiness as he again drifted off into wonderful sleep.

When he awoke again, the dim early morning light peered into the room through the blinds of the window. His eyes opening were met with the stare of dark eyes watching him. He was being watched as he slept. Cynthia smiled at him as he emerged from his groggy state, resting her head on her arm.

"Good morning," she whispered as he focused on her.

"Good morning," he answered. "I didn't realize I was being watched."

She laughed at his early morning attempt at humor as she leaned over and kissed him lightly.

Chad thought, this *is too good! It has to be a dream.*

"What time do you have to be at the church?" Cynthia asked, as she propped up leaning on her elbow.

Even in disarray, hair tousled, and wearing no make-up, Cynthia was the most beautiful person Chad had ever seen.

"Let me think," said Chad rubbing his hand through his hair. "I'm not sure. I had better call the station and find out a little later."

He looked at Cynthia, "How about you? What time do you have to be at work?"

"I have to be there by nine. And, if I'm not mistaken, didn't Jim Stuart tell you that we needed to be ready to meet with Anthony Martin at one?"

Chad answered, "That's right. They are supposed to begin setting up the stage this morning."

Stopping a moment to listen, Chad noted, "It's still raining, isn't it?"

Sitting on the edge of the bed and pulling on Chad's discarded shirt, Cynthia said, "Yes, and I think it is supposed to rain all day."

She got up, then moved towards the living room. Chad couldn't help notice how great she looked in the shirt, nothing but the shirt. It covered the bare essentials, but gave him the view of two very long slender legs.

She would have made a great model for men's shirts. Any kind of shirt!

As she walked through the doorway, she said over her shoulder, "I'll make coffee."

Chad lay for a few moments listening to Cynthia moving about the kitchen. She completed his life in a way he had never felt before; knowing at this moment his life had meaning, and firmly believing there was the reward of an afterlife. God had led him to the two greatest events in his life, the *angels* and Cynthia.

Within a few minutes, Cynthia returned to the bedroom. She carried a tray with coffee and toast. They sat on the bed and ate, enjoying the company of each other. Afterward they held each other again, making love as the night before.

All too soon, they had to return to the work of news and the story of the *angels*. Chad wanted to forget about work and the rest of the world for at least one day, but he knew that wasn't possible. Today would be the biggest day in both of their careers. Cynthia left Chad's to get ready for work. But for the longest time they stood by the door, talking like two teenagers, as if they would never see each other again before finally tearing away from each other.

When she was gone, Chad felt lonely and empty. It was amazing how just her presence made him feel. He also knew that they would have to perform very professionally in public, not allowing anyone to see through their façade or the tremendous magnetism pulling them together. Chad knew it would be hard for him and, selfishly, he hoped it would be hard for Cynthia, too.

By nine o'clock Chad was driving toward St. Michael's. A steady rain continued falling. It still amazed Chad how this small city of Dunning had been transformed into the center of national attention in just a matter of days. Cars filled the streets and people were everywhere, ignoring the rain. As Chad neared Everwine Street, he looked around at the throngs of people standing in the rain in long lines that appeared to stretch for miles. With the street blocked off from traffic, he approached the check point. His WTLA car gained him a nod from policemen standing at the check point as he drove through and on down Everwine.

While there was no vehicular traffic, the crowds of people were huge. The rain seemed to have little deterrence for the many people lined up to visit the church and see its celestial inhabitants. Chad approached the now familiar little church and turned into the parking lot. Police and guard presence was heavy. As he parked his car, Chad noted the construction for the broadcast taking place later that afternoon. A large open tent had been erected complete with wooded flooring, desk, chairs, and lights. Behind it was the white framed church. Walking toward the site he could see workers had begun putting cameras in place for the evening news. The sight of all this gave Chad a feeling of nervousness in the pit of his stomach. Then, the thought of he and Cynthia meeting Jeff Glor and Lester Holt at St. Michael's only enhanced the nervousness and made his stomach almost queasy.

"How does it look?" Chad heard a voice from behind. Turning to face the voice, Chad saw Jim Stuart, the station manager of WTLA.

"Jim, what are you doing out here in this messy weather?" greeted Chad with a question.

He knew very well why Jim was here. He wanted to make certain things were perfect for the appearance of the "big dogs" from CBS and NBC, and he was eager to meet both Jeff Glor and his counterpart, Lester Holt, in person. Not that Chad wasn't looking forward to this as well; he was!

"Everything's got to be just right when the news team arrives from New York," said Jim. "They should be here sometime shortly after noon, unless there's a flight delay."

"Okay." said Chad moving around the desk and sitting in the chair to the right of center. "This mine?" questioned Chad.

"Yes, you'll be on the right. Cynthia Davis of WDDR on the left with Jeff and Lester in the center," continued Jim Stuart.

"Hello," they heard another voice. Chad knew the voice without turning around. It was Cynthia.

Cynthia came under the tent while closing her umbrella. Extending her hand to Jim, she said, "I'm Cynthia Davis and I'll bet you are Jim Stuart."

Jim shook her hand as Chad stood up and came around the desk. Chad thought, *she's good*. With the winning smile, good looks, and the firm handshake she won Jim over immediately.

Jim turned to Chad saying, "Cynthia, I know you're familiar with Chad Simmons from the interviews and tours earlier this week, and perhaps with this broadcast and the days ahead following this story, you can get to know each other better."

Cynthia extended her hand to Chad. Their eyes locked for a moment as Cynthia smiled again. "Yes, Chad, I've enjoyed working with you these past few days. I look forward to working with you in the future and getting to know you better."

Following the script, Chad smiled at Cynthia with his best television smile and commented, "Yeah, I'm sure we'll become better acquainted." Again their eyes locked. Jim could not see how deeply they looked at each other nor could he feel the electricity that passed between them with the brief handshake.

"I'll leave you two for a while," said Jim. "When the rain lets up a bit, the technicians will finish installing cameras. We'll run through the plans for the Dunning segment after the group from New York gets here."

Both Chad and Cynthia nodded.

"Any questions?" said Jim.

"No, not at the moment," replied Cynthia.

"None for me, Jim," added Chad.

"Fine. I'll get back with you both later," he said turning and moving from under the tent and around the large WTLA truck parked beside the tent.

Cynthia opened the folder she held and began to thumb through it. Chad pulled out his notebook and pen and began jotting down some notes. For a couple of moments no one said anything. Then, breaking the silence, Chad spoke.

"I guess you know that I'm very much in love with you, don't you?" Without looking up, he continued to write. Chad paused for a moment, and then added, "I think I have loved you from the moment I first laid eyes on you three years ago."

At that point Chad looked up at Cynthia to find her looking at him. Her eyes were watering as she looked steadily at him.

She wanted to reach over, to touch and feel his warmth. She wanted to say so many things to Chad. He had made her feel human and alive again. He had awakened feelings in her that she thought died in Chicago. It was as if God were giving her a second chance. *She now realized and admitted to herself she had felt the same attraction from the beginning, just as if they were two parts of a puzzle that had finally come together. Were they really made for each other? Was God's Hand in their relationship just as His Hand brought the angels to Dunning?* As these thoughts clouded her head, she just looked at Chad, put down her pen and looked down at the desk. Not wanting her make-up to run, Cynthia blinked several times, her throat felt tight and dry.

"I'm sorry if I spoke out of place. You may not feel that way. I just felt that I had to tell you my feelings, even if it meant you would never speak to me again," said Chad. He continued,

"Sometimes we say things we wish we had never said, but sometimes we wish we had said things, but never say them. I didn't want that to happen. If you never want to see me again, at least, you know how I feel."

Chad felt he had blundered through that moment. He felt that he should not have been so open and he should not have exposed his feelings to her so openly and certainly not so early in their relationship. What was she thinking? Did she see him as a toy, a diversion, as a man that was simply present in this little South Alabama town who would still be here while she moved on to a bigger station in another state?

Chad was ready for her to say something, to let him down easy or maybe say she liked him but was not ready for a serious relationship yet. He just wanted her to say something even if it killed him inside.

She didn't. She sat looking down. Finally, she cleared her throat. Looking up at Chad, Cynthia said very quietly almost as if talking to herself, "I love you and I don't ever want to be far from you."

The only other sound was the rain on the top of the tent. Cynthia cleared her throat again. "Life is too short to play games. I've learned that. Let's just take each other one day at a time. We're not promised more than that, you know."

Her hand moved across the desk to his. Their hands clasped tightly as they looked at each other.

Taking a deep breath and smiling at Chad, while blinking away tears, Cynthia said, "Are you going to be sorry we've said these things?"

Chad looked steadily at Cynthia, then smiled, "Ask me when I'm eighty-five," replied Chad.

This remark broke the trance that had exposed their deep feelings with a warm finish. Laughing, Cynthia let go of Chad's hand and slapped it playfully.

At that moment, one of the technicians appeared from around the side of the mobile television truck. "Is it okay if we finish installing the equipment before it floods again?" he asked.

"Sure, we're just getting some thoughts together and making sure we understand each other," Chad answered the young man.

Suddenly everything turned to preparing for the national news broadcast that evening. Even so, beneath the work and activity, Chad and Cynthia both felt the intoxicating effect of being deeply in love. Not the tension of working with TV's big boys, the rain, or anything else was going to change the sheer exuberance of just being near each other!

Not given space on Everwine Street to set up his mobile unit and stage, William Renfro rented space on an open lot two blocks from St. Michael's. A large mobile truck with *Southwest Evangelical Ministries* painted on its side was parked on the vacant lot and a large, open tent was erected beside it. A stage, cameras, crew, and seating for an audience filled the tent. Reverend Renfro and several of his commentators sat discussing the events in Dunning before cameras set up for his television audience which reached across the South and Southwest. Framing the scene behind them was the roof and steeple of St. Michael's. It stood out above the trees in the gray, rain-filled sky. Stage lights on and the cameras going, Reverend Renfro leaned forward with his elbow on the desk and began:

> *Friends, you've seen the news and our reporting the tremendous crowds here in Dunning, Alabama. Based*

on what I know from studying the Word of God and His Divine promises, this is definitely a Sign of the End Times. God is showing us the opening into heaven by having His Angels preclude His earthly coming! Just as I have predicted for years, the signs are here. Beloved ones, listen for the Trumpets!

His associates on stage nodded in agreement.

"Now friends, we'll take calls on our hot line. Just call the number at the bottom of the screen if you would like to comment on this powerful, unfolding story, or if you would like to contribute to our very important ministry," continued Renfro.

From the board on the mobile truck, lights went on as calls starting coming in to speak to the Reverend.

"Mobile, Alabama. Michelle. Good morning," said Reverend Renfro.

"Brother Renfro, have you talked or made contact with the *angels?*"

Renfro smiled and spoke directly to the camera. "No, Michelle I have not. At the present time it appears that they are not communicating with anyone."

"Caller from Milan, Texas. John, you're on the air," Renfro answering another call.

"Hello, can you hear me?" the voice on the line asked.

"Yes, John, we can hear you. What would you like to say?"

"Reverend Renfro, I was wondering if you could describe the visions that are being seen in the church," the caller questioned.

"John," said Renfro, "Actually, we have not been able to get a tour through the church. The crowds have made it impossible to get our crew in and, unfortunately, the city has not granted us an after-hours tour to bring back to our viewers."

"Joseph, from here in Alabama. Joseph, what have you got for us this morning?" answered Renfro again with his booming announcer's voice.

After a brief silence, an unwavering voice came across the line, "You have no right to be there. This is my task. God called me to bring these events into being."

"I beg your pardon, Joseph; we couldn't hear your entire question. Joseph, are you there?"

Renfro knew the man wasn't still on the line, but he went along anyway. Actually, when he had finished his first statement Joseph had been disconnected. Calls of this nature happened regularly. There were many genuine followers and viewers of Renfro's ministry, but there were also those people on the fringe, in terms of both religion and sanity. Joseph sounded like both.

"It's time for a word from one of our wonderful sponsors," said Renfro. "We'll return in just a moment."

As the camera faded and went to an advertisement for tuna in spring water, Renfro motioned to the producer standing behind the cameras. As he approached, Renfro spoke in a whispered voice, not wanting the live audience of about two dozen to hear. "How did that kook get through to me?"

Angry and irritated Renfro continued. "If one like that slips through again, some heads are gonna roll. Do you understand?"

"Yes, Reverend," stammered the producer. "It won't happen again."

"It had better not!" ordered Renfro.

The camera man pointed to Renfro and counted down with his fingers: three, two, one!

His anger evaporated into a warm smile as the camera lights went on. With a complete change of expression, Reverend Renfro sat smiling and continued, "Welcome back to our morning program coming directly to you from Dunning, Alabama, the city of *the angels*."

The small, bright television screen was in sharp contrast to the outdated, dark, and rundown room where Joseph Turbon had found lodging in the small, seedy hotel. Outside, the half-lit *Lily Hotel* sign flickered, "No Vacancy."

How dare this man say what God has planned! Joseph Turbon knew he had been called to come to Dunning to begin God's work making preparation for the end times. It was his task and not that of some television evangelist like Renfro whose main mission was increasing his listening audience and his receipts. After all, had he himself not been preaching the end times for years? Now he must decide how to carry out God's plan. God had not specifically told him how he was to proceed, but he felt certain in time that He would. The voices that often spoke to him would give him details!

Looking in his small bag laying on the bed, he reached in and pulled out a small chrome revolver. Joseph looked at the gun and whispered to himself, "Sometimes, it requires force when man does not listen to God!"

14

The small private jet which had been parked at the Wiregrass Regional Airport since Tuesday afternoon lifted off at eight-fifteen Wednesday morning. As it gained altitude, circled, and turned north, Michael Stern looked out at the landscape below him. Fields of new crops, woodlands, and small ponds emerged below. Across the narrow aisle of the plane, Steven Howell sat shuffling through the papers that he seemed to always have at hand.

Michael leaned back against his seat and closed his eyes, reflecting over the last twenty-four hours. In just that short amount of time so much had happened. Now, he was on his way back to Washington to convince the President that he should go to Dunning and, perhaps, take with him a small party of world leaders to see the *angels* of St. Michael's. Somehow it all seemed a dream, that this one event stood the possibility of changing our world's thinking, and the relationships of so many people, and how each perceived God, including himself. He drifted off trying to reconcile his own religious beliefs.

Stern awoke to find the plane turning and making an approach into Reagan International Airport outside of the capital. Glancing over at Howell, he saw he was still looking at papers oblivious to anything around him. The plane touched down with only a slight screech of the tires on the runway and taxied to a quiet side of the airport. As it came to a stop, a large black SUV stood waiting. When the door of the plane opened, Stern and Howell deplaned and walked to the waiting vehicle. They would go directly to the White House. The ride through the city would have been any tourist's delight. But Michael wasn't looking at the sights; he was walking himself through the briefing he was going to give President Wallace.

Arriving at the entry gate the SUV paused briefly as a guard went through the check list for anyone coming onto the grounds of the White House. Then the car moved toward the mansion. Stern and Howell got out of the car and walked up the steps to the door of the White House. Inside, they passed one of the many security agents stationed throughout the building. At the information center, an agent sat monitoring calls.

"Morning John," said Stern as they passed. "Is the President in his office?"

"Yes sir. He's been waiting for you, I think," the agent replied.

Walking quickly down the hall they entered the outer office of the President.

"Good morning, June," said Stern and they entered the office.

June Snell sat looking at her computer screen. Glancing up, she smiled and said, "Hello Michael. And how are you today, Steven?"

Both men stopped briefly at her desk exchanging small talk.

June was familiar with just about everyone who "came and went" at the White House on a regular basis. She was an indispensable part of Stuart Wallace's office, having been with the President for many years, going back to his early days as a young lawyer. June didn't miss much. One might be fooled by this grandmotherly-looking lady with gray hair and glasses, but would quickly learn she carried a lot of weight with the President.

"Seen anything lately?" June asked, with a mischievous smile. Picking up her phone to announce their arrival, she waved them toward the President's office.

Stern, smiling and shaking his head at her joke walked toward the office.

Howell winked and said in a low voice as he went past her desk, "June, you wouldn't believe it!"

Entering the President's office, the two men walked to Wallace's desk. The President stood at once to greet them, shaking each man's hand.

"Have a seat. You both must be tired having been up all night but, I do sincerely appreciate the hard work you have done." Both men settled into chairs across from the President and waited for him to continue speaking.

Wallace quickly came to the point. "From your account it sounds as if we have some sort of vision that no one seems to be able to explain. Right?"

"That's correct, Mr. President," answered Stern.

"And you say, along with everyone one else who has witnessed these visions, that you believe they're *angels*, possibly from another plane or dimension, so to speak. Am I correct?"

"Yes sir," answered Stern again.

"Okay. So what are you proposing that we do with this?" asked the President.

"Mr. President, may I suggest that you extend an invitation to as many world leaders as possible inviting them to visit St.

Michael's? May I further suggest that you invite leaders from major religions to this same visit?" answered Stern.

"Let me see if I interpret your report correctly. You think this incident merits invitations of this caliber?" asked Wallace.

"Yes, Mr. President, I do," said Stern.

The President glanced at Howell who sat nodding in agreement with Stern's suggestion.

"You saw them also?" asked Wallace.

"Yes, Mr. President," replied Howell.

Pausing for a moment President Wallace thought. Then he slapped both arms of his chair, stood up and said, "Okay, Michael, we're going to Dunning this evening. We'll fly in the small plane. I don't want anyone to know I've gone anywhere near Alabama. This will be a trip that officially I haven't made. Make it happen! And to everyone involved, it's Top Secret."

The two men rose when the President stood and nodded. Stern now had the task of planning this clandestine visit for the evening.

"As soon as I have the details, I'll inform you sir," Stern said as they turned to leave the office.

"Very good. Until later," said the President, as he sat down and turned to other pressing issues on his desk.

Almost a thousand miles to the south the news media were preparing the special broadcast for the evening. The news groups from CBS and NBC had arrived in Dunning and their meeting with the local news media went well. Both Chad and Cynthia were very much impressed with the New York teams, especially Jeff Glor and Lester Holt. These two men were not only professional, but warm and congenial people as well, which made Chad and Cynthia feel comfortable working with them.

Glor and Holt were not the *prima donna* types, and, to the delight of many on the Dunning team, praised the warm hospitality of the small southern city and the work of the local stations. The atmosphere was one of excitement throughout the afternoon. Descending on Dunning were more and more news media and crowds of people grew larger and larger. The rain continued all day but did not put a damper on anything. Actually, it provided a welcome respite from the heat.

The five o'clock local news was carried by the joint work of WTLA and WDDR with Chad and Cynthia co-anchoring. Glor and Holt stood by complimenting them on their work and their handling of the pressures of such an international story.

During the last commercial break, Chad and Cynthia shifted to the seats on the right and left of the stage while Glor and Holt took the center seats. When the clock moved to five-thirty, a technician pointed to the newscasters counting down the seconds and as the red light came on, he pointed simultaneously to them.

"Good evening, I'm Jeff Glor with CBS News, along with Lester Holt of NBC News, and our host affiliates at WTLA and WDDR here in Dunning, Alabama. We are joined by these stations' anchors, Chad Simmons and Cynthia Davis for this evening's news."

"Our top story, which has grabbed the attention of the nation, and the world, is the *angels* of St. Michael's AME Church, here in Dunning Alabama," continued Lester Holt.

As Holt talked, the camera panned from the stage to the white church with its long line of people slowly entering the church. The camera then moved down the line away from the church to show an even longer line that curved completely out of sight. Turning its angle, the camera then showed the curious crowd across the street which lined Everwine Street.

"For the past few days this story and the people involved has grown monumentally and the *angels* are becoming known to everyone," said Holt.

Glor then spoke, "We want to turn now to our onsite correspondents. Chad, how has this event affected Dunning?"

The camera moved in on Chad as he answered, "Jeff, the appearance of the *angels* has changed the city profoundly in just a matter of days. Dunning advanced from being a small, regional shopping and trading area to the center of news both here and around the world. The population jumped from approximately sixty-five thousand to well over a hundred thousand in just a matter of days due to the influx of visitors."

"Cynthia, what about your observation regarding any effect on Dunning?" asked Holt turning to his left.

"Lester, reiterating what Chad just said, this event has had a tremendous impact on Dunning. What the long range effect will be, we have no idea since no one can really speculate as to how long the visitors will remain," reported Cynthia.

"A question for you both," added Lester. "Will either of you share your own personal insight why these *seemingly heavenly beings* appeared in Dunning?"

Cynthia continued speaking, "I think Chad would agree with me. The authenticity of the beings can be validated, but no one can confirm *why* they chose to appear in this small church in Dunning, Alabama, and no one can assure *how long* they will continue to remain here."

"Yes," continued Chad. "All manner of speculation is out there, but no one really knows."

The discussion continued for several minutes, pertaining mainly to suppositional information, previously discussed many times over. The broadcast also examined how religious sects from other parts of the world might be influenced by the appearance of the *angels*.

Finally, Jeff Glor asked the question many people wanted answered. "Has the government of the United States made any effort to become involved in any of this revelation of the *angels*?"

Chad began, "From what we are able to tell you at this point, there have been reliable inquiries from Washington, but nothing that can be confirmed at this moment."

"Thank you for your extraordinary work, Chad and Cynthia. We look forward to our own visit inside the church and reporting back to you as we continue following this story in the coming days," reported Jeff Glor.

At this juncture of the broadcast, Lester Holt followed, "Continuing with news around the nation and the world, the hot weather has touched off severe thunderstorms and tornadoes throughout the mid-west today."

The remainder of the news went from storms, to the price of gas, to the continuing unrest in the Middle East. The broadcast ended with a sign-off from the joint production of CBS and NBC and with Glor and Holt bidding the listeners a "Good evening."

Local news followed at the home stations' newsrooms as Jeff Glor, Lester Holt, Chad, Cynthia, the staffs, and station managers, shook hands and continued to talk about St. Michael's off the air. Arrangements had been made for a visit into St. Michael's for Glor and Holt and then dinner for the teams before they departed for New York later in the evening. This story had enabled two rival local stations and two major networks to work together, culminating in a successful co-production from Dunning.

Shortly after the broadcast, Glor and Holt visited inside St. Michael's along with other staff members of CBS and NBC. They were quietly and inconspicuously ushered in to see the miraculous beings. Seeing the *angels* in this small, unassuming sanctuary left them moved and awed like the many thousands who, by this time, had also seen them. They felt just as Chad and Cynthia had after first visiting the sanctuary— no story could ever come close to the magnitude of the story of the *angels* of Dunning. They, like everyone associated with this story, knew it was the foremost news maker of modern times.

15

As Tom Weatherman walked away to call his office in Atlanta, Muhammad Harassi punched in numbers on his cell phone. Within a matter of seconds a voice came through his ear-piece.

"Muhammad, how are you?" answered Ishmael Hadi, Muhammad's longtime friend and the Saudi King's Press Secretary.

"I'm good, and you?"

"I, too, am well," replied Ishmael.

Finished with the pleasantries, Ishmael came to the point. "What information do you have for us? Is there any evidence to support the news reports?"

"Ishmael, I am in Dunning, Alabama, now, at the airport waiting for a flight back to Atlanta. Tom Weatherman and I flew in here from Atlanta yesterday afternoon. Last night we were able to make a visit to the church of St. Michael's, after it had been closed for the evening."

"And?" waited Ishmael.

"Ishmael, to answer your question, we saw *angels*. *Angels from heaven* were right above us," explained Muhammad, his voice becoming increasingly excited as he described the vision from the past night to his friend. "It was a sight I thought I'd never see in this life!"

Silence took over the connection for a couple of seconds before Muhammad spoke again.

"At the same time that I was there, a representative of the President of the United States had flown to Dunning under secrecy. It was agreed that nothing of the visit would be made public. I think the government of the United States is likely deciding how to interpret this holy appearance as well. I also think this President will consequently make a call to the King with an invitation to come to the United States, with perhaps a few other world leaders. I think it will be an invitation that he cannot refuse," added Muhammad.

Ishmael looked out the window of his office. It was a few minutes after five, which meant it was just after nine in Alabama. When he finished talking with Muhammad, he would apprise his boss of what he had just been told who, in turn, would speak with the King. Plans for the possible invitation would have to be laid out as quickly as possible, as well as a workable solution to bring the leaders of their faith on board. An opportunity to see God's *angels*, regardless of where they happen to be, cannot be ignored or missed.

"Muhammad, for the present, stay in Atlanta until we decide what we must do," instructed Ishmael.

"Very well," answered Muhammad.

"We will be in touch soon. Goodbye," said Ishmael.

"Goodbye," said Muhammad.

At that moment Tom Weatherman returned to the seating area. He had feigned the need to call his office and instead went over to the magazine and book vendor, where he pretended to browse. He knew that Muhammad needed privacy to touch base with home and describe what he had seen. Tom wished he could have heard the conversation, or at least Muhammad's explanation, of the visit to St. Michael's. But he had waited instead until he saw Muhammad end his phone call before returning to the flight gate.

"Couldn't find a thing I wanted to read. At least, it won't be a long flight," explained Tom.

"No," answered Muhammad, "It is quite a short flight."

Fishing, Tom asked, "When do you think you will have to return home?"

Not wanting to keep his friend in the dark, especially since Tom had made the visit to Dunning possible, Muhammad said, "Tom, I will stay in Atlanta, until I get word from my government regarding how to proceed."

"Great," replied Tom. "You can see the sights of Atlanta and experience a little *southern hospitality*."

"Thanks, Tom, but you have done far more already than I could have asked."

"Don't be absurd, Muhammad. That's what friends do for friends," said Tom with a shrug. He knew full well that he would help Muhammad as a friend; and, there might be a time in the future when he would need Muhammad's help.

At the next moment the voice on the airport public address system announced the boarding of the plane and both Tom and Muhammad moved through the security line toward the gate.

For Michael Stern the day had not been so leisurely. After meeting with the President earlier, he began the job of preparing for President Wallace's undercover visit to Dunning. It was no easy task organizing such a trip in a clandestine manner for the President of the United States. In the present world of satellite news coverage, cell phones, and cell phone cameras, it would be difficult for anyone, much less the President of the United States, to go anywhere unnoticed.

First and foremost, Stern had to prepare Treasury agents who guard the President what should be anticipated once they reach Dunning, and their subsequent visit to the church. His next task was setting in motion preparations for leaving Washington and flying to Dunning with no one being aware. He, then, had to prepare Dunning authorities and coordinate the activities of the local police force with the Secret Service. First things first! He must call Allan Smith to set plans for the visit in motion.

At precisely ten o'clock Mayor Smith's intercom rang. "Yes, Lucy?

"Mayor, Mr. Stern from Washington is on the phone," said Lucy.

"Thanks Lucy, put him through," replied Allan.

"Mr. Mayor, Michael Stern here. How are you this morning?"

"Great, Mr. Stern. How may I help you?"

Stern began speaking immediately without mincing words, "Mayor, the President has requested coming to Dunning to see the *angels* himself tonight." Allan caught his breath as he listened. *No one denied a request from the President.*

"This visit is to be kept completely quiet. No one is to be made aware of his presence except the people who have to know, which I am assuming would include you, Chief Tyler, and just a select few of your people, of course."

Stern allowed this to sink in for a couple of moments before continuing.

"The Secret Service will be in touch with Chief Tyler shortly regarding the particulars of the visit. At this point, do you have any questions?"

Allan thought for a moment then replied, "Not at the moment, other than what time can we expect this visit to take place?"

"We are looking at being in Dunning around midnight," said Stern. "Does that look doable to you?"

"Yes. I certainly see no other problems with this other than informing Reverend Johnson since it is his church," said Smith.

"Certainly, Mr. Mayor, he must be included, but make sure he tells no one, not even his family. After all, this is a very sensitive situation," Stern reiterated. "Can you make this happen, Mr. Mayor?"

Without hesitation Allan answered, "We can do it, Mr. Stern."

"Good," Stern replied. "The Secret Service will be in touch. If you have any questions or anything comes up that I should know about, call me immediately."

"Very good," said Allan. "We'll be awaiting the call from the Secret Service. Goodbye."

The conversation ended. Allan sat for a couple of minutes in his chair, digesting all he had just heard. It was almost more than he could grasp. *Not only had visitors from another dimension rocked Dunning, but now the President of the United States was coming at midnight for a secret viewing! What else could possibly be in store for Dunning?* Again Allan shook his head.

First on his agenda had to be Reverend Thomas Johnson. He must try immediately to get in touch with him. Dialing St.

191

Michael's, Allan drummed his fingers on the desk waiting for someone to answer.

"Reverend Johnson, here. Can I help you?

Allan began speaking, "Reverend Johnson, Allan Smith here. I have some interesting news for you!"

"Mayor, I surely hope the news is good," the Reverend replied.

"Oh, I think you are going to find it's great news, Reverend," added Allan. He paused briefly before continuing. "The President is coming to St. Michael's. He's coming this evening around midnight. This visit is very top secret, of course, and no one else is to know. According to plans by the Secret Service, President Wallace will fly in unannounced with just a small security party." Letting the news sink in, Allan waited for Johnson to answer.

"Mayor, this *is* great news! Who is coming with him?" Johnson wanted to know.

"As I said, it will be a small party with just a select few," replied Allan.

A long period of silence interrupted their conversation as Thomas Johnson mulled over what he had just heard. He was both pleased and shocked that the President of the United States was coming to his small church to view perhaps *the most ecclesiastical sight on this earth since the resurrection of our Lord and Savior, Jesus Christ.* Thomas sat for an indeterminate amount of time, while Allan waited patiently on the other end of the line. He reflected on each event that had transpired at his church since the heavenly spectacle was first discovered by seventy-five-year old Doris Williams, faithful member of St. Michael's African Methodist Episcopal Church and servant of God. Now, to top it all, the President wanted a look himself!

Finally, Thomas spoke, "Mr. Mayor, I am fully aware of how secure we must be to have the President visit, but before proceeding another step, I have a request to make. As you remember, it was Doris Williams, a faithful member of our church, who actually first encountered the heavenly visitors that captured the attention of everyone near and far. I just couldn't help thinking that if anyone had the opportunity of introducing the President to his first glimpse of the heavenly visitors, that person has to be Doris!"

Allan certainly understood the Reverend's request and told him he would immediately contact Mr. Stern in Washington to see if this request could be made possible and would then inform him as soon as he could. Thomas must wait, however, before getting in touch with Doris.

In the several ensuing phone calls that went between Washington and Dunning, it was agreed that the President's plane would be met at midnight by Dunning Police Chief Tyler and the President would be escorted to St. Michael's by unmarked police and Secret Service escort. Being a covert visit, the President would not fly to Dunning in Air Force One, but would instead fly in on a much smaller, unmarked plane. Plans were designed to draw absolutely no attention. At the airport in Dunning, the control tower, which usually closed down by late evening, would be manned by a special crew coming in from Washington. Absolutely nothing would be left to chance. At the church, the President would be met by the Mayor, Governor, and Reverend Johnson to see himself the *angels* of St. Michael's and, of course, Doris Williams!

Shortly before noon, Doris Williams was interrupted in tidying up her small house by the telephone ringing. Her first thought jumped to her daughter, Sarah, and Doris quietly muttered to herself, "She needs me to look after Tyrone today."

But, as she picked up the phone and it wasn't Sarah, she wasn't at all surprised to hear Reverend Johnson's voice: *probably needs me at the church,* she mused. Between the grandchildren and volunteering at St. Michael's, Doris kept busy.

"Doris?" The Reverend asked.

"Yes, Reverend Johnson, and how are you this morning? I hear about all the 'goings on' at the church and I have tried to stay clear of all the crowds over there," Doris went on before Johnson had a chance to continue.

"Doris," the Reverend interrupted, "This is what I want to talk to you about." Speaking of 'goings on' at the church, what would you say to the President of the United States coming to Dunning? Would you be willing to meet with him in the church sanctuary to view the *angels*?"

"Now, Reverend, you just got to let me sit down a minute! You don't mean President Wallace is coming here? I never in my life met a President!"

Reverend Johnson went on to tell Doris about the previously secret visit to the sanctuary by some of the president's staff from Washington, the governor's staff from Alabama, and other newsworthy visitors to Dunning. Doris listened with eyes open wide as he told her about the visit from the President's assistant, Mr. Stern, and about Stern arranging for President Wallace to come to Dunning tonight; and, his own request for Doris, actually having been the first person to discover the *angels*, to be part of the group. The Reverend then discussed with Doris the absolute secretive nature of this visit. She could positively tell no one—no friends, no family! Agreeing on all necessary requirements for being a part of the visit, the Reverend told Doris he would pick her up around eleven to meet the President at twelve, if she wanted to go.

"If I want to go, Reverend? Just try and keep me away! Praise the Lord for this opportunity to see the *angels* again and to meet the President!" exclaimed Doris as she tried to harness her excitement.

Two streets over from the church, the live production continued at Reverend Renfro's mobile studio. Renfro wasn't the least bit affected by the call from the man who had been cut off during the earlier "call-in" session. He dealt regularly with kooks and well knew in discussing religion you had as many opinions as you had people. He took great care screening people who agreed with his thinking, and he was good at it, but occasionally one caller with his own agenda would get through. Despite that, from his obvious success many people agreed with his views of God's plans for the universe! Like many people, such zealots wanted God to act in their time and according to the way they thought events of the world should progress.

The Mayor of Dunning had denied Renfro, as well as his camera crew, a private viewing of the *angels*. Other television news crews had been allowed inside the church and now he had secretive plans of his own; plans that included a surprise visit to the little church once it closed for the evening. Renfro and his crew would travel to the church and simply demand admittance. How could the City risk a confrontation with a well-known religious leader over a visit to a religious shrine? There was no way he would be turned down, risking bad publicity for the City. Neither the Mayor nor this little backwoods town was going to stand in his way of playing a role in this unbelievable, unfolding story. He was owed this. Renfro began preparing for his surprise visit.

Late afternoon found Dunning still under a steady rain; not that rain wasn't needed! Rain was precisely what farmers had been praying for— a steady, soaking rain to provide life-giving water to their crops. Nonetheless, rain didn't stop the enthusiasm of the people who had come to visit St. Michael's. Even in the rain, people waited patiently for their chance to see the *angels*.

As eight o'clock approached and darkness began settling in, people still waited in vain with hopes of getting into the church before it closed for the evening. Most of the TV crews, except for a few skeleton crews maintaining their equipment, had closed their operations. Lights came on in the houses along Everwine Street. The line waiting to get inside the church gradually diminished as people turned away, hoping for the chance to come back tomorrow to see the *angels*. Before long, the only real presence was black and white police cars and national guardsmen standing guard in their ponchos along the street and around the church.

Following a successful national broadcast, Chad had gone home to get dressed for dinner planned with the New York crews. As he stood in his apartment, tying his tie, he gazed out his balcony doors. He thought about the day. It could not have gone better. He had been on national TV with Lester Holt and Jeff Glor, but still that wasn't the best part! He and Cynthia had been totally honest about their feelings for each other. It looked as if this was the beginning of something far more meaningful than he had ever hoped. Staring into the rain, he thought, *God has truly blessed me beyond measure!* He then turned into his bedroom to get his coat.

As Chad, Cynthia, the crews of WTLA, WDDR, plus the groups from CBS and NBC, prepared for a fun evening, Allan Smith sat in his office running through plans for this evening's *hush-hush* visit of the President. Lucy had gone home long ago and now he sat by himself trying to reexamine details to make certain the visit went smoothly. On a typical day being Mayor of Dunning was a busy job for this growing community, but with all that had happened in the past couple of days, it had become overwhelming. Fortunately for Allan, he had a wife who understood his present situation. Sarah Smith was immensely supportive of her husband. She preferred staying in the background, not drawing attention to herself or her family. This attitude was so unlike that of some wives of officials who wanted an equal share of the limelight, or wanted to use their positions to be treated special. She was just Sarah Smith, wife, mother, and support for her husband.

Smith's cell phone rang. Allan glanced to see who was calling as he picked up his phone. It was Bill Tyler, the Police Chief. His watch read almost 11:00 PM, which was still too early for any news from the President.

"Yeah, Bill. What you got?"

Not expecting anything, yet constantly being on his guard, Allan waited for Chief Tyler to speak.

"Mayor, we've got a problem." Tyler's voice was somber.

"What is it, Bill?" asked Allan. He could hear angry voices in the background.

"Reverend William Renfro is here at the church demanding to be allowed inside, along with his crew and cameras. He has a small crew, but says he is not leaving without being allowed inside," added Tyler.

Knowing that in a matter of an hour or so the President would be in Dunning and that Renfro's appearance could possibly ignite other news crews, Allan realized he had to think fast. He certainly did not want the President's visit to be compromised, which could put Wallace in an embarrassing position, as well as the City of Dunning.

"Bill, arrest Renfro and his entire crew for trespassing. That will tie him up until the President is gone," said Allan. "It will take Renfro at least a couple of hours to get out on bail if we're lucky, and if we drag out the process, it might take even longer. We'll worry about the ramifications of this later."

"Okay, Boss, you got it," said Bill Tyler.

After finishing his phone call to the mayor, Tyler returned to Renfro's group still standing in the rain after appearing unannounced earlier.

"Are we going to be allowed entrance into the church now?" asked Renfro, sounding very sure of himself.

"No, Mr. Renfro, you're not. I have orders from the Mayor to arrest you and your group for trespassing. This church is closed now and off limits to you or anyone else for that matter."

Renfro stuttered, his anger rising, "That is ridiculous! I'm the head of a prestigious national religious organization! You can't arrest me!"

"Yes sir, I can, and I will," continued Chief Tyler. "If you will please come quietly with me, I don't think it will be necessary to handcuff you."

Chief Tyler motioned toward the two police cars parked on the street. He was hoping this could happen quietly and quickly; otherwise, in a matter few minutes TV crews would be alerted by the noise and proceed to catch any possible story brewing. Renfro stopped, shocked that he was about to be arrested. He thought seriously about resisting and pressing his demand; but, as several police officers moved closer, he decided not to press the point. Instead, pointing his finger at Tyler, he said angrily, "You'll be sorry for this! You'll pay for this disgrace! Just wait till my lawyer gets here!"

With this last remark, he turned and moved off in the dark and rain with his crew toward the waiting police cars, surrounded by several officers. Tyler breathed a sigh of relief. Renfro had backed down without a struggle and Tyler had prevented another commotion from erupting. Quickly Renfro and his crew were ordered into the cruisers, and soon disappeared in the rain, down the street.

As Tyler stood back and watched the cars disappear, a young man stepped out from the trucks behind him in the parking lot. He was obviously a reporter who was stuck with the graveyard shift. Young, sleepy, and wet, he stood there.

"Chief, is something going on?" he questioned

Tyler looked at him and then glanced back as the cars disappeared down Everwine. "No, just some trespassers, trying to get into the church. You can go back to sleep."

As the young man walked back to the trucks and the humming of the generators, Chief Tyler pulled out his cell phone again. He dialed the Mayor's number. It rang once before Allan answered.

"Mayor, our problem is on the way to the city jail. I'll tell the watch officer to do everything they can to slow down the process." With that Bill added, "I shouldn't say it, but I almost enjoyed making that arrest."

Allan sat back and breathed a sigh of relief. He had dodged another bullet.

"Thanks, Bill, let's just hope that this is our only excitement for the rest of the evening," the Mayor replied.

Glancing at his watch it was couple of minutes past eleven. The President wasn't scheduled to arrive before midnight. Looking out the window, he could see the rain continuing. Based on weather reports, it was predicted all week.

In his hotel at the Hyatt Regency in Atlanta, Muhammad sat with his feet propped on the coffee table. The television was on, but he wasn't watching anything particularly and only had it on to offset the dead silence in the room. Besides that, he had only the rain outside to break the silence as it beat against the window of his tenth floor room. Tom Weatherman had invited Muhammad to dinner on their return to Atlanta, but Muhammad had declined. He was tired from two days of travel. Now, he sat in the hotel wondering what sort of information he would receive from home. His visit to Dunning had filled him with many questions; not just his beliefs, but about others' beliefs. Was it possible that there could be many right answers to God? He wondered himself how God looked at humankind's attempts to understand His Greatness. Muhammad often felt, *Man in his attempt to understand God, completely missed the true reality of God.* He saw in his faith, as well as others, groups who were unbending in their own extreme views. After all, *God was Master and Creator of the Universe, not just the little Planet we call Earth.*

Muhammad also wondered what Ishmael thought about what he had described to him with respect to his visit and the *angels.* Reflecting back to the whole experience, he wondered if he had been too emotional about his visit, if he had been too open about what he saw. After all, for someone who had not actually seen the *angels,* it would be hard to understand. He wondered also how his words would be conveyed to the King. Would the King choose to come to Dunning himself, or simply push it aside as fiction?

Muhammad turned his attention away from his thoughts as he looked now at the television. A late-night talk show was on and the host was talking with one of the many Hollywood personalities, who all looked alike to him. Most were too pretty, too cool, or simply too self-absorbed with his or her own little make-believe world. He drifted off to sleep as the program broke into a commercial break.

16

Prior to coordinating the President's undercover visit to Dunning, Michael Stern barely had time to run home, shower, and change before again returning to the White House. While at home Michael tried to explain to Melinda, his wife, what he had seen in St. Michael's. She stared at him in utter amazement as he described the visions in the church. After listening quietly, she asked, "Michael, what do you think you really saw?"

Looking at his wife, Michael said in a quiet and serious voice, "You know I have never been a practicing believer, but I think I saw *a glimpse of God.*"

Melinda leaned over and hugged Michael, holding him close. "If you are sure that's what you saw, then it is up to you to convince the President the visions are real."

"Oh, I really think he believes me, Melinda. We're flying back to Dunning tonight." He continued, "Please, Melinda, this is top secret. No one is to know anything at all about this. You can't say a word to anyone."

"Certainly not," she replied, understanding the sensitive nature of his position with the White House. "When are you leaving?"

"We will leave later this evening, about nine," he answered. "Everything is already in place for us to go."

Michael returned to his office early evening and rechecked his plans. Looking at the small gold-finished clock on his desk, it showed eight o'clock. Sitting back in his chair, he closed his eyes for a moment. The images of the *angels* came into his thoughts as clearly as they had been when he first saw them the evening before. If their plans went as he hoped, he would see them again soon.

At eight-thirty a caravan of three official, unmarked cars left the grounds of the White House. They drove through the gates and toward the small airport which was kept operational twenty-four/seven and used when necessary to keep governmental movements discrete. There the small, unassuming jet sat waiting for them, its engines idling with a low hum. Another jet filled with agents had left for Dunning at five o'clock to prepare for the President's visit. A third jet idled not far behind the President's plane. It would travel as a companion plane to the President's. All went just as planned. No one had any hint that the President wasn't at the White House, nor suspected that he had even left Washington. Without any notice, the small plane was boarded by the group of men and taxied to a take-off position. Quickly it gained speed and was air-borne south in the direction of Dunning, Alabama. In just over two hours they would be sitting on the ground at the small Dunning airport.

After the incident with Reverend Renfro, Bill Tyler had driven quickly to the airport to await the arrival of the Washington dignitaries under the cover of darkness. By ten o'clock the last of the commercial planes had come and gone. There would be no more air traffic until tomorrow. Only the sound of the steady rain disturbed the silence; only blinking lights at the tower and the blue and white runway lights broke the darkness. This visit was completely out of the ordinary. There would be no presidential limo or special transportation for the group. Plans were to keep it all unnoticeable. The President, Stern and two agents would be riding with the chief, along with a couple of unmarked cars. All along the route to the church cars would be placed on lookout for any unforeseen possibilities. At the church both police and National Guard presence would be strong.

As the President's plane landed, plans were for it to taxi over to the side of the field alongside some of the airport hangars and park beside a governmental plane which had landed earlier that afternoon. Cars would then pick up the presidential party, and make their way into Dunning. It was previously agreed that as the plane landed, Tyler would call the Mayor and inform him.

Allan stayed in his office until eleven. All had been quiet. He spoke several times with Chief Tyler, Reverend Johnson, and Scott Harvard, the agent in charge of the President's security team on-site, as well as agent in charge of arrangements for the President's visit. At precisely eleven PM, Allan Smith left his office, walked outside into the warm, wet night, got into his car, and drove toward St. Michael's. He passed only an occasional car. The Mayor was stopped by security at the road block on Everwine Street before driving on to the parking lot at the church where he was stopped a second time. Parking his car, he walked to the back entrance of the church. Through the window, he could see lights already on and around the church were armed guardsmen. They had been informed that important visitors were coming, but not the identity of the visitors. Allan was greeted at the door by a young guard officer and a policeman. Entering the church,

Allan saw Reverend Johnson standing with another police officer and two men he assumed to be agents from Washington.

Walking up to the group, Allan spoke first. "Good evening, Reverend Johnson."

Thomas Johnson smiled and extended his hand to Allan. "Good evening, Mayor Smith. I'm sorry we didn't have better weather for our visitors from Washington, but I guess this will have to do. May I introduce to you an important church member accompanying me tonight, Mrs. Doris Williams?"

Extending his hand to the other men and to Mrs. Williams, Allan shook their hands.

"Mr. Mayor," continued Thomas, "this is Officer James Webb, and special agents, Scott Harvard and Adam McCord."

"Happy to meet you," said Allan. "Everything's in place, I suppose," he added.

"Yes sir, everything is ready for the President," answered Harvard.

"Have the agents seen our visitors, Reverend?" asked Allan.

"We have, and I'm tremendously happy the President decided to make this visit, Mayor. There is no way to describe it," added Harvard. "Their presence is truly amazing. Unbelievable!"

"That is the way most people feel when they see the figures overhead," added Reverend Johnson. Everyone nodded in agreement so no one needed to say anything else.

"Let's go into the conference room while we wait for the President," said Thomas.

They followed him into the room where a variety of snacks and drinks were on the table and coffee brewed on the counter.

"Gentlemen, make yourselves at home. Have something to eat if you wish," instructed Thomas. Two of the men helped themselves to the sandwiches and other snacks on the table. After taking a drink of hot coffee, Agent Harvard said, "This really is good. It throws off the dampness. I might even go so far as to say this is the best coffee I've had in a while."

As the men laughed, the Reverend added, "It's nothing special, just A&P coffee and water from the well here at St. Michael's."

Enlightening the conversation Allan joked, "You mean this isn't city water, Reverend?" Taking another sip from his cup, he went on, "You're sure it's safe to drink?"

Everyone smiled again as Johnson said, "It's been safe for over a hundred years. Maybe that's why it tastes so good." He continued on, "Before the church had electricity water was pumped by hand for its needs. With electricity, water was piped into the church, but it's the same well that has been with the church all these years."

As the men waited, they talked about the *angels* and the potential long-term effect on Dunning; and, the thinking of the American people and the rest of the world. Time passed quickly as they waited. At precisely eleven forty-five, Allan's phone and Agent Harvard's phone rang at the same time. Allan, glancing at the screen on his phone saw it was the call for which he was waiting. Agent Harvard turned away and answered his phone.

"Hello," Allan answered.

"Mayor, the President's plane just landed. We should be at the church in about half an hour," reported Chief Tyler.

"Thanks, Bill, we'll be waiting," said Allan, ending his conversation.

Twenty-five minutes later a young officer entered the back door and reported to Mayor Smith that the President's car was driving into the parking lot. A couple of minutes later the door opened and the Chief of Police, along with Michael Stern, plus several other men, eyeing the surroundings cautiously, entered the church. With them was the President of the United States, Stuart Wallace.

Michael Stern spoke as the door closed, "Gentlemen, President Wallace."

As President Wallace shook hands around the group, Stern introduced each of them. The President, in turn, repeated their names while shaking their hands.

It was now Allan Smith's turn, "Mr. President, speaking for everyone, this is truly an honor! We are happy to have you with us, even if it's not a public visit. I don't think you are going to be disappointed."

The President nodded in agreement.

Smith continued, "Mr. President, Reverend Johnson, fellow church member, Doris Williams, and I will take over here. Reverend Johnson, would you like to say a word?"

"Thank you, Mr. Mayor," then turning to face the President, Johnson added, "It is such an honor and a privilege, Mr. President, to have you here, Sir. In just a few minutes you're going to witness something that will impact you for the rest of your life. These other men have been witnesses already. I think they will attest to what I am saying. We have no idea why these *angels* are with us. We only know that they are here. Many people may try to explain their recent appearance here at St. Michael's, but I won't attempt to read into God's mind. Maybe it's God's way of saying to the modern world, *I am here and have always been here. Don't ignore Me!* And, just maybe, it will bring some sort of peace between all who claim to be God's people."

For a moment it was quiet and those present waited for the minister to continue. The quietness was perhaps the result of each man trying to pull together his own conclusions. This quiet was broken by an abrupt rumble of thunder as the rain which had fallen all day turned into a storm with both wind and rain.

Without any further comments Reverend Johnson said, "Mr. President, if you will follow me, please."

Walking from the conference room and down the hallway, they approached the sanctuary. The door was guarded by policemen, which had been the case since the *angels* were first sighted. Tonight, however, additional police officers and two National Guardsmen were on duty. As the group approached the sanctuary, one officer opened the door. A carpet runner had been placed the length of the hallway to protect the red carpet from all the traffic of the past few days. Walking through the doorway, Reverend Johnson paused and looked upward. The President stood beside him; the others stood slightly behind both of them.

President Wallace looking upward spotted the *angels* immediately. They remained just as others had seen them, their forms clear and silvery in a peaceful, resting state, appearing completely unaware of the mortals looking at them from below.

The President like all of the others who had visited the church before him gazed upward in awe, realizing that he was seeing a glimpse of something truly unworldly. Stuart Wallace felt weak, shaky, and almost as if he had just stepped out of a scene in the Old Testament. *Only he wasn't Jacob wrestling with an angel, he was standing in this small church looking up at them.* Turning first to Thomas Johnson, and then to the others, his look sought verification. But they, like him, stood gazing upward trying to understand the vision they saw above them. The others stood silently looking fixedly into this '*tear in time*' which allowed them to see beyond their own dimension. Only the sound of the rain and accompanying thunder broke the silence. After a few minutes Reverend Johnson turned and led the silent delegation back down the hallway and into the conference room.

Entering the room, Reverend Johnson was the first to speak. "Mr. President, now you've seen what we've seen. I'm sure others have reported to you how impossible it is to describe this scene to anyone. My only explanation being, it's simply a *miracle!*"

The President, visibly moved by the images, nodded. "Reverend Johnson, I'm glad that I came here tonight. You're right, it can't be explained. I am thinking, perhaps, we should invite not only our own people to come and see this, but others as well. Maybe, world leaders, religious leaders, and anyone else who wants to see a miracle."

The President continued, "I, like you, have no idea what this means, but it is a miracle, a modern day miracle. When we get back to Washington, we'll begin to issue special invitations around the world. I hope that will be acceptable to you and St. Michael's, Reverend."

Reverend Johnson smiled, "Mr. President, anytime that I, or anyone, at St. Michael's can extend God's word, it is certainly acceptable."

"Mayor Smith, Chief Tyler, thank you for assisting in this visit," said the President.

Allan answered, "It was all our pleasure Mr. President."

"We will be back in touch with you either tomorrow or the next day as invitations are issued and our office can begin to coordinate visits," said President Wallace.

"And, we will gladly assist in any way possible, Mr. President," answered Allan.

"Very good," said the President. "I guess we had better get back to Washington now. We have lots to do putting all this together."

With those words, the President shook hands with all those present and, with his escort, left St. Michael's. The contingency from Dunning, headed up by Chief Tyler, led the President back through the dark city streets to the airport where his plane was waiting. Within minutes after boarding, the plane with its flashing lights was airborne, and disappeared into the rain-filled night over South Alabama.

Doris Williams left St. Michael's as well, driven home by one of the guards. This was a night that would long be remembered by this humble, middle-aged Christian woman whose discovery shook this small community, along with a nation's leader, to its very core.

Once the President had departed, the church was quiet. Reverend Johnson and Mayor Smith went into the pastor's office and sat for a few minutes, exhausted from the very busy day and then the night visit to the church.

"Reverend, I thought it couldn't get any more interesting," began Allan, "but it looks like it is about to."

Thomas smiled and nodded. "The President of the United States coming here to St. Michael's—I wonder if he will now make it public that he came here and why. If he does, what do you suppose he will he say?"

"Reverend, I think he is going to say that St. Michael's in Dunning is *where God's angels have chosen to visit*," said Allan.

President Wallace was back in Washington and in the White House before daylight. He went quietly into the White House where he found Barbara Wallace in bed and still awake. She turned over and sat up upon his entering their bedroom.

"I'm sorry, I didn't mean to wake you," said the President.

Presumably, as is the case with most Presidents' wives, she was his chief advisor, critic, and sounding board. Stuart called her shortly before his plane landed in Washington and, understandably, she had a multitude of questions for him, which he promised he would answer upon returning to the White House.

"It's okay, I wasn't asleep. I know you're tired but I want you to tell me all about it," said Barbara, as she sat up in bed, motioning him to sit beside her.

He loosened his tie, took off his coat, and pulled off his shoes before getting onto the bed and propping up some pillows behind his head.

They sat for almost an hour as he told her about the *angels*. Barbara asked many questions about the church, about Dunning, and the *angels*. She was convinced after hearing his story that they were real and this could be a major influence in world relations especially between the nations of the Western and the Eastern worlds. Barbara agreed with Stuart that he should make a statement to the news organizations which would be followed by invitations to many religious and political leaders around the world.

Friday morning dawned clear and hot in Washington D.C. By nine AM, Michael Stern arrived at his office in the White House, being scheduled for a ten o'clock meeting with the President to plot out a plan of action to notify specific leaders who would be invited guests of the United States for the purpose of viewing the *angels* in Dunning. The presidential office had put out an early morning press release stating that the President would make a one o'clock announcement to the press of extreme interest. No further mention was made regarding the topic of the announcement, or of his overnight visit to Dunning.

17

By nine o'clock central time on Friday morning, Chad had climbed out of bed, got ready for work, and was on the mobile site of WTLA at St. Michael's. The previous night, dinner for the visiting CBS and NBC groups had gone wonderfully. He could not have been more impressed with both Jeff Glor and Lester Holt, as individuals and as news professionals. Even with the excitement of working and dining with national television anchors, Chad was not in the least distracted from his awareness of Cynthia. He thought about her continually, even though she looked gorgeous and every bit the professional, he now felt this special bond between them would not fade. He felt it was a bond that would last a lifetime. He had never been happier in his life.

While he went about his chores on-site, he constantly kept an eye out for Cynthia's car to appear in the parking lot. When she finally did drive up, he again felt the excitement of being in love for the first time. It seemed that just being near her was enough. Getting out of her car, she spotted Chad sitting under the WTLA awning and instinctively smiled, waved, and pointed to the WDDR staging area as she headed in that direction.

Chad thought to himself, I must be careful about how this relationship between Cynthia and me appears to our fellow co-workers. We can't let people know of any possible connection between us that might compromise our professionalism. He resigned himself to keeping the "just friends" charade, and returned to his work.

Cynthia settled into her chair and began to put together her schedule for the day. As she did so, she thought about Chad. After dinner last night, she had wanted to take his hand, to leave with Chad. She wanted to lie in his arms again and wake up with him close beside her. Logic sustained itself, however. At the end of the evening she got into her own car and went home, alone.

This Friday morning also found Allan Smith in his office at City Hall and Reverend Thomas Johnson at the church. Due to the increased activity in Dunning and at St. Michael's, both men were busier than usual. As the morning warmed under a cloudy sky and light rain, traffic began to snarl, and crowds continuously grew along Everwine Street, lining up to see the visitors. By eight o'clock the church started allowing people to enter and pass by the sanctuary in an unending procession.

In room 227 at the Lily Motel in the center of the old part of Dunning, Joseph Turbon sat watching the television screen. When TV cameras panned the street, Joseph saw the tremendous crowd lined up and down the streets in the vicinity of St. Michael's to get a brief look at the *angels* in the church sanctuary. Joseph shook his head and mumbled to himself, "Don't these people know what is about to happen? In just a matter of days all of this will end as God destroys it all."

In Joseph Turbon's mind, no one was capable of understanding what God had planned. No one except himself, that is! Joseph now believed, heart and soul, that this was what he had been called to do. He was to usher in the "end of days" and the beginning God's kingdom. False teachers such as Thomas Johnson, William Renfro, and all other ministers had no right to try to tell their followers what God wanted. They, like all of the people who had abandoned him, were wrong! Even his own family had been wrong to criticize him and his work. But now, he would show them. He wasn't exactly sure how, but he would show them. God would certainly tell him and, in the process, he would punish those people who stood in his way and in God's way. "I will punish them all," said Joseph to himself as he looked at the shiny pistol which lay on the dresser beside the bed.

Since his arrival in Dunning, Joseph had sat in this room rarely leaving except for that one attempt to go to the church. The large crowds had stopped that. His call to Reverend Johnson and then to Reverend Renfro gave him a feeling of being in control. *Now he must wait for God's voice to direct him.* But, after several days, no voice had spoken to him in word or dream. Still Joseph was determined to wait for God's directions. He sat back on the bed, propped up against the pillows, and gazed at the television screen. "Soon they will see God's plan," Joseph said to himself. He didn't doubt it at all. "Hadn't the scriptures said as much?"

The phone rang in Michael Stern's office. "Yes, Mr. President, everything is set for one o'clock. I'll be there in just a moment," continued Stern as he gathered up the papers from his desk and walked toward the door. Walking quickly down the hall to the Oval Office, Stern nodded to several people he passed in route, and upon reaching the outer office, he found June standing guard as usual.

"Good morning, Ms. Snell," said Michael, as he walked to her desk. It was wise to always stay on the good side of the President's self-appointed guardian.

"Good morning, Michael," she replied warmly. "I think the President is expecting you."

"Thank you," said Stern as he walked toward the President office. *Yep, stay on her good side,* thought Stern.

Entering his executive office, Stern found the President looking over a multitude of papers on his desk. President Wallace working in shirt sleeves, looked up over his readers, and motioned for Michael to have a seat.

Leaning back in his chair and taking off his glasses, President Wallace said, "Michael, I know you're as tired as I am, and after this news conference, you can rest. But, for now we have to push ourselves a bit further. Take a look at this and tell me if it pretty well sums it up our state of affairs with regard to the *angels?*"

Taking the paper from the President, Michael began reading what he had written. After studying it closely for several minutes, Michael handed the proposed conference material back to the President.

"Mr. President, I believe it's exactly what you need to say," said Stern. "The nation and the world need to know what we saw at St. Michael's."

"Michael, do you have that list of the names that I need to contact after the press conference?" questioned the President.

"Yes sir, I have it right here," said Michael, opening the folder he had on his lap and passing the sheets across the desk to the President.

The President studied the list. "Looks good, Michael. I can't think of anyone that you might have left out."

"No sir, I tried to include anyone whom I felt would want to be a part of this news for whatever reason." He then added, "I have even included the leadership of Iran and North Korea, even though their interest remains to be seen."

"Be back here at twelve-thirty and we'll go over any last minute changes," directed Wallace.

"Okay, Sir," said Michael standing to leave. "Anything else I need to check on?"

"I think for now, we have it covered," the President answered, looking back at the papers on his desk as if double-checking his notes. Without further discussion Michael walked out of the room and back to his office. It was only a short time before the President's news conference.

By one o'clock the White House press room was filled with reporters, recorders, and cameras. The room was abuzz as reporters tried to guess what the President was going to say. It also bristled with cameras and equipment as well. At precisely one o'clock, the door to the side of the press room opened and President Wallace, Michael Stern, and Steven Howell walked in. Everyone stood as the President entered.

"Please be seated," instructed President Wallace. With everyone settled into their chairs, notebooks in hand, the President began:

> *I have called this press conference this afternoon as a way of talking not only to the American people, but to the nations of the world. As most of the public in this country are aware via way of the many news reports on all the networks, there have been some unusual appearances in Southeast Alabama, more specifically, at St. Michael's African Episcopal Methodist Church in Dunning, Alabama. After having sent representatives*

*to Dunning to examine the reported appearances,
my advisors suggested that I, too, travel to Dunning
and see things for myself. I did so last evening. To my
downright amazement, the reports and information
you have heard are true.*

This statement brought about muted sounds of whispers
throughout the room. The President continued:

*As a result of my visit, I have deemed it an "act of
generosity" from the United States and an "act
of responsibility" to invite other world leaders to
witness......*he paused for a moment, *"to witness
firsthand, the angels.*

At this point the somewhat muted whispers escalated to a
louder murmur. The President moved ahead:

*No president or world leader in modern times has been
able to make such a claim. I can assure you that had
it not been so irrefutably clear to all who witnessed
these Holy Images, this press conference would not
be taking place. As a result, invitations are being
extended to many Heads of State, as well as religious
leaders throughout the world. I certainly hope that all
will respond and accept our invitation to view these
hallowed visitors.*

The President then paused and said with a slight smile, "At
this time I will take questions." Holding up both hands he added
with a bigger smile, "Just please remember. I'm not a religious
scholar."

This last remark brought about a wave of laughter as the President began to acknowledge different reporters in an attempt to answer questions.

"Mr. President," began a young woman sitting in the middle of the group as the President accepted her question.

"Ms. Darby, I believe," as he acknowledged her.

"Mr. President, why was your visit unannounced?"

Wallace nodded with her question. "My advisors and I felt it prudent in order to keep confusion to a minimum while I visited St. Michael's, the site of the *angels*. If it were not a credible sighting, then the government would not be seen as taking a wild step into make-believe. Ms. Darby, if I may continue, please, not only did I travel to St. Michael's, but I saw the *angels*. And, I may add, that I am convinced beyond any doubt that is precisely what these beings are, *angels!*"

Many questions followed with the President attempting to answer each as best as he could. Some questions he answered by merely saying, "I don't know." He answered others as honestly as possible for about ten minutes before saying, "I have some other pressing business at this time. Thank you for coming."

Turning, he exited the room followed by Stern and Howell.

Once out of the press room, President Wallace walked back to his office followed by the two assistants. Entering the office, President Wallace turned to Stern. "The invitations have been sent?"

"Yes, Mr. President, we should begin receiving replies later today or tomorrow," answered Stern.

"Good. Let's hope that we get the response we want," Wallace acknowledged.

Walking to his desk and removing his coat he sat down. Picking up one of the papers on his desk he added, "Thanks

Michael, and you, too, Steven, for all the hard work for the past couple of days. I know it has been very demanding."

As the two men left, Stern stopped at the door, turned and said, "Mr. President, this was something that needed to be investigated. You were correct to carry it to the American people and to the rest of the world. As President, it has made everyone aware of the importance of this seemingly unreal, yet "real" event.

The President looked at Stern. "I hope you're right, Michael. I hope you're right. Thanks again."

At the same time Michael was leaving the President's office in Washington, Muhammad Harassi sat working on his laptop in Atlanta. He had spent most of the day working in his hotel room. He wanted very much to hear from Ismael, but there had been no call.

Abruptly his phone rang. Even though he was expecting a call at some point, he was startled by the ring. Picking up his phone, Muhammad answered, "Hello?"

"Muhammad," the voice on the other end said, "This is Tom. Did I catch you at a bad time?"

"No, Tom, I was just working at my computer and hoping that this call might be from my boss, Ishmael Hadi. I wanted to hear something from my government."

"Then, I suppose you saw President Wallace's new conference just a few minutes ago," said Weatherman.

"Actually, I did not. I have not had the television on today. I've been trying to get some work done while I waited for word from Ishmael."

"In light of the President's news conference, you should be getting some sort of information from your State Department very soon as he announced that he was extending invitations to many world leaders." Tom quickly added, "And, I'm sure that included Saudi Arabia."

A beep on Muhammad's phone led Muhammad to say, "Tom, I'm getting another call. Let me call you back, please."

Tom answered, "Sure. Bye."

"Yes," said Muhammad picking up his cell phone to answer the call.

"Muhammad, this is Ishmael. The King is planning to make a trip to the United States this weekend. He should arrive in Washington on Saturday and will be leading a delegation of not only clerics, but leaders from several of the nations closely connected to the Kingdom as well."

Muhammad breathed a sigh of relief. He had been taken seriously; but, needless to say, the invitation from the President made it easier for the King and other Middle Eastern leaders, to embrace a visit to St. Michael's.

Excitement began to build again in Muhammad. The king of his nation and leaders of other Muslim countries were coming! The possibilities were immense. Was this an opportunity for opposing religious ideologies to find common ground and, possibly, end almost fifteen hundred years of strife over whose views of God were right or wrong?

"We will begin making arrangements today," Ishmael said. "You should fly to Washington and meet us as we arrive. I will call you again soon and advise you of the completed arrangements."

"I look forward to your call," said Muhammad. "Goodbye."

"Goodbye," said Ishmael.

Immediately, Muhammad redialed Tom Weatherman. The phone rang several times before Weatherman answered.

"Tom, good news. That was the call I was expecting. The King is coming Saturday by invitation of the President."

"That's great!" said Tom. "Is there anything that I can do?"

"Not that I can think of. Tom, you have already done more than I could ever thank you for; but, one thing more, if you will, please keep this to yourself until the Kingdom makes the announcement public," replied Muhammad.

"Certainly, Muhammad," answered Tom.

"I will be flying to Washington to meet the Saudi delegation and will keep in touch."

"Goodbye, Muhammad," said Tom.

The conversation over, Muhammad got up and begin getting his things together.

While Muhammad had not seen the President's press conference on television, Joseph Turbon had. He had sat and listened to the President make his announcement about his visit to Dunning and the foreign visitors who were coming to see the *angels*.

This must be the sign. Joseph thought. *This is what I am supposed to do. I will start the "beginning of the end" by eliminating all the leaders of these false nations.*

It all seemed to come into focus to Joseph now. God had sent him as his soldier to bring an end to the evil leaders who had been trying to prevent God's plan from coming into fruition with their constant fighting over issues of land, economics, and faith instead of listening to what God was saying. In his own mind, he knew what God wanted. Now he would show them. He would show all those people who had been unwilling to listen to his message. He would show them that he was right and, the voices that he was hearing came from God.

Joseph smiled to himself as he touched the small shiny revolver. *Yes, he would carry out the vengeance of God.*

18

The rain finally relented and the sun came out with only a few scattered clouds and by noon the temperature and the humidity both soared. Weather forecasts called for rain in the afternoon and evening for the next several days. As Chad sat looking over the outline for the day's afternoon interviews and the evening report on the activities from the church, he glanced across the parking lot at the ever-growing multitude of people. For the past several days, the long line had coiled around the church from down the street, under the covered walk, and to the side door of the little white church. Chad felt as if he were watching a story being revealed that could have come from the Old Testament in the Bible. Technicians were now busy with the cameras and lights on the portable stage set up for the evening news. A vibration and then a ring caused Chad to take his phone from his belt. Before answering it, he glanced at the screen and noted the call was from Jim Stuart, his boss.

"Hello, Jim, whatcha need?" said Chad.

Without his usual lighthearted banter, Jim went directly to the point. "You've seen the President's press conference?" asked Jim.

"Yes, Jim, I did. Which means we have visitors coming tomorrow, right?" continued Chad.

"Exactly. You and Cynthia will be the only two TV broadcasters handling the interviews and questions for the President and his group on Saturday," continued Jim. "Lots of folks aren't really happy about this. They feel like they're getting cut out, I suppose. But, by now everyone is accustomed to seeing you two carrying this story. So that's the way it will be."

Taking a breath Jim continued, "We have it on good authority that a number of leaders have already accepted; namely, the Prime Minister of the UK, the Presidents of France and Italy, and quite possibly the Kings of Saudi Arabia and Jordan."

"Whew," breathed Chad. "Doesn't get any better than that!"

"Well, maybe it does," continued Jim.

"You wanna explain what that means?" asked Chad.

"It means that if all the names on the list turn out to be the same ones on the list of people coming, then the Russian President and the Chairman of the People's Republic of China might also accept invitations." Having said that, Jim paused to let this information sink in with Chad.

"Wow again!" said Chad. "We might as well have the whole body of the United Nations charter a bus and come down!"

"My next statement, it could happen, Chad. You up for it?" said Jim.

"Has WDDR been informed about any of this?" asked Chad.

"Yes, I've spoken with them as well. Cynthia Davis will be coming over this afternoon to talk with you about it. Then we can initiate plans with the networks to work out the particulars."

"Chad, do you think you can continue to co-anchor this with Cynthia? I know in the past it hasn't always been easy, with the competition between you two."

Chad smiled over the phone with that question. "Jim, I think we can make it work for the good of both stations and the networks."

Jim laughed, "I'm glad you said that, Chad. Who knows, the two of you might even become friends after all!"

Resisting the temptation to say something, Chad said, "Jim, maybe you're right. I guess it could happen."

"Great. I knew I could count on you, Chad," said Jim.

"Sure. You know me, Jim. Always the professional."

"Let's stop here. I wouldn't want to go that far!" laughed Jim. "Check with you later. Bye"

"Bye," said Chad, pressing the "end" key on his phone's screen.

Sitting back, Chad began to think about how all that this could develop. Suddenly the whole thing made him nervous. The fact that he and Cynthia could not only be on national, but international, television with the President and many heads of state gave Chad a case of the nerves. His life had changed beyond belief in just a matter of days. Last week his top story had been hot weather and now it was world leaders and *angels*! Not to mention his growing relationship with Cynthia.

Chad looked up from the desk to find Cynthia standing at the foot of the stairs to the platform. She had walked up noiselessly and was watching Chad as he sat pondering the evolving situation.

When he saw her, he stood up and asked, "Been there a while, have you?"

Cynthia smiled and said, "Actually only a couple of moments. I was just watching you." Cynthia walked up the stairs and onto the stage. Chad's eyes immediately gave away his feelings. Cynthia knew from his unguarded look how he felt about her. It made her feel very happy.

"Am I disturbing your work?" she asked.

"Absolutely," said Chad looking around to make sure no one was watching before adding, "Yes, but who cares?" They both laughed.

"Have a seat," Chad said motioning her to sit with him. "I guess you have heard about tomorrow."

Cynthia smiled and nodded her head in excitement. "I can't believe all this is happening."

"Yeah, it's pretty incredible," said Chad. "You ready for it?"

"I think so," she replied.

"After we finish here this evening, you wanna come over and maybe let's fix something to eat?" Chad playfully quizzed.

Cynthia shook her head "no." But before Chad had the chance to try and hide his disappointment, Cynthia continued, "I want to return the dinner favor, although mine may not be as good as yours."

Chad's face lit up with Cynthia's proposal. Jokingly he said, "And you can cook?"

"Certainly, silly. Actually I'm a pretty good cook."

"Okay then, what time should I come over?" asked Chad.

"Let's see, if we can get things wrapped up here by seven, be at my place at eight-thirty, "said Cynthia.

"Okay. One other thing," said Chad stopping to look at Cynthia.

"What?" she asked.

"Your address? Where do you live?" asked Chad playfully smiling.

"Oh yeah, I forgot. The Pagoda Tree Apartments, just west of town on Willow Lane. Apartment 210," responded Cynthia.

"Okay then, dinner at eight-thirty," said Chad. "I'll bring the wine."

With plans for dinner made, Cynthia returned to the WDDR mobile unit to prepare for the evening news and Saturday. The afternoon proceeded, filled with organizing and planning meetings for both Chad and Cynthia. This visit by both world and religious leaders was going to require a tremendous amount of security, which was already arriving in Dunning and, particularly, around St. Michael's.

By the time the President made his public announcement via television with respect to the *angels*, several planes had already landed and began unloading to make preparations for the number of dignitaries who would soon be appearing on the scene in Dunning along with President Wallace. Security would be as tight as any that this nation had seen away from Washington, DC. It would include not only Dunning police and National Guardsmen, but also Secret Service agents, and Military Police from the nearby military bases of Fort Rucker, Alabama, and Fort Benning, Georgia.

A block away at the *Southwestern Evangelical Ministries* mobile studio, the Reverend William Renfro was still boiling over his arrest. The process had purposely taken Renfro a lengthy amount of time to post bail and be released from jail. Renfro threatened the police the entire time he was held that upon his release the city of Dunning would end up broke after paying the charges he planned to file against them. He had been so irate at the police station that officers had to threaten to restrain him.

Renfro was released by one o'clock and went to the Holiday Inn where he had previously rented a whole floor of rooms for his staff and crew. It was the same Holiday Inn where

Stern and the late night visitors from Washington had stayed the night before. Ironically, if Renfro had tried to return to St. Michael's following his release, he might have been witness to the President's motorcade leaving! The arrest had truly provided a good cover for the President's visit.

On his Friday morning broadcast, Renfro unloaded the unfairness of his arrest and the violation of his civil rights; however, he made no attempt to explain that he had been arrested trying to gain entry into the church after hours. Renfro vowed to his television audience that he would see the *angels* before leaving Dunning.

As the five-thirty news aired, all networks were reporting invitation acceptances by each of those countries whose leaders had been invited to join the President in viewing the *angels*. Additionally, invitations had been accepted by the Pope, the Orthodox patriarch, various protestant leaders from around the world, the Dali Lama, as well as religious leaders from the Muslim faith, and a Hindu delegation. It turned out to be later than Chad and Cynthia thought originally before they were able to leave St. Michael's.

Chad made a mad dash home to shower and change clothes before driving to The Pagoda Tree Apartment complex. By the time he arrived, it was almost nine as he nervously rang the bell at Apartment 210. It wasn't totally that he felt uncertain about how Cynthia felt, he was just plain nervous. "Shoot," he said to himself, shaking his arms as if to get rid of the nervousness. "Why does she affect me this way?"

The door opened. Cynthia was standing there smiling, her hair pulled back in a pony-tail and wearing white shorts and a dark blue top. Chad caught his breath. She looked wonderfully cool and relaxed. There wasn't the slightest hint that she had been working all day in the heat. Her slightly tanned legs made the summer outfit perfect. Cynthia extended Chad an invitation to come inside. As he walked into the room, Cynthia reached her arms around his neck and kissed him. It was a kiss that released the pent up emotions of being together all day and unable to release suppressed feelings generated by the closeness of their working relationship. Chad responded by pulling Cynthia close to him and returning the long, deep kiss. He could feel the electricity that flowed between them. Had anyone been able to store it, the electricity could have lit up the entire apartment complex!

Chad and Cynthia had to be so careful at work to keep their feelings disguised, he was honestly afraid that the electricity between them would give them away and everyone would be able to see!

Parting, Chad smiled and said, "Now that's a hello."

Cynthia laughed, pulled away, and playfully hit his shoulder. "You're going to embarrass me."

Glancing round the room, Cynthia's apartment, like Chad's, was very neat. Hers was decorated with a more modern flair, with the focal point being a low red couch and coordinating patterned chairs. From the kitchen he could smell food. Chinese he thought.

"I can't believe you had time to come home, cook and look so . . ." he gestured toward her, "so breathtaking." Cynthia laughed again with that wonderful smile that Chad found so enticing.

"Before you go too far I have to tell you, I cheated. The dinner is takeout Chinese from the frozen department at Publix."

"Oh, no!" Chad responded in mock surprise. "You've ruined the whole evening!"

Again Cynthia playfully batted Chad. Then she took his hand and led him into the kitchen.

The kitchen was modern, very clean, and neat. There was none of the visible clutter of Chad's kitchen. On the counter was the Chinese take-out.

"Here, you open the wine and I'll fix the plates," said Cynthia handing Chad a corkscrew from a kitchen drawer.

"That's fine," said Chad as he opened the bottle. It made a little pop as it opened.

Chad said, "Actually I'm surprised you had time to do this. You have to be tired from today."

"Yes, it's been a pretty busy day, but this is nice." Cynthia turned to Chad. "Just being here, together without all the action at the church is quietly comforting and rejuvenating."

Chad poured two glasses of wine and handed one to Cynthia. "Mmm, this is very good," said Chad as he touched his glass to hers. "Very good!"

Looking into each other's eyes, they leaned closer together, their lips meeting again, just a light, tender touch. Then, picking up their plates and glasses, Chad and Cynthia walked into the small dining area in which they sat and began to eat.

"You really do make good Chinese," joked Chad.

Shaking her head with a serious expression, Cynthia said, "It takes lots of practice."

Laughing, while eating, they talked about the day, and what Saturday was going to bring, plus all the preparations necessary for it. They would have to be on-site by nine and along with everyone else, prepared for the visits of many heads of state. They had rehearsed how the group from Washington would arrive; the President speaking to the television cameras, and then, short interviews from Cynthia and Chad. Afterward the entire group would visit the church, guided by Reverend Johnson and Mayor

Smith. Being mindful of security and huge crowds of people, the visit having been coordinated ahead of time, was estimated to take no more than two or three hours. Upon completion of the tour, the group in its entirety would return to Washington.

"What do you suppose will happen?" Chad asked.

"Happen?" questioned Cynthia, "What do you mean?"

"With the *angels*—do you suppose they will stay in the church?" asked Chad.

"I don't know," answered Cynthia thoughtfully. "It is still a mystery to me why they are even visible to us."

Taking a sip from his glass, Chad thought a moment before shaking his head and adding, "I'm certainly not one to second guess God, but who knows, maybe it's God's way of saying, *I'm still here.* Or, *Stop fighting over stupid things. Be still and listen!*"

Taking a breath, Chad continued this serious part of the conversation. Putting down his fork, he looked at Cynthia. "What about us? Where do we go after all this?"

Cynthia looked at Chad. "I don't know, Chad. I know that I love you." Going from seriousness and trying to lighten the tone of the conversation, Cynthia leaned across the table and placed her hand on Chad's. "Let's just take each day, one at the time. Let's enjoy the moment."

Chad smiled and nodded.

After dinner they moved into the living room. They sat on the couch, but this time not at opposite ends. Cynthia sat close to Chad, his arm around her shoulder. She leaned her head against his chin. Chad could smell the freshness of her just washed hair. Everything was too perfect.

For what seemed hours they sat not talking or moving, simply enjoying being there, together. The darkness of the night and the light of the one lamp made the room cozy and relaxing. Finally, Cynthia turned her head to look up into Chad's eyes.

For a moment she sat there as if searching; trying to read his thoughts. Then she moved closer and kissed his lips, turning her whole body into his.

Chad responded to her kiss and they moved deeper into a hypnotic spell. Their passion became more and more intense until close was not enough. Cynthia arose from the couch and took Chad's hand. Nothing needed to be said. Her room was dark and the bed felt soft and cool to their touch.

Across town at that moment, the area around St. Michael's was buzzing with activity. The number of guardsmen had been dramatically increased. Barriers had been placed to further control the flow of traffic and crowds that were expected the next morning. A greater police presence was there as well; only now, the security included those from Washington who were assigned the task of planning and providing additional protection for Saturday's distinguished visitors. Mayor Smith and Chief Tyler had been on-site the entire evening, along with various other technicians, crews, and secret security details. Many others were there as well, working to make sure such a visit would go off as smoothly as possible. Allan Smith received a call from Governor Bayer saying he would fly in from Montgomery and be present for the arrival of the President and his party of distinguished dignitaries.

Just a block over from Everwine Street, a figure walked along the darkened street. Joseph Turbon walked silently in front of the houses as lights and the flickering of televisions offered the only illumination in the dark night. The street lights along the quiet street were almost obscured by the trees that lined the street, giving the whole scene a ghostly appearance.

Turbon walked to the end of Everwine Street. Here, he turned and walked down the sidewalk on the opposite side of the tree-lined street blending into small groups of people who were there observing the security buildup. Even into late evening, still people were standing all along the sidewalk, although police barriers prevented anyone from crossing the street to the church.

As Turbon walked, he began to develop a plan. In his mind, he would become the *"Angel of Death."* He would be *"the Messenger"* sent to start the chain of events that would lead to the unfolding of God's greater plan. It all seemed so simple to him now. He would be *"God's Avenger," as well as his own, and it would play out at the same time.* Those people who had ignored him were going to feel his wrath. Walking back the way he had come, Joseph Turbon disappeared into the summer evening, into the shadows of the large trees.

19

S aturday morning was hot, but with scattered clouds that promised rain. By seven o'clock Dunning was already bursting with activity. It wasn't every day that this small town was going to be visited not only by the President of the United States, but a host of world leaders from great nations as well. There were leaders from smaller nations, too, plus religious leaders from Muslim, Christian, and Jewish faiths. Included, too, was the possibility of leaders in the delegation from Buddhist and Hindu groups. The events of the past few days were bringing kings, presidents, prime ministers, and even a couple of theocrats to this otherwise virtually unknown small southern city.

Allan Smith got up early having had only a couple of hours of sleep. He, along with Chief Tyler, had worked the night before and on into the early morning hours. Now, they were making the rounds with the Chief of Security of the President's security team—visiting the airport, checking the motorcade route leading into Dunning, scanning neighborhoods around the church, and even the church grounds. Guardsmen, military police, state troopers, and Dunning police were stationed everywhere. Airplanes transporting the dignitaries from Washington were scheduled to arrive by noon. All other flights had been temporarily postponed until the Washington delegation and guests had come and gone. Governor Bayer arrived at seven insisting on making some of the rounds with Smith and Tyler.

When it was time for Chad to leave Cynthia's, they stood at the door of Apartment 210 refusing to allow themselves to be apart for any length of time, simply holding each other as if they would not see one another again. In reality, it would only be a short while before both would arrive at St. Michael's, carrying out their roles as reporters and not lovers. Finally, Chad left Cynthia's embrace and hurried home to get dressed for the day. At nine-fifteen he rolled into the parking lot of the church, prepared for probably the busiest day of his reporting career. As he closed the door of his car, Chad spotted Cynthia's car already parked. Walking to the WTLA site he casually looked hoping to see her. She was nowhere to be seen. Disappointed, he walked to the WTLA pavilion where he found a flurry of activity at the desk. Even Jim Stuart was there directing the activities. Seeing Chad approaching, Jim motioned him to the desk.

"Chad, we are going to have a direct link with New York including Jeff Glor and Lester Holt before the interview and will be examining the visit by the President and his group of foreign VIPs. You and Cynthia Davis will conduct all of this together as we planned yesterday."

Without waiting for any sort of comment, Jim continued. "Here is a list of questions that you and Cynthia should direct to the President and any other members of his party, if at all possible."

Stopping, Jim waited for Chad to say something.

"How long is this going to take?" asked Chad, rubbing his hand across his forehead which was already starting to perspire. "Are we going to have the opportunity to ask any real questions, or is this basically going to be a photo op?"

Pausing as he picked up another paper from the desk, Jim said, "I have no idea. You will have to play it by ear."

Jim continued, "Our station and WDDR will have our cameras set up with feeds going to all of the other networks. And, as we did before, you and Cynthia will represent all of the networks."

Smiling at Jim, Chad commented somewhat sarcastically, "I'm sure they all really like that."

"Yeah," was Jim's reply, "They've complained the whole time. But, it's here in Dunning and the space is limited. So, they have no choice. I can feel the polite resentment. But, that's the way it is."

In Washington, DC, Air Force One sat on the tarmac, its engines running at an idle. Behind it sat an identical plane idling. The number of foreign dignitaries who had accepted invitations from Washington to come to view the *angels* in Dunning was somewhat larger than expected, and consequently, was divided into two groups for security purposes. Cameras from news networks around the world were positioned to catch sight of this group arriving in an unusually large motorcade. A podium and a microphone were placed near the planes for the President to speak before departing for Dunning. Not only were there hundreds of reporters and cameras, but a huge crowd of spectators had gathered behind the fences to see the group off. All morning reporters had been reporting into their microphones while on cameras, feeding pre-event observations to the public before the distinguished leaders arrived. As in Dunning, a large security presence was in Washington as well. No one wanted anything to go wrong with so many of the world leaders gathered together in one place.

At ten o'clock AM, headlights from the huge motorcade were spotted by the crowd. Cameras followed the line of black vehicles rolling onto the tarmac. Black limo after black limo pulled onto the red carpeted area at the podium and unloaded the passengers. The first one getting out was the President of the United States. President Wallace stood and welcomed each one of the guests individually as they exited the cars. Stern and Howell stood behind him, and behind them were other notables from Washington. Stern's place was immediately behind the President with a list of the names of those in attendance, making sure President Wallace addressed each of them correctly.

The Prime Minister of the United Kingdom, followed by the Presidents of France and Russia, the Chancellor of Germany, and the Chairman of the People's Republic of China were next to exit the limos, and lastly, a host of others which included leaders from Canada, Brazil, Mexico, and Israel. The list of dignitaries went on. The world's Catholic leader, the Pope, arrived with a dozen officials, dressed in red robes. The Dalai Lama and his small group dressed in bright reds and oranges arrived next. The arrival of the King of Saudi Arabia, followed by the Presidents of Egypt, Morocco, and rulers of several smaller Gulf States, represented the Muslim states. They were each welcomed by the President and other members of the distinguished gathering. The Saudi King led his delegation to the podium. Muhammad Harassi and Ishmael Hadi walked behind the King, plus a long line of men wearing the traditional dress of the desert kingdom.

Muhammad had been informed previously that both the King and Hadi wished to meet with him before meeting with

President Wallace; therefore, he met with the Saudi party early Saturday morning at Reagan International Airport. In this meeting, Muhammad detailed with the King his own experience with the *winged visitors* residing in rafters of the small church. The King appeared pleased at his story and felt reassured by his coming to the United States and the trip south to Dunning.

After all of the black limousines unloaded and departed, President Wallace stepped to the microphone and delivered an official welcome from the United States.

> *Distinguished guests and leaders of the family of nations and leaders of the world's religions, as the President of the United States, and on behalf of the citizens of the United States, we welcome you!*

There was a large applause from the crowd as the cameras rolled and photographers clicked historic pictures of the gathering. President Wallace continued.

> *Today is a historic occasion as the people of the world gather to witness such a truly amazing spectacle, a sight so unbelievable that it has brought together many nations. It is our hope that because of this miracle, we can begin to bring all people together in peace and understanding. Others will have to judge for themselves what it means, but I personally believe this is a way of the Great Creator communicating to us: **I am present always.** Through this miraculous visit to our small blue planet, and with God's help, maybe we can put an end to the misery and war that has plagued mankind for thousands of years. Thank you.*

After this very brief welcome, the President turned to the gathered group engaging in conversation with some of them. Then, within moments they began boarding the two planes that were waiting. The cameras continued to roll as the two large presidential planes had their ramps removed and their doors closed. Slowly the engines revved to a roar as they taxied onto the runway, taking position for departing. Air Force One taxied out first followed by an identical second plane. With a loud roar, the President's plane was airborne. It was soon followed by the second blue and silver plane. Within minutes both planes became specks in the pale blue summer sky of Washington as they turned and headed southward.

While the two planes were making their journey southward, back in Dunning, Joseph Turbon gathered his belongings and placed them in his old truck. Climbing into the cab he turned the ignition key, coaxing the old engine to start up with a roar and a puff of gray smoke. Driving out from the old motel, its neon welcome sign only half lighted with just the "**Mo**" flashing, the result of a short in the wiring, Joseph turned east toward the congestion around St. Michael's. Instead of driving to the head of Everwine Street, Joseph turned onto Houston Street, two blocks north from the church. On the right was the group of tents that formed the site of the *Southwest Evangelical Ministries*. There were a number of cars and trucks parked along the side of the large production tent.

Joseph glanced upward at threatening rainclouds beginning to gather as he pulled his truck onto the grass of a make-shift parking area. From his truck he could see *SEM*'s daily broadcast in progress. Several cameramen and technicians monitored the live broadcast. William Renfro was speaking on camera with one of his producers about the expected group of distinguished visitors coming from Washington. Joseph got out of his truck and walked to where a small crowd of people, Renfro's studio audience, sat on folding metal chairs watching the broadcast. William Renfro was speaking in his usual pious manner, filled with criticism of anything that wasn't in line with his beliefs and still smarting from the refusal by the City to allow his team to enter the church.

"We are being discriminated against by the government and the religious factions that are puppets and in the good graces of the government. We, as representatives of the religious outreach, are completely kept out." People in the audience nodded their agreement as Renfro continued with somewhat of a smirk in his voice, "They won't allow us to carry our cameras or ministry into the church, but they will allow foreign agents and false religious groups to visit, personally invited by the President of the United States, nonetheless."

Renfro's enthusiasm increased as he sensed his words were being met with agreement from his live audience and television viewers. Joseph Turbon walked into the tent and sat down on a folding chair at the end of the front row. As he sat down, a plump older lady with gray ringlets in her teased hair smiled and nodded to Joseph, but showing no notice of her or anyone else, he simply kept focused on Renfro.

All night Joseph had carefully thought through what he must do. It had come to him that God wanted him to stop these impostors who blasphemed God's will. He should silence them all and start the wheels turning for the "beginning of the end." It was God's will, not his. He was only God's instrument. The fact that these television ministers had large followings and brought in lots of money angered Joseph because he knew they were false prophets.

As Renfro continued speaking, Joseph slowly rose. The table where Renfro sat in front of the camera was only feet away on the raised one-foot stage.

"You are the voice of evil," Joseph Turbon proclaimed as he stood up.

At first it was too low for anyone to hear. Still standing, Joseph spoke again only this time much louder.

"**You are the voice of evil**!" he shouted.

Hearing this, Renfro stopped in mid-sentence as the filming crew turned to look at Turbon. Immediately everything stopped with the exception of the cameras.

For a third time and still much louder, Turbon cleared his voice and shouted, "**YOU ARE THE VOICE OF EVIL**!" William Renfro glared at Joseph Turbon, his surprise turning to anger which was evident to those around him. A member of Renfro's security team, always on the outlook for trouble makers, moved from the side to stop him. In an instant Joseph Turbon pulled the shiny revolver from under his shirt and pointed it at the security officer. There was a flash and a loud noise as the man dropped to the ground. Turning to face Renfro again, Joseph mounted the small stage. Screams and cries echoed from the terrified audience as many began to run and seek cover, turning over chairs along the way. The crew on stage had fled with the shot.

Now only Joseph Turbon, William Renfro, and his frightened producer remained on the stage. All three men stood frozen in the moment. Then Turbon pointed the pistol at Renfro.

Disbelief covered Renfro's face. Without a word Turbon pulled the trigger. With the jerk of the shot, a flash and noise again erupted. Renfro looked surprised for a moment as if not realizing that he had been shot. A red stain slowly became visible on his white shirt and gray suit jacket as he stared at Turbon and then down at his wound, not fully comprehending what he was seeing. He fell hard, face first on the floor and lay unmoving.

Joseph Turbon pointed the gun at the frightened young man standing beside the fallen Renfro. Fear caused the man to fall to his knees where he waited for the next shot to take him. It didn't come, however, and Turbon coolly turned and walked away from the tent and back to his truck. Getting into it, he started the engine, backed out, and onto the street.

Turbon drove unhurriedly down the street and turned into the alleyway which ran between the streets of Houston and Everwine. It was a narrow passage used for garbage and trash collection. Midway down he turned into the back driveway of a small yellow house he had staked out the night before. The drive ran all the way through to Everwine. As he drove slowly beside the neat, yellow house, Ms. Sally stood in her yard watering the summer flowers as she did daily. The elderly woman looked up at the sound of the truck as it drove slowly by and at the man sitting in the cab. Putting her hand on her hip and frowning, Ms. Sally thought, *Now what's that man doin' comin' through my drive like that? He's up to no good, for sure.*

She received no acknowledgment from him and he took no notice of her, driving slowly through the narrow lane, looking neither to the right nor left. As he reached Everwine, Joseph Turbon suddenly gunned the engine and turned in the direction of the church at the far end of the street. As he did, he caught the soldiers on guard completely by surprise. Before they could unshoulder their weapons, he was gone, accelerating quickly down the street.

—⁓—

Chad, Cynthia, Jim Stuart, and Allan Smith stood on the stage of WTLA looking over proposed details for the impending visit. Police and guardsman were everywhere now in anticipation of the Presidential party. They were determined nothing would happen to upset the President's visit, scheduled in less than an hour. Chad stood close to Cynthia pretending to read as she held the papers. She knew he probably wasn't looking at the papers, but simply trying to be as close as possible to her, which brought a quiet, secretive smile to her face.

Jim was saying, "As soon as the Washington group arrives......" when they heard a loud crash followed by a couple of gunshots, followed by another series of more shots. Joseph Turbon had turned out of Ms. Sally's driveway and accelerated the old blue truck down Everwine and toward the church. A military Humvee was blocking the street with a group of soldiers standing beside it. Hearing and seeing the accelerating truck approaching, the soldiers flagged the truck to stop. It did not! In an instant, Joseph accelerated, hitting the front fender of the Humvee spinning it around, and sending soldiers scurrying out of the way. As the truck moved rapidly past the guard vehicle, they opened fire to try to stop the truck. People on both sides of the street ducked for cover at the sound of the shots.

The WTLA group could see people along the street moving back away from the curb and ducking to find cover at the sound of the gunfire. More shots could be heard closer to the church. Policeman, Secret Service, and guardsmen could be seen drawing their weapons and looking in the direction of the shooting. Chad, Cynthia, Jim, and Allan all looked intently in the direction of the gunfire, but could see nothing until the old blue Chevy truck wheeled into view at a high rate of speed and turned into the parking lot, just barely making the turn. Turning the old truck caught the front fender of one of the black and whites parked there, knocking it up on the curb. More shots were fired at the truck as police leveled their weapons toward it. Two of its tires were flat and its body was peppered with bullet holes. All the windows were shattered, but still the old truck continued to move forward across the parking lot toward the news trucks and cameras. The truck rocketed like a missile toward the WTLA booth as the group stood staring in amazement.

"Get out of the way!" shouted Chad as Jim turned and ran, followed by Allan. Instead of running Cynthia looked at Chad and froze. Just before the truck hit, Chad pushed Cynthia off the stage to the right beside the large mobile truck.

The old truck struck the stage hurling and crashing cameras, lights, and desks. The stage collapsed as did the tent over the stage where the truck finally came to a stop. It stopped where the WTLA News stage had been earlier. In seconds policemen were swarming over the scene of the crash. The ruined truck's engine was still running, covered with rubble of the crash. An officer pushed back the tent and opened the door of the truck, his pistol drawn. There was no need. Joseph Turbon sat slumped over the steering wheel, dead. He had been hit multiple times. The officer reached across his body and switched the truck's engine off.

Suddenly, a voice from the side of the collapsed tent was heard from under the debris. "Help! Help! Get me out!"

More officers rushed over and quickly dug Cynthia out from under the debris. Helped to her feet, surprisingly she was unhurt except for a small bleeding cut on her forehead and one on her arm. Frantically, she looked around where the stage had been. By now Jim Stuart and Allan Smith were there.

"Are you okay?" asked Jim, visibly shaken by the sudden attack.

"Yes, I'm fine, I think. Where's Chad?" asked Cynthia, looking around, becoming frantic when he did not appear.

Not seeing him, both fear and panic gripped Cynthia. "Where's Chad?" she asked again, her voice shaking when she didn't see him.

The men looked over the broken stage. There was no sign of Chad. Impulsively, Allan said, "Let's push this truck back."

Everyone around the collapsed tent came together and began to push the crashed, bullet-riddled truck away from the ruined stage. Once it was out of the way, they saw Chad. He was lying where the truck had struck, covered in broken bits of wood and equipment. He lay motionless.

Cynthia rushed to Chad, only to be stopped by Allan. "Let the police see to him first. If he's hurt we don't want to move him and make it worse." Allan knew instinctively Chad had not made it. As several officers bent down over Chad, another of the officers dashed back to the street to get medical assistance. In less than a minute the officer was running back followed by two emergency workers. As they knelt over Chad, tears streamed down Cynthia's face as she watched the emergency personnel work. Jim had his arm around her for support.

"He's breathing," called out one of the EMTs. "Get an ambulance here! Quick!" At that instant, an ambulance was already moving into the parking lot and up to the scene of all the chaos.

Carefully they moved the debris away from Chad and slid a portable stretcher underneath him. He lay unresponsive. The emergency personnel gently lifted him from the remains of the broken stage and equipment and placed him in the waiting ambulance.

Many of the other network teams had gathered closely around. Robert Wood and Bob Silver were among them. They were standing with Jim and Cynthia. While the obvious feeling of helplessness engulfed them, each one continued standing hoping to be of some assistance.

The attendants adjusted Chad in the ambulance; Cynthia began to climb in beside him.

Jim Stuart stopped her by asking, "I know this sounds cold, but what are you going to be able to do? Someone has to stay and cover the President's arrival and the interviews. Would Chad want you to go? You can't do anything to help him at this time. Let the emergency staff do their job."

Cynthia, her faced smeared from tears and mascara, stopped and turned to Jim. "I don't care! If he had not pushed me out of the way, I'd be the one on that stretcher and not him. Someone else will have to do it. He's more important," said Cynthia looking back at Chad.

Jim could see the determination on her face and knew that he wasn't going to change her mind. Rubbing his hand through his hair, Jim tried to think. He was in charge of seeing that the interviews went as scheduled. Now he had to face the situation with neither Chad nor Cynthia being here.

"Excuse me." It was Robert Wood's voice.

Jim turned to face him.

"If there is anything that we can do," Wood pointed to Silver, "we'd be glad to help. If Cynthia will let us, we'll go with Chad to the hospital."

She shook her head, tears streaming down her face. "I lost someone very close to me once. I won't let it happen again, not if I can help it."

"Okay, okay, Cynthia," said Jim. "Go with Chad. Call me as soon as you know something about his condition."

She climbed into the ambulance and the doors closed. Quickly, it pulled out of the parking lot and rolled down Everwine, its siren and lights going.

Jim Stuart turned to Wood. "You can help. With Chad and Cynthia not here, someone has to conduct the interviews. Would you and Bob do it?"

"Jim, I feel like we're stealing this from those two," said Robert.

Bob Silver nodded in agreement. "It's just not right."

"Look, we don't have time to make other arrangements. It's only a matter of an hour before the President is here. We don't have time to do anything else. Will you do it?" pleaded Stuart. "Will CNN allow you to work with Bob and ABC? Besides, we're gonna need cameras and equipment, YOUR cameras and equipment, to replace the mess we have here."

"Looks as though we have no other choice." said Wood looking at Silver. "This will really have to be a combined job with all of our networks."

"Great!" replied Jim Stuart. "Let's get moving."

In the ensuing hour before the arrival of the President of the United States and a select group of international representatives, necessary preparations were pushed into high gear. Everyone at the scene worked together. While the news crews cleaned up the mess and set up cameras and equipment, various law enforcement agencies cleared the large crowd of people from Everwine Street fearing others might be involved in the attack. A perimeter was then drawn around St. Michael's. No one was allowed inside the perimeter except the news media and those people who lived in the neighborhood within the perimeter. These people were instructed to remain inside their homes for their own safety. They, like the rest of the world, could follow the events as they played out on television. Going from the huge crowds that had previously stood waiting on Everwine, the street immediately evolved into a ghost town, security being the only presence. To thwart any further attempt to carry out an attack at St. Michael's, the police and army were on highest alert. No one, not anything, was going to get by them!

—◦◦◦—

Aboard Air Force One, the President received the news of the tragic events that had just played out in Dunning. He, like his advisors, concluded that too much was at stake to call off the visit now. With added support from security in Dunning, it was agreed the visit would not be cancelled. The planes landed not to a large crowd, as expected earlier, but to an empty airport. Chartered red and blue striped buses provided by a private concern, Southern Coaches, met the large group of dignitaries. Driving into Dunning, the delegation of political and religious leaders met with an almost uncanny silence. The route from the airport to the church had been cleared completely and all traffic had been diverted away from the processional route mapped out for the distinguished visitors. The airport and the town wore the appearance of a scene from a science fiction movie in which the whole town had been evacuated. The only clue this really wasn't the case was the huge number of people and cars well away from the motorcade, several streets away. This security feature had all been arranged in an astonishing one-hour endeavor, thanks to the cooperation and appearance throughout the city of the local police, State Troopers, National Guardsmen, and Military Police, who could be seen everywhere near the route of the motorcade.

At the Dunning Medical Center, Cynthia sat in the emergency waiting room unable to function. She sat alone. As she sat, she quietly offered a prayer:

> *Father God, through the angels You allowed us to see a glimpse of the other side. You changed my life with this. Then, with Chad, You gave me another chance to have someone to live for in this world. Oh, God, please don't let Chad die! Don't let him leave me now.*

Tears flowed and flowed as she spoke to God. Having voiced this last prayer, a feeling of peace washed over her. Cynthia felt that God was allowing His presence to be with her and take away the unrelenting fear of losing Chad. Cynthia believed that God would protect Chad. She began to believe in her heart and soul the *angels* were in some way a message from God. Why had He sent them to Dunning? There had to be a purpose, still unrevealed perhaps.

In the waiting room, Cynthia glanced up at the television and saw the motorcade driving through Dunning. She watched the President, the Pope, the King of Saudi Arabia, and numerous other world and religious leaders exiting the buses at St. Michael's. She watched as they moved into the church. She watched when they came out and immediately detected from their faces how the event had moved and transformed them all. She watched as Robert Wood and Bob Silver interviewed the President and listened as others in the party made comments about the miraculous visions they had witnessed, and then speculated as to what effect this phenomenon would have on the world and its people. But, while she felt happy and inspired that maybe, just maybe, the world was going to change for the first time in thousands of years; none of it seemed to matter so much if Chad wasn't going to be here to see the impact of this miracle with her. Her life had undergone a *miraculous* change in just the span of a week; first, by the *angels* in St. Michael's, and then by Chad Simmons, and lastly, but more importantly, Cynthia learning to rely on God again. Since losing John back in Chicago, she had given herself totally to her work, resigned herself to never love again, and basically had not given her spiritual life much thought either. God had not answered her prayers for John, so she pretty much gave up on turning to Him in times of need. Yet, today Cynthia was not experiencing the hopeless feelings she felt before moving to Dunning—about her work, or love. She was completely trusting God to heal Chad. Regarding her work, Cynthia didn't feel the slightest pang of loss not being there and interviewing all those important people before an audience of billions of people. That simply didn't matter now.

Cynthia listened when Wood and Silver talked about the attack before the Presidential party had arrived and recounted why Chad and she were not there because he had been injured saving her life. She smiled as they, along with all of their viewers, wished that Chad would come through safely from his injuries sustained during the attack.

"Ms. Davis," a caring voice brought her back to reality.

Cynthia turned to see a doctor in blue scrubs standing in the doorway.

She stood, waiting for him to say something. His expression gave no hint as to Chad's condition.

"Yes, I'm Cynthia Davis," she answered.

"Ms. Davis, Mr. Simmons was broken up very badly," began the doctor. "He has sustained broken legs, a broken arm, a serious concussion and a collapsed lung." He stopped here.

No thought Cynthia as she felt a pang of fear grab her, it can't end like this, not again! It just can't. Fighting back tears, she went cold and numb bracing herself for the doctor's inevitable words, words she had dealt with before. *Oh Father God, please. I'm trusting You.*

The doctor continued. "He should not be alive, but he is. The trauma his body experienced was tremendous. Some power I can't explain is working here. He is heavily sedated right now and will be for a while. But, I think he is, perhaps, going to survive if he can get through the next couple of days. How? I'm not sure. Let's just call it a *miracle.*"

With these words Cynthia began to cry again, only this time it was out of relief. God had answered her prayers. The God that she had witnessed through the appearance of the *angels* had acted in her life.

"When can I see him?" Cynthia asked fighting back more tears.

"Maybe by tomorrow he will be able to talk with you," the doctor replied. "Until then, he needs to rest allowing his body to get over the shock of the injury."

"Thank you, doctor. Thank you so much," Cynthia said. The relief was evident in her face.

"He is a very fortunate man, Miss Davis. I'd say he had *more* than luck on his side," added the doctor with a tired smile as he turned and walked out the door and down the hallway.

Cynthia took a deep breath, went to look for a phone, and dialed the number for Jim Stuart. It rang a couple of times before she heard, "Yes, Cynthia, how is Chad?"

She felt emotions rise in her voice again as she said, "He's going to make it if things go well for the next couple of days. The doctor said he was injured very severely and he shouldn't even be alive. But I know he is going to make it."

She could hear a sigh of relief on the other end of the call. "Thank God. I'll be at the hospital as soon as we can tie up things here. By the way, the President heard about Chad and what happened. He commented in his remarks to the audience about his heroics."

Jim paused a few seconds then said, "There is one other thing I probably should mention to you, Cynthia. My secretary was able to reach Chad's parents by telephone for me a short while ago and she gave them details of Chad's accident. Being a parent myself and knowing they had already lost one son, I felt it my duty as his employer and friend to apprise them of the seriousness of Chad's condition. They are driving up from Panama City, Florida, as we speak and should be here within the next couple of hours or so.

"Thanks, Jim," Cynthia replied. "I will explain to them how Chad saved my life and that I simply could not leave him alone in the hospital."

As Cynthia settled down to wait for any further news about Chad, she pondered how she should approach Chad's parents about their relationship. No one at the station knew anything was going on between them, even though Jim might now suspect something. Whatever anyone thought at this point, she was not going to leave Chad. It was apparent that she just might have to be the one to explain to his parents the seriousness of their new relationship and the love they felt for each other. It would be a long wait and a tough couple of days ahead, but she didn't mind, just as long as he was alive. It was nearly eight o'clock when Jim Stuart came to the hospital. Walking in, he was not alone. Both Robert Silver and Bob Wood were with him. Cynthia hugged them and thanked them for coming.

Wood brushed off Cynthia's thank you with, "We had to come! After all, you and he are not just fellow reporters, but friends."

They sat down to talk about Chad and his injuries and the attack earlier in the day.

"From what we have been able to piece together, the attacker, Joseph Turbon, was a religious extremist and mentally unbalanced as well. It appears that he had driven from Arkansas to be a part of the events in Dunning," Robert Wood explained.

"Speaking of which, bet you haven't caught the latest on the news?" probed Bob Silver.

What news?" questioned Cynthia.

Bob continued, "Before attacking the press at St. Michael's, this Joseph Turbon drove to the mobile unit of the Ministries of William Renfro and killed Renfro and a security guard."

Surprised, Cynthia said, "The guy with the huge evangelical group in the Southwest?"

"The same one," said Robert Wood.

"That guy must really have been disturbed and totally out of touch with reality," commented Cynthia.

"He definitely had some issues," Jim concluded, shaking his head, and then adding, "But, there are lots of people totally out in left, or right field trying to push their ideas on others."

They sat and visited for about an hour when a young nurse in scrubs stepped in the doorway and said, "Ms. Davis?"

"Yes," said Cynthia standing with her arms folded across her chest.

"Mr. Simmons is awake and reasonably lucid. He's not really supposed to have company, but he keeps asking for you. The doctor said to let you in for just a couple of minutes."

"Cynthia, go and check on him. We've got to go," said Jim. "Call me if anything changes."

Cynthia hugged each of them 'goodbye' and turned to follow the nurse.

As she did, Jim Stuart added, "Tell Chad not to take too long getting over this. We don't want him taking advantage of the situation and thinking he's special or something!"

She sniffed and laughed as she turned telling Jim, "I'll make sure he hears that."

Cynthia followed the nurse down the hall and through the double doors, into the intensive care unit. She caught her breath when she saw Chad. Chad was literally bandaged from head to toe. Both legs and his left arm were immobilized. He was taped around his chest. His face was bruised and he had a black eye. He lay still with his eyes closed, breathing ever so lightly.

Cynthia reached his bed and stood beside it, saying nothing. Chad did not notice anyone was there until the young nurse said quietly, "I think he's drifted off to sleep."

Chad opened his eyes and saw Cynthia. He smiled a very weak smile, and moved his good right arm toward her.

She took his hand in hers. He squeezed it tightly. Cynthia resisted the urge to cry.

"Boy, you certainly look good for television cameras," she joked, trying to smile and at the same time not letting him see how much she wanted to cry.

In a very weak voice he responded barely above a whisper, "Yep, all I need is a little powder and I'll look great. You got some?"

Cynthia smiled and sniffed at his attempt at humor. *He looks terrible*, she thought. But then, he had come as close to death as one could and still survive.

"Your boss, Robert Wood and Bob Silver were just here checking on you," Cynthia said as she stroked his hand.

"Oh yeah," in the same weak voice, he said, "Trying to get me to move to the big time, I'll bet."

"Exactly," said Cynthia. Smiling again, she one-upped him by saying, "They plan on offering you a multimillion dollar contract to anchor the news on national television."

"I hope you told them it wouldn't be enough," he whispered.

"I told them they would have to double it," smiled Cynthia.

"Good," said Chad.

Looking at her with a bruised and puffy face, Chad said, "How are you doing?"

"Much better now that I know that you're okay," she replied looking into his eyes. "I was afraid I had lost you."

Chad replied, "Sorry I had to get rough and push you, but then you wouldn't move."

"Yeah, about that. You can expect a call from my lawyer about the shove," said Cynthia, trying to keep the conversation from getting too heavy and starting the tears again.

Again Chad tried to laugh, but the pain was evident when he did.

"Are you hurting now?" said Cynthia still holding onto his hand.

"No, I'm okay," he lied. "In fact I was going to ask if I could come over to your place this evening."

Even with the injuries and his obvious pain, Chad continued trying to joke and make light of his condition. It made Cynthia smile to watch him try so hard. She knew he didn't want her to know he was hurting.

"Good, I'll look for you about nine. You can recognize me easily. I'll be the one in the leopard nightie who answers the door," smiled Cynthia.

Smiling weakly Chad said, "Cynthia, if I could move, I'd be there. I'm just afraid I will have to get rid of some of this baggage first." Squirming, he added, "Especially this catheter."

Cynthia smiled and shook her head at his attempt to joke.

The young nurse came up and said, "I think we need to let Mr. Simmons rest for a while."

"Yes," said Cynthia softly.

She leaned over the edge of the bed and lightly kissed Chad's lips. "I'll be back later. Don't go anywhere."

The look in his eyes showed the love he felt for her. He didn't have to say anything. He just nodded.

"Bye," said Cynthia. In a whisper she added, "I love you."

He mouthed the words, "I love you."

She turned and left the room, walking back down the hallway to the waiting room; she would spend the night there, even knowing that there was nothing she could do. She just wanted to be there, to be near him if he needed her.

As Cynthia reached the waiting area, Chad's parents appeared. She immediately recognized them from the photograph in Chad's living room. She approached them and introduced herself, surprised somewhat to find out that Chad had already told them that he had met a "girl who had completely turned his life around and was very much in love with her." Cynthia smiled through misty eyes and related how she and Chad had come together viewing and reporting the *angels* at St. Michael's. She further explained the Joseph Turbon incident and the ensuing accident wherein Chad had pushed her from the stage, saving her life and endangering his own.

Cynthia and Chad's parents spent the rest of the night in the small hospital waiting room getting acquainted, praying, and just being near the one who meant so much to all of them.

20

had's stay in the hospital lasted for three weeks. When he left, he did so in a wheelchair and wearing three casts. Cynthia went to the hospital daily to sit with him. After he was discharged, she was with him, too, leaving only to perform a needed chore here and there, or go in to work as needed, or when his parents came for brief visits. WDDR was generous in letting her have so much time off from work. Most of the news was still devoted to the story of the unexplainable appearance of the *angels* at St. Michael's and the continuous influx of people in Dunning, sometimes by the thousands, each trying to get a glimpse of the celestial visitors. People poured in from across the nation and around the world. The town of Dunning was far from settling down. It just seemed to get even busier even after the visit of the President and various dignitaries from around the world. Dunning was becoming a shrine for almost every possible religious group, whether Christian, Muslim, Jew, Hindu, or Buddhist. The *angels* with the shimmery wings had touched everyone. Still, there was no spiritual, theological or even logical explanation for their presence. They were simply there quietly resting in the rafters, seemingly oblivious to all activity beneath them.

On a Friday morning, eight weeks after the *angels* first appeared and were discovered by Doris Williams, Reverend Johnson sat working in his office. Church services had been moved from St. Michael's to the Civic Center in Dunning for as long as the *angels* continued to remain in the sanctuary. Attendance in Reverend Johnson's services had risen dramatically. It was as if people had suddenly awakened to God, the Lord Almighty, and His Presence, in a very busy world that too often had forgotten about the Earth's Creator. Maybe it took an event like the *angels* to make people realize that there was more to life than work, material things, and competing in the rat-race of modern society. Attendance dramatically increased at religious churches and temples elsewhere as did donations to many relief agencies around the world. Thomas Johnson was very happy with the events that had evolved as a result of the *angels,* even if he were unable to explain their presence which had truly impacted the lives of millions of people, those who had seen, as well as those who had only heard, about the *angels of Dunning.*

Crowds of people continuously moved through the church at a pace that showed no signs of letting up. Day after day as Thomas Johnson sat working in his office, a glance out the window revealed the long, continuous line that traveled down the street and out of sight. Many churches wrote letters inquiring about the *angels* or offering to send money to help with the upkeep of the church. As usual, he refused. One particular day in late summer, Thomas sat at his desk, white shirt sleeves rolled up, working on such correspondence when he was interrupted.

"Reverend Johnson, something is happening in the sanctuary!"

As Reverend Johnson looked up he saw a young policeman standing at his door looking seriously bewildered. Getting up quickly from his chair, he followed the young man down the hallway toward the sanctuary. A crowd of people still moved slowly by the open doors, looking upward. Only now, they were pointing and speaking in hushed whispers.

When Thomas looked up, he saw why the officer was so excited.

Above them, the *tear in the dimension of time* still revealed the *angels*, but now they were beginning to move as if awakening from a long sleep. A low "oooh" came from the people below as one of the beings above them spread its wings, showing the ethereal, unearthly beauty of the beings. Something was happening. A woman bolted from the doorway and hurried out the door. Others followed suit. After watching for a few moments, Thomas hurried back to his office. He sat down and began pushing the buttons on his desk phone.

"This is Thomas Johnson at St. Michael's. Is Mayor Smith in?" he asked.

In Allan Smith's office Lucy looked down at the Mayor's calendar before saying, "Reverend, the Mayor should be in the office in just a few minutes. May I give him a message?"

"Oh, please," replied Thomas, "Tell him to come to the church as soon as possible. Something is happening."

"I will Reverend. Thank you. Bye."

Hanging up the phone, Lucy began dialing the Mayor's cell number. It rang only once before she heard Allan's voice.

"Yes, Lucy, what is it?"

"Mr. Mayor, I just got a call from Reverend Johnson." Lucy continued, "He said something is happening at the church and that you need to get over there as quickly as possible. There was a sense of urgency in his voice."

"Thanks, Lucy," Allan replied. "I'm on my way."

Hanging up, Allan dialed Chief Tyler's number. "Bill, I'm headed to St. Michael's. Reverend Johnson just called and said something is going on over there."

Tyler questioned, "Did he say what was happening?"

"No, just that I needed to get over there," said Allan.

"I'll meet you there. I should be there in about ten minutes," said Tyler, hanging up.

Allan Smith arrived at the church first and walked in the back door. Everwine Street and the church still remained under close security. Having had no more threats or incidents, the work around the church now just involved crowd control rather than security. Inside the door, Allan walked past an officer and stopped outside Thomas Johnson's door. Before he could knock Thomas saw him and rose to greet him.

Shaking hands, Allan said, "What seems to be our problem, Reverend?"

"Come with me, Mayor Smith. It's better that I show you," said Thomas leading Allan out of the office. Allan could detect the sense of urgency in his voice. As they hurried down the hall, Bill Tyler came rushing through the back door. Without a word, he followed them, all walking at a quick pace down the hallway. Bypassing the people in line waiting for a glimpse into the sanctuary, they reached the doorway and looked upward. They saw the movement just as Reverend Johnson had seen it earlier. Neither Allan nor Bill Tyler had seen the *angels* in any manner of active stance before. They stood motionless, mesmerized by the size and growing activity.

After what seemed like several minutes, Allan spoke, "What's going on?"

"I have no idea," answered Reverend Johnson. Then he added, "It looks as if the *angels* may be going somewhere."

"Yeah, but where?" said Allan as he continued looking upward. "I think I need to call some people."

"What do we do?" questioned Tyler.

"I don't know that we do anything," Allan replied.

"Should we continue to allow people to come through?" asked Tyler.

"I guess so, Bill," said Allan. "For the time being, anyway."

Turning to Reverend Johnson, Allan said, "Can we go back to your office. I think we need to make a few phone calls."

Once inside the Reverend's office, Allan dialed WTLA studio and after a few moments started speaking with Jim Stuart. "Jim, we've got some sort of activity here at St. Michael's."

Then listening for a moment said, "I'd have no idea. Can you get someone over here now? Great! Thanks."

Disconnecting his phone he began to dial again. "Yes, this is Mayor Allan Smith. Is Cynthia Davis there? Okay. Give me that number. Fine. Thanks."

While Allan Smith was making calls, Reverend Johnson also began making calls. His calls included the Bishop and his close circle of church members. After informing Bishop Brown of the change in the appearance of the *angels*, he then dialed Raymond Dickens, his wife, Elizabeth, and Doris Williams.

Allan waited as he heard the phone ring. Cynthia answered.

"Cynthia, Allan Smith here. I have some interesting news, and I thought you might want to be party to it."

Cynthia had stopped by Chad's apartment to check on him on her way to cover a story about limited hotel accommodations in Dunning. With Chad being home from the hospital now, Cynthia spent most of her time with him, leaving only to do work when she was needed.

"Yes, hello, Mayor. It's good to hear from you. What news?" asked Cynthia.

Chad watched Cynthia as she sat listening to the voice on the other end of the conversation. Her eyes widening, went to Chad as she listened to the Mayor and he was following her conversation very closely.

"Thank you. We'll be right there," said Cynthia ending the conversation.

"*We'll?*" said Chad.

"We'll! Get into your chair, we're going to St. Michael's," said Cynthia.

As quickly as she could get Chad into his wheel chair and into her car, they were heading to St. Michael's, driving downtown and through the heavy traffic was now commonplace in Dunning. For weeks it had been like this with people coming from all over the states and even some countries abroad. Reaching the roadblock at the head of Everwine, Cynthia stopped briefly to show her press badge. Motioned on through the checkpoint, she drove down the tree-lined street, past the long lines of people waiting to get the opportunity to enter the little church. They were waved into the parking lot by a police officer and immediately spotted the long line of people slowly and quietly entering the church. Though most of the television network trucks and equipment were gone, some had been left to follow continuing events. At the exit door, it was a different story, however. As people exited the church, they showed not only the quiet amazement of seeing the *angels*, but sheer excitement, exchanging comments as they walked through the church yard and back down to the street by the exit.

Getting out of the car and helping Chad into his wheel chair, Cynthia rolled him to the back door of the church where two policemen standing guard motioned for help from inside. Two guardsmen appeared and lifted Chad and his chair through the door and into the hallway. Reverend Johnson and Allan Smith appeared from inside the Pastor's office joining them.

"Hi. Man, you've come a long way in the past few weeks," greeted Mayor Smith, all smiles.

Chad flashed a smile back and a hello as he shook hands with Smith, Johnson, and Tyler, asking in a somewhat lighthearted manner, "Reverend, what have we got going on here?"

"It appears there is some sort of activity going on with our visitors," was Johnson's response.

Allan Smith said, "Yeah, some sort of *unusual* activity, I'd say."

"Is it possible for us to take a look, Reverend?" Cynthia asked.

"Most certainly, I think you will want to take a look!" he replied.

Mayor Smith turned to one of the young policeman standing there and said, "Close the door for a few minutes and let this group of people clear the building. Tell them the doors will be reopened in just a few minutes."

"Yes sir," obeyed the young officer disappearing around the corner and down the hallway. Five minutes later he returned. "It's all clear, sir."

"Thanks," replied the Mayor.

The small group proceeded down the now empty hallway. The crowd was gone, except for the few remaining policemen, who were always there to maintain order.

Reaching the doorway to the sanctuary, Chad and Cynthia saw immediately what all the commotion was about. There was activity above them! Looking up, they could see the *angels* now flexing their huge shimmery-looking, majestic wings as if in preparation for departing. No longer were they sitting quietly in the space above the altar. There was now movement along with an audible sound of wind rushing through the rafters, similar to that of a storm blowing in. The group stood watching in amazement as the *angels* took flight one after the other, with the almost deafening sound of a blowing wind. Within a matter of seconds all three were gone and '*the tear in the fabric of time*' closed completely, leaving nothing but the quiet, dark sanctuary.

Astonished, the group stood and continued to stare upward, only now there nothing to see.

Allan, first to speak, asked, "What just happened?"

"I don't know," murmured Chad, looking upward, still mystified, and hoping to see something to explain the *miracle* they had all just witnessed. Only now, there was nothing to see and no sound either, only the light streaming through the stained glass windows into the still and silent room.

In a low, husky voice, and looking misty-eyed, Reverend Johnson commented, still staring upward, "Our *angels* have gone."

21

Crowds continued coming to St. Michael's to see where the *angels* had been. Because of the widespread fascination with the *angels*, Reverend Johnson and the congregation decided that the church would allow visitors to come and see the place where these *angels of Dunning* had just appeared one day and stayed for two months. Tours continued Tuesday through Saturday, but the church decided to close once again for services on Sunday. Monday still remained the day to clean the church from the busy week and forever a day of remembrance for Doris Williams, who was the first person to actually view part of *heaven's realm on earth*.

In a matter of eight weeks, St. Michael's had become a site considered **Holy**. It was now one of the holiest of religious sites in the world and sanctioned by all religions. The fact that many religious leaders from all faiths had visited and witnessed the *angels* gave great credibility to this small, unassuming, southern church. The *angels* were no longer present in the rafters at St. Michael's but Christians, Jews, Muslims, Buddhists, and Hindus could often be found waiting in line to see the former, brief *resting place of the indisputable heavenly angels.*

Other than being the former site of the *angels*, a major draw to this small, unassuming church in Dunning, was realized the following Monday after the *angels* had gone.

Doris had always been responsible for maintaining the sanctuary. When a cleaning crew was called in to clean where the many pilgrims had walked, she insisted on overseeing the crew. She had done this task for many years as a labor of love and was not about to let it go to a professional cleaning company. The sanctuary would remain hers as long as she was physically able to do the work. Doris arrived Monday morning as usual and seeing the Reverend's car parked in the back, she went on in through the back door and into the janitor's closet gathering up cleaning materials and tools. She then walked into the empty sanctuary.

As was Doris's Monday morning ritual before starting to clean, she walked up to the altar to pray. Closing her eyes she could still visualize the majestic *angel*s and imagined she could still feel their presence in the room. She finished praying and began dusting and polishing the railing and podium. As she did so, something caught her eye. Behind one of the red-cushioned chairs where the pastor sat, she saw something that looked like feathers. Doris moved in closer and knelt down to examine the objects. It was feathers, large white feathers! A tingle of excitement ran through her body. Getting up quickly, Doris walked out of the sanctuary and practically ran toward Reverend Johnson's office. Pausing at his door somewhat breathless, she saw him sitting behind his desk.

Rapping gently on the door frame, Doris made her presence known. "Reverend, I have something you need to see," she began.

Thomas Johnson looked up over his glasses.

He sat up and looked at Doris. Laying down his pen he said half-jokingly, "You haven't seen something again, have you, Sister?"

Doris slowly nodded "yes." He hurriedly got up and followed Doris out and back to the sanctuary of St. Michael's. There was none of his questioning this time about seeing shadows, being ill, or taking an early morning drink! This time, he just followed!

On a Tuesday morning a few weeks later as the crowds began to form, there was talk not only about the *angels* who had been seen by thousands of people in St. Michael's, and millions, if not billions, on television; there was also talk about what had been left behind. Now, in a place of honor, enclosed in a glass case with gold framing, on a red velvet pillow, lay three large white feathers that had been left by the *angels.* St. Michael's was now truly one of the most important pilgrimage sites in the world. Neither St. Michael's nor Dunning would ever be the same again.

Six months to the day from the time the *angels* were first seen, a wedding was performed in St. Michael's by the Reverend Thomas Johnson. It was the wedding of Chad Simmons and Cynthia Davis.

Feathers
Sometime Appear When Angels
Have Been Near

CPSIA information can be obtained
at www.ICGtesting.com
Printed in the USA
LVHW111608130919
631008LV00001B/80/P